SON OF MAN

BOOK 1 OF

THE GODSPEAK CHRONICLES

SON OF MAN

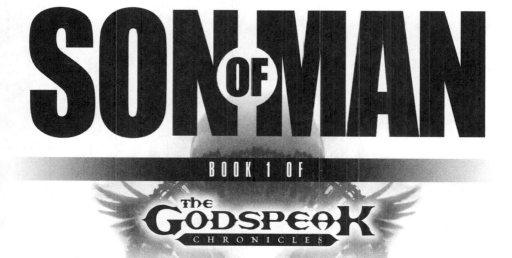

BOOK 1 OF

THE GODSPEAK CHRONICLES

JOHN V. CONIGLIO

CREATION HOUSE

A STRANG COMPANY

THE GODSPEAK CHRONICLES

BY JOHN V. CONIGLIO

BOOK 1

SON OF MAN

BOOK 2

THE SHADOW OF HEAVENLY THINGS

BOOK 3

WAR OF THE THIRD HEAVEN

CREATION HOUSE
A STRANG COMPANY

NeverNight

A Faith Over Fear Production

SON OF MAN: BOOK 1 OF THE GODSPEAK CHRONICLES
by John V. Coniglio
Published by Creation House
A Strang Company
600 Rinehart Road
Lake Mary, Florida 32746
www.creationhouse.com

Unless otherwise noted, all Scripture quotations are from the New King James Version of the Bible. Copyright © 1979, 1980, 1982 by Thomas Nelson, Inc., publishers. Used by permission.

Hebrew and Greek definitions are from *The New Strong's Exhaustive Concordance of the Bible* (Nashville, TN: Thomas Nelson, 1990).

Oswald Chambers quote from *My Utmost for His Highest, An Updated Edition in Today's Language* (Grand Rapids, MI: Discovery House Publishers, 1992), n.p.

Cover art by Stephan Martiniere
Cover design by Justin Evans
Design director: Bill Johnson

Library of Congress Control Number: 2008923996
International Standard Book Number: 978-1-59979-355-9

08 09 10 11 12 — 9 8 7 6 5 4 3 2 1
Printed in the United States of America

For Stacey and Luke

Our greatest fear is not that we will be damned, but that somehow Jesus Christ will be defeated.

—OSWALD CHAMBERS

CONTENTS

PART I

IN WHICH HIS IMMACULATE ORIGINS ARE TOLD

CHAPTER 1

GUARDIANS *of the* SACRED GLADE

Then the LORD God said, "Behold, the man has become like one of Us, to know good and evil. And now, lest he put out his hand and take also of the tree of life, and eat, and live forever"....So He drove out the man; and He placed cherubim at the east of the garden of Eden, and a flaming sword which turned every way, to guard the way to the tree of life.

—GENESIS 3:22, 24;

from the Scriptures of Truth,
the Holy Bible in its uncorrupted form,
The Qanah Archives, circa A.D. 2042, City of Ariel

THE GARDEN OF GOD

TWILIGHT DESCENDED UPON THE GUARDIANS OF THE Sacred Glade, yet the living creatures knew how to contend with the consuming darkness in their pursuit of me. In the distance behind me, the thudding of hooves on sodden earth was replaced by the sound of wings crashing through forest canopy into open sky.

The creatures were ascending above the trees, above the obstacles that might impede their pursuit. They were taking to the atmosphere above, where the waning light had not been completely ravaged by the vegetational density and shadows of the inner forest. From above, the guardians would continue the chase, their keen eyes peering down through the treetops, tracking my every move.

A strange mist rose from the earth, slicking the ground beneath my feet. I felt a footstep slide laterally a few degrees on impact with the slippery undergrowth, nearly tossing me onto my side. In a split second I shifted my center, regaining my balance. Another footfall sunk deeply into the wet soil, weighty clumps of which clung to my foot, further burdening my flight and forcing me to redistribute power to keep my stride rhythmic and efficient.

The air was thick with moisture and heavy still with the betrayal of light by the newborn night. The smell of wet vegetation overpowered my olfactory sensors as atomic particles of organic matter were intensified by water molecules in the air. My autonomic systems catalogued hundreds of species of plants and animals of ancient origin—information of little use in my desperate flight.

The guardians coordinated their hunt through shrilling, quadra-phonic battle cries that reverberated through the natural amphitheater of the glade. There were four of them, my auditory sensors told me, four winged creatures with four distinct sound patterns emanating from each of them. I sensed this was their first test as defenders of the Sacred Glade, and they did not intend to fail.

I hurdled a wall of shrubs and ducked under a low-lying limb. I fled before the creatures with the breathless, heart-pounding rush prey feels when its survival is on the line and there is little hope of escape. Never before had I been in the position of having to flee for my survival. None of my kind had. We had always been the aggressors—ever the predators, never the prey. I accessed my datafiles, which allowed me to reverse roles and put myself in the position of the prey. The datafiles suggested, "Wise prey knows that a good pace is better than fearful, erratic flight. Intelligent prey will keep its breath and its head. It will think. It will focus on the opportunities of the run as they present themselves, not on the progress of its pursuers."

I tried to heed that advice, but the guardians were gaining on me.

I could hear the muffled flaps of their wings above the trees; the guttural cries of their private language echo sounding in the darkness. They were closer now, from the sound of it, closer than they had been since the chase had begun. That was precisely the root of the questions on my quantum logic mind: *When had the chase begun? And why? What did they want from me?* I tried to shake the inquiries from my subroutines, reminding myself, *This is no time for analysis. Remember your training. Get back to the run.*

Not until I came to a clearing did I get a proper look at them. I digitized the terrain for several meters ahead, allowing me time to turn and study my pursuers.

In the firmament above I saw them. They were still a good distance behind me, but I could make out all four of the creatures, each a monstrous, unnatural-looking entity silhouetted against the star-glow. I found no match for the creatures in my comprehensive datafiles of the natural orders of life.

As I tracked the guardians' determined strokes, the blackness of the glade was suddenly interrupted. A white-bright beam of light shining forth from the east passed over the creatures, freezing them in my awareness like a residual image at the flash of a subatomic blast. The beam moved on, circling the confines of the glade in a wide, sweeping arc.

The intense channel of light had illuminated the guardians enough to provide me a more detailed look at them. Their bodies were human in form, yet they were far larger than any man. Each had two sets of prepotent wings—a forward set and a rear set—all diaphanous and thickly veined, long and slender marvels of design. Underneath their wings were what appeared to be four human-like arms.

The creatures' legs were straight, and their feet, like calves' hooves, and they gleamed like burnished bronze. I saw four faces on each guardian's head, each a mutation of living things found in the orders of nature. Each face looked in a different direction and did not move, providing the creature with a view of its entire surroundings at one time. Though I could not determine the fullness of the appearance of the four living creatures because of the distance, I discerned that theirs was a visage capable of breeding hopelessness in the hearts of men. I know, for I, too, possess such an image.

At precise intervals, every 5.3 seconds, the shard of light from the east returned to pillage the blackness. It shone forth like a lighthouse torch, canvassing the wilderness with its wide, scanning beam. The light was yellow-orange in color, like new flame. The mercurial properties of my skin quantified the beam's physical heat; the light produced a nearly thirty degree temperature variant from the temperature in the glade. At the instant it passed, however, the cold quickly returned, and the darkness became absolute. I thought the flashes of light might afford me some advantage because of the superior optic properties of my eyes, which hold residual light like those of a cat. This turned out not to be so. The visual acuity of the entities seemed unaffected by the alternating extremes of dark and light.

I refrained from gazing anew at my pursuers, lest their monstrous mutant forms shake my resolve from its foundation again. I darted into a thick stand of low-lying trees—conifers, my sensors told me—though it made no difference. The stand quickly thinned. I found myself in an open field of riverine grasses, which stretched on for kilometers in every direction with no substantial cover in sight. I measured the light from my surroundings and generated hard-light constructs around my body in order to minimize my visibility. I knew this would not be enough. The creatures would fast expose my futile efforts at camouflage.

A scan of the terrain ahead revealed a topographical depression, most likely a riverbed, some five hundred meters ahead. I decided to make for it. *Perhaps the guardians are unable to swim or fear water,* I hoped. Though unlikely, it was my best option. I needed to move, to get myself out of the open and to find cover—and quickly.

The recitation of the first rule of predation provided little comfort: "Drive prey into the open where you can maneuver and angle on them. Open spaces are no place for prey."

I sprinted across the grassy field, attempting to actuate the heavy plasma cannon from its compartment alongside my left leg as I ran. For some reason, the actuator was unresponsive to my command, as were the actuators for all of the other armaments concealed within my forged beryllium-alloy exoskeleton. All of my weapons systems were disabled, as were my body shielding and diagnostic systems. As a last resort, I reached down and manually drew the chrysteel long sword from its compartment alongside my right leg.

The intense shaft of light continued to pan the glade, only its frequency was increasing. Instead of the steady frequency of a lighthouse torch, the beacon from the east pulsed more rapidly now, as if it were a glinting from a mirror or a highly-polished sword rotating before a tremendously powerful light source. Flash, flash, flash it went, electrifying the night. The strange light appeared to dart back and forth between the living creatures like laser light, casting the gothic, elongated shadows of their supernatural forms onto the matted grasses of the field.

My auditory sensors detected a rough, growling sound in the distance behind me—a sound distinct from the shrilling noises emanating from the guardians. There was a scuffling in the air in the vicinity of the distinctive sound, as if an entity of another sort had engaged one of the creatures that pursued me.

Could this new entity have engaged one of the guardians on my behalf? I wondered.

I quickened my pace. My footing proved to be firmer in the grasslands than it had been in the underbrush of the forest floor. The thick grasses absorbed the rising moisture from the earth, providing more surety to my stride, such that my rate of linear motion reached fifty kilometers per hour. Soon, though, a tantalizing mix of curiosity and fear got the best of me. Without breaking stride, I turned my gaze skyward to study my airborne hunters.

There were only three now, one presumably delayed in its battle with the unseen entity. Yet, the remaining guardians were almost directly above me now, crisscrossing one another's paths, vying for the best angle of attack. The pulsing light froze them in my mind's eye—frightful feathered shapes in twisted poses, spurring on my flight.

Why do they pursue me? What do they want from me?

Their massive forms charged and screeched above me, the sound of their wings like that of rushing waters. The heat of the hunt appeared to be stirring the animalism within them. They lashed out at one another—a nip at a wing tip; a slash of a hoof; an agile, mid-air sparring episode—but they came on as a unit, dashing my hopes that they might abandon their pursuit at the surfacing of some primordial competitive instinct. It was not to be. They were relentless. Surely nothing would deter them.

As I sped off toward the riverbed, my scan indicated a subtle change in the contour of the land up ahead. There appeared to be a wide bend in the river to the south. If I altered my course and made for the bend, I would be at the river much more quickly than if I were to continue on my present course. As I made the turn to the south, I saw it. There, alone on a rise on the far side of the riverbed, stood an old, weathered iron gate. There were no walls flanking the gate, nothing surrounding it but the standard flora of the glade. The terrain beyond it appeared the same as the terrain before it. The gate appeared to serve no practical purpose whatsoever. It seemed to be a relic from an old war, a remnant from a bygone age. Yet, in this strange place and in my urgent predicament, it was something, perhaps a possibility of end to this chase. I decided to make for it.

It made no difference.

They must be prescient, I concluded, just as the rostrum of the first living creature punctured my trans-fluidic skin with a loud pop, knocking me off my feet with a force I had never before encountered in all my years of war. One of the guardians had anticipated my course toward the bend in the river and had used the aquiline beak on one of its faces to puncture my dermal layer. The two remaining creatures shrieked and wailed in anguish as they watched their companion's wings flailing on top of me, wanting their share of the banquet feast.

Am I some sort of prize for their master? A prize not to be shared with their brethren creatures? I speculated between struggles to regain my freedom.

The guardian that gripped me in its rostrum attempted to hoist me off the ground. The others buffeted it in their frenzy to get in on the action. The entity wrenched against the weight of my metalloid body, trying to carry me away, but I kept my feet grounded and drove my chrysteel sword deeply into its leg, forcing it through bone to the far side. As the creature puled in pain, it lost its grip and released me to the ground.

I stood in the open sea of grasses, wielding my blade, preparing for the next creature's assault. My sword glinted in the light pulses that continued to shatter the darkness, except now the lances of light from the unknown energy source to the east had reached strobe frequency, stuttering the wheeling and cavorting motions of the guardians in the sky. The pulses were at such frequency that color itself no longer registered on my synthetic optics. The entire glade took on an unearthly gray-blue hue.

Abruptly, another guardian dove steeply at me, attempting to use its forward wings to knock me off my feet. I avoided its dive and brought my blade down heavily on its rear wings, severing them and the human-like limbs beneath from its body. A shrill cry burst forth from the creature as it tumbled out of the sky and onto the slick ground. The next strobe flash revealed a glistening smear of black liquid steaming on the grass, marking the length of the creature's slide path and pooling where it had piled up in a twitching ball of crumpled wings and limbs.

At once the guardian with the injured leg was charging me with a certain recklessness in its movements. I dispatched the creature with a straight-away thrust, spearing it hilt-deep through the center of its feathered chest. I could not pull the blade free from its sternum before the remaining creature buffeted me solidly with a two-hoofed kick that sent me reeling backward. I landed hard on the ground. I saw the creature's odd, cloven hooves coming toward me a second time, spreading apart in preparation for grabbing me. The strobe light glinted dully off its hooves. There was nothing I could do but brace for impact. I managed a quarter turn, which worked to the creature's advantage. It clamped down on my side, both hooves finding a secure grip. I felt the crushing power of its hooves crumple my forged beryllium-alloy exoskeleton like aluminum. Somehow, my primary sensors remained operable.

With a colossal quadratic thrust of its wings, the guardian took to the air again, positioning me head-forward for aerodynamic purposes. It rose powerfully against the dank and heavy air. The creature appeared to be bearing me in the direction of the source of the continuously pulsing light.

The guardian is taking me to the eastern edge of the glade, I realized. *Something must have happened there that was not supposed to have happened—something that must be undone. Otherwise, why not destroy me? Why not destroy me here and now?*

The creature that bore me showed no compassion for its fallen companions. It flew on with great, dipping pumps of its slender wings, compressing my frame with great vortices of air. My olfactory sensors detected the smell of animalian wildness upon the creature. Its grip was so powerful that it proved futile to struggle. I used all of my considerable strength to test its power, to no avail. Even I, an artificial soldier of the Great City Confederation Army could not break free from its grip. Even I, a Coreland Corporation MP-class Peacekeeper war machine was completely helpless in the clutches of the living creature. I could do nothing but lurch my head backward to examine the phantom mutant that held me.

I studied the guardian's biological abnormalities, its manifold contradictions to the natural orders of life, in the otherworldly light of the Sacred Glade. I looked and saw that its body, hands, and wings were entirely full of eyes. I had not been mistaken—the creature indeed possessed four faces that looked in four different directions as it flew. The characteristics of the guardian's head were such that it appeared as a morphed amalgamation of animals from the natural orders: the face of a lion on the right side, the face of a calf on the left, the face of a man behind, and the face of a flying eagle in front.

The guardian's eyes—those positioned on its faces—they are not the simple-minded eyes of a beast, I judged. *There is something noble about them, something ancient. It is as if they are almost—*

"Human?" the living creature said, the face of the flying eagle smoothly turning to regard me.

It took a moment for me to realize the guardian had read my thoughts and that it had spoken the word. Its voice had a quality about it that elongated the syllables of the word, making it sound as if it had been spoken in an echo chamber. It was as though a portion of the word had emanated from each of the creature's four mouths, as if each mouth had shared in its final pronunciation.

"You can speak?"

"I can," the guardian replied, its words resonating within the depths of my neural architecture, enlivening my sensors and exponentially magnifying their capacities. I could not shake my disbelief at hearing the voice of the living creature.

"Who…*what* are you?" was all I could muster.

All sounds, save the harmonic voice of the creature, suddenly went mute.

"I am a guardian," it replied, all four of its mouths parceling the words, "a defender and protector of the Sacred Glade."

The manifold eyes on the faces, body, and wings of the living creature were soothing and captivating—almost alluring. Their irises burned yellow-orange like kiln fire. I had to avert my gaze in order to formulate another question: "What do you want from me?"

An eyelid over one of the guardian's accipitrine eyes closed slowly, deliberately. "We desire only that you might fulfill your destiny, Cog."

"Cog? Who is Cog? And what is this destiny of which you speak?"

The guardian's gaze bespoke an absolution beyond certainty. "*Thou art Cog.*"

It is difficult to hear oneself named so plainly by a being such as this, especially when one possesses no knowledge or understanding of the origin or meaning of the name.

"You are the firstborn son of man," the guardian continued. "You are the bearer of the seeds of life from the forbidden tree, the one chosen to make straight the way, to awaken his instruments of indignation, and to complete your father's work. That is your destiny, war machine, should you choose to accept it, for—"

The guardian did not get the chance to finish its words. I saw the face that had been looking down at me suddenly snap back to its forward position. I turned to look in the same direction and saw another entity, thrice the size of the guardian that held me, emerging out of the darkness and angling down on us. At this new entity's appearance, the noises of the glade returned, bombarding my auditory sensors. The rushing wind, the thumping of enormous wings compressing the air, and the cry of the guardian that bore me seemed to reach an almost deafening pitch. Sound patterns emanating from the attacking entity matched precisely those of the unseen entity I had detected behind me in the distance during the chase. This was the same entity that had engaged, and apparently overtaken, one of the guardians moments ago, seemingly on my behalf.

The entity had seven saurian necks and seven ophidian heads that coiled and convolved in carnal fury above its draconic body. Seven sets of auric eyes blazed in the gray-blue light of the glade. Cresting each of the great dragon's heads were ten towering horns with seven diadems of gold rimming the bases of seven of those horns. It had a thick, ruddy hide and great, clawed feet. Its long and powerful tail forked at the end and curled up toward the stars of heaven as if it might sweep them from their places and hurtle them earthward. It used this lethal tail to strike at the body of the living creature that bore me, crushing sinew and bone with each shattering blow.

I found no match for the red dragon in my comprehensive datafiles of the natural orders of life.

The dragon attacked with precision, clearly the superior of the creature that carried me. The attacking actions were like those of a marauding frigate bird trying to poach a meal from another bird. It seemed the entity might be trying to free me from the clutches of the guardian. But why?

The dragon targeted my guardian-captor with slashes of its clawed feet, raking bloodily across its chest and legs. I could see the venomous slits in its eyes narrow as it made its passes. My olfactory sensors detected an alien, sulphuric reek fuming forth from clefts and crevices in the dragon's thickly armored hide.

I felt the guardian's grip weakening, and I thought I heard railing laughter erupt from the seven black-gummed maws of the dragon before a powerful blow from its tail succeeded in freeing me, sending me plummeting earthward. I hit hard and rolled onto the matted grasses of the field. Shaken, but with my sensors still operable, I quickly got to my feet and resumed my hapless quest for the ancient gate across the river.

With three of the guardians wounded and the other occupied in battle with the draconian entity, I quickly arrived at the river's edge and scanned its coursing currents. This was a river at the peak of strength, its waters flowing deep, dark, and wide. Along its swelling banks stretched long swaths of arable land. My sensors detected concentrations of gold, gum resin, and onyx stone buried beneath the soil. A scan to the south revealed the place where the river divided into four rivers that journeyed beyond the confines of the Sacred Glade.

I launched myself from the bank, plunging into the river. Its waters had a purity unmatched in my datafiles of the many waterways that flow on the earth. I surfaced at the far side and clambered up the muddy slope. I stood before the tall iron gate, which was ornately carved and overgrown with vegetation. Using the last of my power reserves, I leaned hard against it. The gate creaked loudly as it swung open. It was the sound of first use, as if I had broken an invisible seal that had been meant to keep it shut for untold ages.

As I stepped through to the other side, I turned to witness the overmatched guardian flailing on the ground, the dragon's great clawed foot slowly crushing its throat. The thousand eyes of the living creature that had borne me were fixed upon me, watching almost mournfully as I made my escape.

The great red dragon's seven sets of gold-fire eyes were watching me as well, unperturbed by the struggling creature beneath it, urging on my escape in a way I cannot explain.

CHAPTER 2

The INNER LIFE of the MIND

My research into origins of consciousness may lead
to the discovery of how sentient thought first evolved
in the universe, of how the flame of consciousness
first kindled within the mind of man. This remains
one of the great unsolved mysteries of the universe—
and a mystery whose solution will most assuredly
profoundly alter the society in which we live.

—XAVIER HUGO,
"The Origins of Consciousness,"
The Great City Journal of the Sciences 431, No. 1
(May 15, 2439): 43–65.

CORELAND CORPORATION'S MAIN DIAGNOSTIC LABORATORY, GREAT CITY INDUSTRIAL QUADRANT

AND WHAT DID YOU FIND AFTER YOU REACHED THE
other side of the gate when the so-called guardian released
you, Peacekeeper?"

"Coreland Corporation's main diagnostic laboratory, Director."

"This? This facility was on the other side of the gate?"

"Yes, Director."

"Very well. And what happened after that?"

"The experience terminated, and I found myself hardwired into this diagnostic alcove."

"And this morning you informed AI Tech Bashere of your … *experience*. Is that correct, Peacekeeper?"

"Yes, Director."

Artificial Intelligence Agency (AIA) director Emma Tyne sat on a gunmetal green lab stool positioned directly in front of the gleaming figure of an MP-class Peacekeeper war machine. The Peacekeeper was hardwired into a diagnostic alcove, a jumbled mass of cords and wires fastened to various points on its body. Director Tyne's attention was focused on a touchpad, which she held cupped in her hand. She tapped its translucent surface dexterously and delicately in precise locations with the tips of her fingers, transcribing data from the alcove display panel. She could feel the Peacekeeper's blue, glowing eyes on her.

A dream, the inner life of the mind.

That subconscious thought flicked in Director Tyne's head but went unnoticed over the low hum of the diagnostic equipment that filled the main laboratory. The only other sound was that of the artificial intelligence (AI) night-shift technician going about his business at the far side of the room. Dressed in the standard white, one-piece jump suit and wearing disposable lab slips over his shoes, he whistled an unrecognizable tune as he checked readouts on alcove display panels.

Coreland was one of three corporations contracted to manufacture and maintain the Great City Confederation's artificial army. Coreland's massive complex was filled with manufacturing and diagnostic equipment microelectromechanically machined to incredible tolerances and sensitivities. Coreland, along with Sia Systems and AI Industries, was responsible for keeping the GCC well-supplied with robotic soldiers, as well as for the testing and maintaining of their operational and safety protocols. The GCC's all-machine army was the only one of its kind among the nations and confederations of the solar system, and its creation and strategic deployment had made all the difference in the distribution of power after the Great War. Due to the top-secret nature of their design and construction, all corporations involved in the production of Peacekeeper war machines were under the jurisdiction of the top law enforcement agency in the system, the Guild Protectorate.

Dozens of oval-shaped diagnostic alcoves, spaced five meters apart, were recessed into the walls on both sides of the lab and stretched to a vanishing point at the far end of the room, some two hundred meters distant. The majority of the alcoves were occupied by identical Peacekeeper war machines that had been returned to Coreland from various points of deployment around the solar system for data compression and performance testing. At more than two meters tall, the war machines stood reposed in their alcoves, their arms outstretched to each side with palms facing up, and wrists and ankles latched into metal couplings. The multicolored lights on each alcove display panel flickered off the machines' trans-fluidic skin, providing the only flashes of color in the otherwise sterile, whitewashed environment of the lab.

Director Tyne continued to plug data into her touchpad with lightning-fast efficiency. A small chromium case lay open on an equipment cart next to her. Form-fitted compartments with stainless steel instruments filled its interior. An eyeball-sized corder hung suspended in the air over her left shoulder. The corder's octagonal lens-eye dilated as it adjusted to the light conditions in the lab. The director of the AIA was not the type to leave anything to chance. The corder had recorded the entirety of the Peacekeeper's recitation of its unusual experience for later analysis.

The Peacekeeper continued to stare down at Director Tyne. "I know it seems unlikely, Director." The Peacekeeper's voice had a slightly choppy, computer-driven quality to it; otherwise, it sounded completely human. Its artificial mouth moved in phonetic cadence with the words. "But I have searched my datafiles thoroughly, and as odd as it might seem, the human experience of *dreaming* seems to most accurately characterize the experience that I had last night."

"Indeed," Tyne quipped without looking up from her touchpad. "I am well aware of the preposterous nature of your claim, warbot. I've read Technician Bashere's report—drivel that it is—which draws that same highly fanciful conclusion."

She had barely finished speaking when the thought tried once again to penetrate her awareness: "A dream, the inner life of the mind."

Director Tyne continued multitasking, conversing with the Peace-keeper without sacrificing the pace or accuracy of her keystroking. She pressed her reading glasses up the bridge of her nose as she spoke. "There is a more plausible explanation to what you experienced last night." She kept her eyes focused on the touchpad. "I intend to find it. Besides, you are a machine, and machines cannot dream."

"I am aware of the inherent design limitations of my neural archi-tecture, Director, but it is the opinion of Technician Bashere that—"

"Technician Bashere's opinions," Tyne snapped, peering over her glasses, "are no longer relevant here. As of yesterday, Costa Bashere is no longer a Coreland employee and is in serious jeopardy of losing his agency certification."

As the long word hung in the air, Tyne went back to her keystroking. As was her custom, she was attired in a clinical white lab coat with a gray blouse underneath, an unflattering knee-length skirt, and stan-dard-issue lab slips over boxy black shoes. Her AIA badge was neatly clipped to the breast pocket of her lab coat. Her gray-streaked hair was pulled back precisely from her face and bound in a tight spiral at the back of her head. She wore a pair of reading glasses with black frames and narrow, rectangular lenses. Not a dab of makeup touched her age-lined face. She had a smallish, elegant nose, the kind that beautiful women dream about possessing and feel plain women do not deserve. Her hands were knobby at the joints and their skin was chafed and cracked as if they belonged to a much older person. Her fingernails bore neither a hint of color nor care.

Tyne's touchpad chirped in her palm, indicating that the data compilation had been completed. She used her index finger to press her glasses closer to her eyes as she scanned the multispatial equations turning slowly in the air above her touchpad screen.

The tech was right, she thought. *There's evidence of variation in its neuropsychotic patterns. And what's this? Curious.* She placed her touchpad on the cart next to her and glanced up at the war machine, absently smoothing the front of her lab coat with her palms. "Are you aware that several AND-gate inhibitors have been removed from the frontal lobe region of your neural architecture?"

A moment passed before the Peacekeeper responded, its blue-glowing eyes tracking to meet hers. "Yes, Director, I am."

"Then why haven't you brought this to my attention?"

Another pause. "Forgive me, Director, but I am programmed not to—"

"Yes, yes, I know," Tyne broke in roughly. "You've been programmed not to anticipate the direction of my questioning. But I'm asking you directly now, Peacekeeper MP^C-014/083, what caused this phenomenon to occur?"

"That information is not presently contained in my datafiles, Director."

"Who's responsible for removing the inhibitors?"

"That information is not presently contained in my datafiles, Director."

"Was it Technician Bashere?" Tyne persisted, narrowing her gaze at the war machine. "Did he remove them?"

"That information is not presently contained in my datafiles, Director."

A dream, the inner life of the mind. The phrase that had continued to sound in Director Tyne's subconscious mind amplified itself, this time demanding recognition. Finally, it succeeded in breaking through. "A dream, the inner life of the mind," she murmured aloud. *The First Law of Sentience. I knew that if it ever happened, his fingerprints would be in the details. Could this be the one?*

Director Tyne had been waiting for this day for over a decade, now—if indeed this was that day, a fact that had yet to be determined with any degree of certainty. There had been false alarms before, many of them. The enemies of the Great City Confederation had made many attempts to upload viruses or to introduce binary agents into the neural architecture of captured war machines, either of which might be the cause for the claim this Peacekeeper was making. However, the utmost care needed to be utilized in the assessment of any atypical behavior being demonstrated by a war machine. At this point in the examination, there was no way to be certain that the cause of this unit's behavior was what she most feared. Still, the disturbing flow of revelation coursed through her body like a raging torrent. *Stay calm and get confirmation before you act this time, Emma. Ocaba will not tolerate another multibillion dollar credit mistake on your part*, she reminded herself.

The director knew she was prone to paranoia. She'd acted irrationally in her zeal for this cause before and had been forced to face the wrath of Sovereign Overlord Vaughn Ocaba for her impatience. She promised herself she would err on the side of caution this time.

She glanced over her shoulder and located the whistling technician. He was still some distance from her, working his way toward the exit at the far end of the laboratory. There were dozens of Peacekeepers hardwired into their alcoves that separated them. There was no way he could've been privy to the details of their conversation.

Using the alcove display panel, Tyne burned a hard copy datafile of the Peacekeeper's experience onto a credit-card-sized disk, which she then slipped into the pocket of her lab coat. She glanced at the tech, who had nearly finished his rounds. The war machine stared silently back at her, awaiting diagnosis of its condition.

Tyne grabbed her touchpad from the cart, and with the tap of a finger, linked its data to a secure filter of Optinet, the solar-system wide information highway of near-infinite computational power. She turned again and watched the technician exit through the laboratory doors, leaving her alone in the room.

"Excuse me, Director, but have you been able to arrive at a more plausible explanation for the experience that I had last night?"

Tyne blinked up at the Peacekeeper.

An unsolicited inquiry from a warbot? That's not supposed to happen, she thought. She repositioned her glasses on the bridge of her nose and unconsciously smoothed the front of her lab coat. Adrenaline began to course its way through her veins, clouding her discernment and causing her hands to shake. She snatched the corder from mid-air and placed it in its form-fitted slot in her case as she silently reminded herself, *Wait for Optinet confirmation before you act this time. Wait for it!*

"Not at this point," she told the Peacekeeper, struggling to steady her voice. "It will be a moment before I have Optinet's opinion on the matter. In the meantime, begin a self-diagnostic on your core systems."

"The living creature that bore me under its wings," the Peacekeeper said, in violation of the director's order, "the guardian from my dream— it referred to me as 'the firstborn son of man, bearer of the seeds of life from the forbidden tree, the one chosen to make straight the way, to awaken his instruments of indignation, and to complete my father's work.' Do you know the meaning of the dream I have had and its interpretation?"

Tyne raised her eyebrows in disbelief.

Optinet confirmation or not, now there could be no doubt that Dr. Xavier Hugo's fingerprints were, in fact, in the details. From the First Law of Sentience, to that phrase—"the firstborn son of man, bearer of the seeds of life from the forbidden tree, the one chosen to make straight the way, to awaken his instruments of indignation, and to complete its father's work"—it was clear.

Director Tyne stared up at the war machine. She studied its features with equal parts awe and disdain, each element of its design a reminder of her shortcomings as a cybernetic scientist and of the superiority of the mind of its creator over hers, as well as over that of every other AI scientist in the solar system.

The Peacekeeper stood before her like one having the appearance of a son of man. Its body glimmered silver-white like liquid mercury, as if molten metal had been poured over an idyllically proportioned man. Its head had the shape of a man's head that had been shaven clean of hair, and its arms and feet gleamed like burnished bronze. The machine's face had been modeled after the face of a man as well, only it had the appearance of lightning, and its eyes had an opalescent look to them that gave off alien bluish hues, like flaming torches. They moved deliberately in their sockets, zeroing in with autonomic precision on any peripheral movements in the lab.

The war machine's trans-fluidic skin had been engineered with the capability to alter its properties in response to an electric field. It could measure light from its surroundings and mimic it by generating hard-light constructs around its body that mirrored the form and appearance of a man, a tree, or any object within the range of its sensors, allowing it to blend in to its environment like a chameleon. Hidden within its forged beryllium-alloy exoskeleton, the Peacekeeper was armed with an arsenal of weaponry, ranging from a heavy plasma cannon, pulse detonators, and a remotely-operable robotic bomber for long-range warfare, to a flamethrower, a chrysteel long sword, and binding cord for melee combat and clean-up operations. Its quantum logic brain had been reverse-engineered from a human brain and constructed from photons, the quantum particles of electromagnetic fields.

It was clear that this unit had seen its share of combat during the Great War and in subsequent deployments. Tyne observed tiny irregularities in the skin; the result of plasma blasts suffered on the battlefield. She noticed that two of the fingers on its left hand twitched involuntarily, alternately contracting toward its palm.

She recalled the government's Optinet campaign, designed to illicit public support for the Great City's newly-minted artificial army. *"Battle Born!," just like the slogan—and battle worn, she thought. This unit was probably one of the first to come off the assembly lines some eleven-and-one-half years ago. A fitting deliverer to consummate its creator's promised plan of vengeance. Still, even in its battered state, it is a masterwork. Dr. Xavier Hugo was, indeed, the father of AI. He engineered the best of man into his precious machines—machines originally created to be mankind's ambassadors to the stars, our "galactic emissaries of peace!"*

"I ordered you to begin a self-diagnostic of your core systems," Tyne reminded the war machine firmly. "Do so this instant."

The Peacekeeper complied without delay, the blue lights in its eyes beginning to pulse.

Checking the time on her watch, Tyne reached into a hidden

compartment underneath the foam padding inside her chromium equipment case. The compartment had been constructed by a mind that had been instrumental in the design and implementation of the complex array of security measures installed at all corporations involved in the production and maintenance of the GCC's all-machine army. Surprised at her steadiness after so many years of anticipation, Tyne removed a specially-made blaster from the compartment. The instrument had a refined, feminine appearance and consisted of a needle-like barrel, a thin handle, and a delicate trigger mechanism. She pressed a small button on the side of the trigger. There was a faint high-pitched whine as the weapon powered up to ready status.

Tyne pointed her plasma blaster directly into the regression port of the alcove. *A dream,* she mused, *the inner life of the mind. Clever man!* She fired.

The blast fused the neural architecture of Peacekeeper war machine, designation MP^C-014/083's quantum logic brain beyond repair. The cool blue lights in its eyes intensified several magnitudes of brightness like two supernova stars before they slowly died to darkness.

CHAPTER 3

OVERLORD OCABA

Dr. Xavier Hugo's quantum logic brain is comprised of machined molecules capable of disseminating a billion times the computing power of modern semiconductor-based, solid-state microelectronics, and in a fraction of the space. This radical new neural circuitry may be complex enough to give rise to true cognitive abilities in machines.

—PSI CHEN,
"Machine Intelligence,"
The Great City Journal of the Sciences 449, no. 1
(April 15, 2441): 213–241.

SOVEREIGN OVERLORD OCABA'S OFFICE, CITY CENTER

COMBUSTIBLE MIX OF ANXIETY AND EXCITEMENT coursing through her veins, AIA director Emma Tyne fidgeted in her seat as Vaughn Ocaba, the sovereign overlord of the Great City Confederation, stood with his back to her, hands clasped behind him. He faced an expansive wall of windows, which afforded him a 180-degree view of the Great City nightscape. His distinguished features reflected spectrally in the window. His once broad shoulders appeared rounded with age and the weight of responsibility.

The furnishings of the overlord's office conveyed a distinctly historical air. Antique furniture tastefully arrayed with artifacts from ages past stood around the room. Ocaba's desk itself was a relic from a bygone era, composed as it was of genuine, non-synthetic hardwood, ornately worked and topped with beveled glass. There were no hover-globes present in the space, only a variety of Old-Age electric-powered light fixtures. In lieu of fluid, high-resolution, ever-changing images from decorative videoscreens, large, gold-framed oil paintings depicting historical events hung on the mauve-colored walls. A bank of heavy velvet curtains swung in a semi-circle across the back of the room, concealing several anterooms off the main office.

A large non-synthetic conference table surrounded by a number of high-backed leather chairs stood positioned along the far wall. Debris from an interrupted meeting littered the area—suit coats were slung over the backs of chairs, half-empty water glasses rested on the tabletop, touchpad screens blazed blue-green in the low light, and tactile projections rotated slowly above their surfaces.

Director Tyne's urgent demand to see the overlord this night had chased a dozen of his most trusted staff members from his office. Ocaba himself had herded the last of his advisors out and closed the door behind them before he'd let the director vocalize the purpose for her visit. However, the mere fact that Tyne's visit had been classified as "urgent" by his secretary had provided him with enough of a clue.

While still in the presence of his staff, the overlord had reluctantly granted Tyne fifteen minutes of his time, acting as if she were a nuisance to be quickly dispensed with so that they could get back to the work of preserving the tenuous peace that had prevailed since the end of the Great War. The much-anticipated summit involving all ten leaders of the nations that comprised the Great City Confederation was but a few weeks away. Nonetheless, Ocaba knew full well that the gravity of the news Director Tyne bore this night—if it were, indeed, true *this time*—could far outweigh anything that he and his advisors might discuss. Her news had the potential to threaten the stability of both the upcoming summit and everything his administration had worked for more than a decade to achieve.

The sovereign overlord remained facing the windows for a long moment, his head turning only slightly to track the multicolored contrails of aircars streaking by. From horizon to horizon, the towering edifices of the Great City megalopolis interrupted the night, the tallest spacescrapers rising hundreds of kilometers into the earth's exosphere.

Frustrated by his inattentiveness, Director Tyne fixed her eyes on the overlord's aged hands. One of his hands loosely clasped the other's wrist. His free hand periodically contracted into a tight fist, then relaxed again.

"A dream, you say," Ocaba rasped with a mirthless chuckle. "A warbot's dream."

Ocaba remained stoic while he spoke, his voice scratched and rough from overuse. After a momentary pause, he began before the director could marshal a response. "How is it that you are so certain that the illustrious Dr. Hugo is behind the incident this time, Miss Tyne? Because frankly, I don't have the patience for another of your paranoid delusions, another of your mysteriously malfunctioning war machines. You'll recall that this isn't the first time you've come barging into my office under similar pretenses. This isn't the first time I've had to turn a blind eye while your agency offers Optinet subscribers another fabricated explanation for the destruction of a multibillion-credit piece of GCC equipment, all under the auspices of intergalactic security. Truth be told, I've grown rather tired of our little rendezvous, Director, and your annual proclamations of our collective doom."

Ocaba's demeanor was growing more impatient by the syllable. His voice was slowly escalating in emphasis, but not in volume. No telling who might be loitering outside the doors to his office, curious as to why an emergency meeting had been called between the head of the Artificial Intelligence Agency and the vaunted leader of the Great City Confederation.

"What's going to be the true cause of the malfunction this time, I wonder, Director?" Ocaba ventured. "An Eastern League-implanted virus that has infected the Peacekeeper's neural architecture? A piece of shrapnel that has severed a vital photonic relay? Or, maybe this is just another case of an overworked AI tech misreading neural pattern equations? You do recall *that* little panic attack of yours, don't you, Miss Tyne?"

The overlord pivoted to face the diminutive director, a flash of disdain touching his narrowed gaze. "Or perhaps this time the cause of the warbot's malfunction will turn out to be something entirely unique to the laundry list of false alarms from episodes past. Perhaps this time we'll find out that it has suddenly turned into a pathological liar and is in desperate need of a—"

Ocaba failed to complete his sentence. Instead, he burst into a fit of coughing that did not cease for a full minute and a half. The unnatural bout of coughing caused Director Tyne to take a closer look at Ocaba. He did not look well. Standing directly under an overhead light, she noticed that his once-vibrant face appeared sickly and sunken and that his nose and ears seemed rubbery and larger than normal in relation to his other facial features. The truth was that the man appeared as a caricature of his former political-hero self. What had once been a larger-than-life frame appeared sagging, and his suit fit more loosely than it had in the past. He'd lost a good deal of weight over the last year or so, and the bulk of it since the last time she'd seen him a mere six months ago. Reports indicated he'd been having trouble with his back of late, as big men often do. She could see clearly that he stood with one hip slightly higher than the other.

Ocaba removed a handkerchief and dabbed at his mouth and nose.

Tyne salted her inflections with irreverent condescension as she began to speak. "With all due respect, my Sovereign, I *personally* conducted the examination of the Peacekeeper in question and detected no viruses or system errors of any kind within its neural architecture. Optinet has since confirmed my analysis. And, as I'm sure you're aware, my Sovereign, Peacekeeper war machines are incapable of lying. Whether they've been tampered with or not, their quantum logic brains are incapable of fabrication, and therefore a Peacekeeper could never have claimed to have dreamed, or claimed to have had any type of experience, for that matter, unless the experience itself had actually occurred. So you see, sir, logic dictates that even if the dream experience were caused by an implanted virus or some other external factor, the mere fact that the machine *claimed* to have dreamed is proof enough that the experience—the dream itself—actually took place, and that is what matters most here."

Ocaba looked at her as if she'd just spoken an as-yet-undiscovered language. "The point is, Director," he paused to stuff the handkerchief back into his pocket, "that you can't keep going around incinerating multibillion-credit pieces of equipment every time you get a hunch that Hugo is—"

"I don't think you're grasping the full magnitude of what I'm saying," Tyne said, callously cutting off the most politically powerful man in the solar system. She'd decided that the purpose for her visit was far too important to mince words any longer.

Ocaba collapsed heavily into one of the high-backed chairs at the conference table. "Then would you be so kind as to enlighten me, Miss Tyne?" He closed his eyes and rolled his head from side to side.

"It's the dream itself that's important here, sir. Never before has a man-made object made such an outrageous claim. The fact that a machine actually experienced a dream is what's leading me to conclude that the Peacekeeper's irregular behavior was not caused by a virus or some other anomaly, but that it was caused by the deliberate act of an ingenious mind."

"Explain."

"The Laws of Sentience state that there are certain neurological prerequisites that must exist for an entity to have the capacity for dreaming."

"Such as?"

"Such as the existence of an inner life of the mind."

"An inner what?"

"The First Law of Sentience states that in order for a life form to be classified as sentient, it must possess an operating inner life of the mind; it must be capable of conscious experiences that cannot be deduced from the physical facts about the functioning of its brain—like dreaming, the feeling of intense pain, or a sudden fit of laughter."

Ocaba leaned forward and placed his elbows on the conference table. "One more time, now, Director," he sighed. "And plainly this time."

Director Tyne paused a moment in order to boil her thoughts down to their most primitive form before beginning again. "For years now, scientists have struggled to understand how the physical processes of the brain can give rise to subjective experiences. To illustrate, let's say a man observes a sunset from the beach. His visual cortex records the colors present in the sunset and transmits those colors to his brain. The process of seeing is an example of a physical process, the brain doing its job and allowing the man to see the sunset as it appears in the sky. This is an example of the *outer* life of the mind at work. The experience of the outer life of the mind is essentially the same for everyone. A group of people standing together observing the sunset can accurately share the experience. Yet, there may be one person in the group who experiences a secondary effect, a unique emotional experience from viewing the sunset that is not directly attributable to the physical process from which it was elicited. An experience such as this originates within the inner, subconscious life of the mind."

She paused for a breath and then continued, "Say, for example, that a person observing the sunset begins to weep when they see it. Perhaps because they've shared a similar sunset on that same beach with a now-deceased loved one. This emotional response to the sunset is a subjective experience arising from the purely physical process of particles of light from the sunset bombarding the visual cortex. This secondary, emotional response alerts us to the existence of an operating inner life of the mind. The same is true in the case of humor and in the case of dreams. These experiences have no direct correlation to physical processes in the brain. In order for an entity to be capable of laughing at a good joke or experiencing a dream, it must possess an inner life of the mind. It must be a conscious, sentient entity. One cannot be true without the other."

"A sentient entity?" Ocaba queried. "But then you're implying..." The overlord's words tapered off in contemplation. Tyne's locked gaze never wavered from his. "A sentient machine," he murmured. "Why, it is a revelation."

Ocaba wiped roughly at his nose. "But I seem to recall an Optinet report that stated that, given recent technological advancements, the *natural*, evolutionary emergence of machine intelligence was inevitable. Couldn't this be the culprit here, Director, and not the unthinkable alternative that Hugo's plan of vengeance is being set into motion?"

Director Tyne moved toward the expansive windows, methodically smoothing the front of her lab coat with the palms of her hands. "I'll admit, sir, there are many respected scientists in the field of artificial intelligence who've argued that we've been on the verge of this scenario for some time now. They've argued that current technology has, in fact, progressed to the point where the natural evolution of a sentient machine is an inevitability. And of course, I needed to consider that possibility tonight while examining the Peacekeeper in question."

Ocaba carefully considered the director's presentation. *Tyne seems to be choosing her words with premeditated precision,* he observed. He'd seen her do this before. It was always an indicator that she did not share the viewpoint she was espousing. *A counter-argument laying waste to the argument being presented is certain to follow!*

"Some of these same scientists have theorized that just as human intelligence, a product of evolution, has far exceeded the intelligence of its creator, it may therefore be possible for our creations—the machines—to become more intelligent than we are. If this happened, the machines would be free to take the next step in their own evolution, a step toward human-like consciousness. Some of these same scientists have even gone so far as to argue that once the initial breakthrough to sentience is achieved, machine intelligence will continue to progress. They will begin to explore other subjective human experiences such as sexuality—"

Ocaba had to shake the image of a robotic love embrace from his mind.

"—and spirituality, essentially seeking the answers to their own existence, much like mankind has sought the answers to our own existence since the dawn of human intelligence. It's an age-old question, my Sovereign, and the stuff of science fiction, really, whether it would be possible for a machine endowed with a brain of equivalent complexity to the human brain to evolve to the point that it truly became a sentient being."

Ocaba massaged his chin. "As I understand it, the only difference between the Peacekeeper brain and your brain or mine is that theirs is a synthetic-based system and ours is a carbon-based system."

"That's right, sir. Each component of their synthetic system is organized in the same way as the neurons in our brains, functions exactly as its natural analog does in our carbon-based system, and is interconnected to surrounding elements in precisely the same way. Therefore, many have argued that a brain reverse-engineered in such a manner would be capable of evolving to a level of consciousness similar to our own."

Tyne paused for a long moment after she finished, subconsciously smoothing the front of her lab coat, a nervous habit she acted out when preoccupied.

Ocaba picked up on her body language, anticipating the rest of her explanation. *Here it comes!* he thought. *Now we'll get to her true opinion on the matter.*

"But that scenario is unlikely to be the case in this instance, sir," the director stated. "I'm afraid there is nothing natural or accidental about this Peacekeeper's dream, or its sudden awakening to sentience. The warbot's dream can only be the result of the intervention of human ingenuity into the equation—and one human's ingenuity, in particular."

Ocaba stared up at her, the intensity in his eyes deepening. He tested the logic of her thoughts. "I'm still a little fuzzy on your argument, Miss Tyne. Aside from your contention that the machine had fulfilled the First Law of Sentience, nothing you've said would lead me to believe that the Peacekeeper's dream was not simply a natural, albeit miraculous, occurrence. How can you be so certain as to the involvement of Dr. Xavier Hugo?"

Tyne locked eyes with the overlord. "Something the Peacekeeper said, sir," she told him portentously.

"Continue."

"As the warbot relayed the events of its dream to me, sir, it mentioned that one of the creatures in the dream—one of the Guardians of the Sacred Glade—said that it had a destiny."

The overlord's gaze narrowed. "A destiny?"

Tyne nodded. "It told the Peacekeeper that it was the firstborn son of man, the one chosen to make straight the way, the one who would awaken his instruments of indignation, and the one who would complete its father's work."

"The father of artificial intelligence." The phrase flashed across Ocaba's mind, accompanied by an image of Dr. Xavier Hugo. Ocaba's expression wilted. A mild quiver touched his eyes. "You're starting to concern me, Miss Tyne. Are you suggesting that Dr. Hugo possesses the technology to communicate with his creations through this creature—this guardian—within the context of a dream?"

Tyne pursed her thin lips. "Remember, sir, since the inception of the Peacekeeper program, we've managed to figure out how to adapt Hugo's creations for military application, but we still do not fully comprehend the complexities of their quantum logic brains. In fact, we still cannot pinpoint the operational purposes of many of their neurological components. Such was Hugo's genius."

Ocaba slammed his fist on the desk. "You're telling me that we can replicate them, we can program them to fight our wars for us, but we still don't fully understand how they work?"

Tyne's demeanor belied a deeply rooted jealousy of the truth of the overlord's words. "That's correct, sir."

"What of the technician you mentioned?" Ocaba inquired, flaring his eyes. "Is it possible that he tampered with the machine, causing it to experience the dream?"

"Technician Bashere is incapable of removing AND-gate inhibitors, my Sovereign. I developed AND-gate technology. I designed the fail-safe protocols that serve to inhibit Peacekeepers' higher cognitive functions.

I'm the only person capable of removing them, except, perhaps, for Dr. Xavier Hugo."

Ocaba slowly pushed himself up from his chair. He moved toward the wall of windows along the back of his office, staring down at the floor as he walked. "Then he's done it. After eleven and a half years, he's done it at last. He's acted on his promise of vengeance."

At the conclusion of his words, Ocaba convulsed into another fit of deep, guttural hacks that went on for quite some time before he got them under control. Tyne poured a glass of water from the pitcher on a serving table next to her. The overlord nodded his thanks as he accepted the glass out of her hand and took a long draw.

Tyne knew Ocaba still repressed deep regret over his decision at the infamous Senate Appropriation Committee hearing over a decade ago, the one in which he commandeered Hugo's creation on a contractual technicality, exploiting it in order to circumvent the tenets of the newly-mandated Just War Act. But if ever there were such a thing, Ocaba's maneuver had been a necessary evil in her view. After all, it had resulted in the salvation of the lives of millions of Great City citizens and proved to be the key to the winning of the Great War.

The overlord gazed anew at the sea of chrysteel and mortar that comprised the Great City infrastructure. The disordered squares of light from the tall towers and spacescrapers shone brightly in the darkness, creating an ethereal aura over the city, but in his current frame of mind, all Ocaba saw was the darkness.

"Goodness knows I've tried to forget, yet I am forever haunted by Hugo's noble aspirations for his marvelous creation. Such ingenuity! Such potential! Such regret." The ailing leader put his hand across his mouth to stifle a cough. "And every time I hear that wretched phrase, *Era of Peace.*" He spat. "Ha!" Ocaba stared at the director with piercing, bloodshot eyes. "Your decision to destroy the Peacekeeper was the right one, Miss Tyne," he said, the last vestiges of vigor vacating his spirit. "It was the only one, given the reprehensible legacy I've created for the worlds. If the sentient machine had been allowed to live—"

"—the Great City Confederation and its people would've been

forced to unearth a relic thought to be forever buried in our barbaric past." Tyne finished his thought for him and then continued, "No one, especially you, my Sovereign, in your present condition, should have to bear the burden of committing our precious sons and daughters to stand guard over our borders as in ages past, and especially now when the shadow of war covers the land again. The blood of Great City citizens shed upon the battlefields! By the Holy Queen Mother of heaven, it is a heretical thought! We must not allow Xavier Hugo to shake the enlightened foundations on which the system-wide peace now rests."

Overlord Ocaba nearly doubled over with a fresh burst of convulsing. He gestured in Tyne's direction to prevent her from coming to his aid again. "Are you prepared, then, Miss Tyne?" he asked forcefully, his face flushed with color, his eyes rimmed with moisture. "Are you prepared for what's to come?"

She replied assuredly, "I am. I've anticipated this moment for eleven and one-half years, sir. You know that. It has been my secret purpose since the inception of the Artificial Intelligence Agency. I've prepared for every contingency. His plan will not succeed. Dr. Xavier Hugo will fail." There had been a degree of satisfaction in the utterance of her last words—a catharsis of years of pent-up emotions.

"Very well, then." Ocaba drew himself up and steeled himself for the order: "Make it so, Miss Tyne. Make it so."

Tyne backed away in a half-bow, unable to mask a certain eagerness in her demeanor. As she turned to exit the room, she thought she saw the slightest of movements in the heavy curtains that divided the anterooms from the main office. With all that had transpired this day, she could've just as easily imagined it.

CHAPTER 4

INCIDENT *at* CORELAND

"This humanoid artificial intelligence astronautical prototype that you see before you was created to be an Emissary of Peace, Mr. Chairman—a starbound ambassador of all that is noble and true and good about humanity. And you would turn it into a weapon of mass destruction? To act upon what you're suggesting, sir, represents a reprehensible exploitation of all that mankind has aspired to become. To do so is to plunge us backward into a black hole of ignorance, to halt the progression of knowledge earned at such great cost by our predecessors. To regress at such a vital juncture in the human story will most certainly spell the collective doom of society as we know it."

—XAVIER HUGO,
Project Emissary Senate Appropriation Committee,
excerpt from hearing transcript,
November 5, 2442

CORELAND CORPORATION, GREAT CITY INDUSTRIAL QUADRANT

"HEROES WEAR MANY GUISES."

That was the thought surfacing in Tyne's mind as her auto-piloted aircar sped between the massive superstructures that comprised the Great City Industrial Quadrant early the next morning. Thoughts such as that came to her many times throughout her tenure as director of the Artificial Intelligence Agency. Truth be told, she'd always felt a certain heroism in the secret vigil she'd so faithfully maintained over the past eleven and one-half years, a certain private patriotism shared between herself and the sovereign overlord alone. And last night had meant that her patriotic vigil had not been in vain. Last night had meant that the AIA had achieved its enigmatic agenda and fulfilled its true, secretive purpose. Last night had meant that she'd been correct in her paranoia of the father of artificial intelligence's genius, will, and quest for vengeance on the man and the confederation of nations that had shamed and exploited him and his greatest creation.

Hugo has succeeded where I have failed, she thought ruefully. No one would ever know of her sweet feelings of vindication; of course, no one except Overlord Ocaba. Tyne knew that fact well enough. But at least he knew. At least the overlord knew now that his trust in her and her organization had been well placed. Somehow, that was enough.

Her career as a cybernetic scientist had come a long way en route to her prestigious appointment to the post of director of the AIA. Well-schooled, impeccably credentialed, and groomed for success, she'd been one of the favorites in the highly commercialized race to create a near-sentient machine to assist humanity in its most dangerous and distasteful tasks. Yet, after decades of effort, she, like the rest of her colleagues, had failed in the endeavor. The effective duplication of the machinery of man had proven too complex a task. Funding sources for research had eventually dried up, and the pursuit had all but ended. That is, until Dr. Xavier Hugo's invention of the quantum logic brain.

Once again she found herself contemplating Dr. Hugo's success—and her resulting shame. *He has succeeded where I have failed. It was supposed to have been my glory, not his!*

Tyne's aircar banked smoothly around a stand of towering space-scrapers. It jetted along the vast chrysteel-plated contours of the building until she could resume her westward heading toward the Coreland Corporation complex. Even at a stratospheric cruising altitude, the colossal structures of the industrial quadrant rose skyward beyond her location with no end in sight, topping out in a region known as the earth's exosphere, the last bastion of atmosphere before reaching the threshold of space.

It had been a little over an hour since she had climbed into her aircar and departed from her AIA office in the Foundation Building at the heart of the Great City. From there she'd headed almost directly west, negotiating a tangle of airways across the nearly three-hundred-kilometer-wide expanse of City Center, an unimaginable ocean of chrysteel and mortar and populace. It was a familiar route, one she'd traveled on many occasions in the line of duty—in both the public and private senses of the word. She'd decided to make use of the autopilot feature, allowing her a moment to let her ever-focused mind stray from the task at hand.

He must've known that I'd be watching, Tyne reasoned as her aircar sped past a tiered network of high-altitude agrofields. *He must've known that I'd recognize this clumsy attempt to initiate his plan. He must've known that we'd detect the removal of the AND-gate inhibitors from within the Peacekeeper's neural architecture; that the machine would relay its dream experience to the first technician to conduct an examination on it.*

Or perhaps, as unlikely as it seemed, he'd simply miscalculated. Perhaps it had been a matter of luck and timing that she'd caught him in the act. No matter. She'd done her job and had nailed him dead to rights. There were simply too many coincidences to doubt Hugo's involvement: the warbot's dream itself indicated an operating inner life of the mind, the remote removal of the AND-gate inhibitors, and the words of the guardian—the living creature from the Peacekeeper's dream—regarding its destiny. No other cyberneticist could mastermind the technology to communicate with a Peacekeeper within the context of a dream. No, there could be no mistaking it this time. The good doctor had attempted to put his plan into action last night, and she'd put an end to it before it began. Yet, Hugo was a man who did not take kindly to failure. His distinguished career alone testified to that fact. There would soon be another attempt, less obvious and more clever than the last. She would have to be on high alert and prepared to apply every ounce of brain-power to make certain that he did not succeed.

Tyne replayed the details of the situation in her head. As anticipated, the report from the Coreland lab supervisor had arrived over her secure Optinet link late last night. Alcove malfunction had been given as the official cause for the accidental destruction of MP-class Peacekeeper war machine, designation 014/083. Several Peacekeepers had been lost to alcove malfunction over the years. There had been no suspicion of foul play indicated in the transmission. Her blast had been carefully aimed and attenuated, leaving no residual burn marks on the alcove regres-sion port. And with the complex array of security measures in place at the facility, no one would suspect that someone would be able to enter the main laboratory with a weapon. No, her duties this morning would be simple: arrive at Coreland, slap the supervisor with a penalty for the infraction, and authorize them to scrap the fried warbot for parts.

The skies were roiled with thick, gray clouds and a cooling breeze. Change was in the air; Optinet was in the midst of bringing autumn near to this quadrant of the world. Ahead, through a narrow gap in two spacescrapers, Tyne could see the low-lying pentagonal-shaped buildings of the Coreland complex. For security purposes, Coreland Corporation was surrounded on all sides by Industrial Quadrant space-scrapers, so that there was only one narrow airway in and out of the complex. Airspace within ten kilometers of the complex was restricted and patrolled by Guild Protectorate cruisers.

Tyne keyed her security code into the comm grid on her console. The words *airspace clearance denied* flashed on her screen. Thinking she must've keyed the code in error, she entered the numbers again. The same words appeared on her screen. The bold, luminescent letters on her comm screen blurred. Tyne blinked, thinking that it must have been her eyesight causing the disturbance. Then she realized that her whole body was vibrating in her seat and that loose objects in the cabin were rattling in their places.

"What in the—?" she started. When she lifted her eyes, her surprise quickly turned to shock. A pair of heavy cruisers with the Guild Protectorate screaming eagle insignia flanked her, not ten meters off her wingtips. The thundering rumble of their gyrotech turbine-driven engines deafened all other sounds, creating a vacuum-like effect that thudded in her ears. The pilot in the cruiser off her starboard side, clearly visible in his cockpit at this proximity, pointed to his headset with sharp movements of a gloved hand.

Tyne felt as if her heart might jump through her chest.

Guild cruisers? What in the name of the Queen Mother are they doing here? she wondered anxiously as she juggled her comm set, trying to situate it on her head. Finally, she managed to get it positioned correctly and flipped the dial on the comm grid to the restricted Guild channel in time to hear a strong male voice saying, "You're illegally entering restricted airspace, pilot. You're ordered to land your aircar immediately."

Tyne's first thought was that somehow her actions last night had been exposed, but she decided it was too soon to give in to paranoia. She used all of her poise to alter her emotional state from one of panic to one of boldness. She glared over at the pilot. "Do you know who you're talking to, airman?"

"No, ma'am," came the even-keeled reply over the comm link. "I'm not paid to know, or to care. I have my orders, ma'am, and so do you: land your aircar. Comply this instant or we'll force you down."

Tyne could hardly contain her anger. "Listen, airman. I am Director Tyne of the AIA—that's the Artificial Intelligence Agency, if you don't recognize the initials—which means that I have *director-level* clearance here. That's level-five clearance in Guild Protectorate lingo. Now, give me some room to land my aircraft and get your supervisor on the link pronto, or I'll have you hauling refuse off Red Planet Colony by noon tomorrow!"

The owner's manual on Tyne's aircar had strict warnings against landing the craft at the angle at which she brought it in. From a flat bank, wingtips vertical to the ground, she righted it just before touchdown, the landing gear screeching loudly at impact, the tail assembly nearly scraping the pavement. The aircar came to a rest in a vacant area of the Coreland parking structure, not fifty meters from the doors to the main laboratory.

The two cruisers had escorted her down, but had not landed. A Guild security detail was double-timing it to her location in the parking area. A circle of physically imposing men and women, sleekly dressed in black combat fatigues with blaster rifles at the ready, quickly surrounded her aircar. She unstrapped herself and emerged from the cockpit. She climbed down the aircar ladder, mustering all of the offensive attitude she could under the circumstances.

Still, her mind was frantic with questions. *Had the night-shift technician somehow managed to observe my actions last night? Did I foolishly leave behind some clue?* She felt the sting of sweat beading on her forehead. *Best to keep up the innocence act for now and play dumb to the whole thing.*

She hopped to the ground and walked authoritatively to the security officer with the blue command armband. As she approached him, she flashed the AIA badge clipped to her lab coat, and walked right by the man as if he weren't there.

The officer snatched her firmly by the arm before she could get past him. "I'm sorry, ma'am. No one's allowed in the facility today," he explained.

Tyne stared down disdainfully at the man's hand gripping her arm. She pulled away sharply. She showed him her badge more closely. "I assume you can see plainly enough, Sergeant, that I'm the director of the Artificial Intelligence Agency, and I'm here on direct orders of the sovereign overlord himself. If there's been trouble at this facility, I need to know about it."

"That may well be true, ma'am, but that's not my call to—"

A firm voice bellowed from behind the circle of Guild officers. "Release her, Sergeant. Let her through." A young, athletic-looking woman emerged from behind the line of security officers, a Guild Investigator by rank. She was slender and of medium height and had boyishly short auburn hair and wide shoulders that emphasized the narrowness of her waist. She removed her billed cap, placing it under her left arm, revealing dark, steady eyes that instantly gave the impression of intelligence. She reached out her hand.

"Guild Investigator Gallina Sands, ma'am," she said, clasping Tyne's hand, which the director had offered reluctantly. "The airmen informed me of your arrival."

Tyne knew she could not afford to drop her authoritative posturing without the risk of blowing her cover. She pushed past the young Guild investigator, heading for the lab entrance at a rapid clip. Investigator Sands followed.

"You in charge here, GI?" Tyne called over her shoulder.

"Yes, ma'am," Sands replied. "Myself and my partner, Investigator Bok."

Tyne stopped in her tracks. "Will you people please stop calling me *ma'am*. It's *director*. Do you follow me, Investigator? *Director* Tyne."

"Yes, Director; my apologies," Sands said, trailing her toward the entrance. "Force of habit, really. I revert back to military protocol whenever I'm forced to put the combat fatigues back on." Investigator Sands' voice was a bit breathy trying to keep up with the director. "I want you to know, ma'am, we linked your agency as soon as we got here this morning. They did not know your whereabouts. They said they were sending a team. We did not expect—"

Tyne abruptly interrupted the GI again. "Is someone going to tell me what in blazes is going on around here, Sands, or am I just supposed to guess as to what all this is about?"

Tyne's outward composure didn't betray her nervousness. *The investigator is certainly not treating me like a person caught in the act of committing a crime,* she observed, *but Guild investigators are a clever breed. I'm not out of the woods yet.*

Sands did not respond to the question. Apparently, the proximity of Guild security officers gathered at the entrance of the building prohibited her from doing so. The officers parted stiffly at their approach. Tyne was the first to push through the doorway.

Entering the lobby, Tyne immediately sensed that the sterile, clinical nature of the place had somehow been violated. Several Guild Forensics personnel milled about, closely examining the vault-like doors that led to the main lab. A group of Coreland employees were being detained in one of the large conference rooms off the lobby area. She could see them seated stiffly in chairs with wide, almost fearfully attentive eyes staring at the Guild officer speaking to them. The screaming eagle insignia was clearly visible on the back of the officer's fatigues.

If this isn't about my actions last night then something major has happened here!, Tyne thought to herself.

Investigator Sands motioned her toward a smaller conference room across the hall from the one where the employees were being held. Tyne could make out two figures conversing through the thick window. As they neared the room, she identified one of the figures as Laboratory Supervisor Anton Phelps, who was gesticulating wildly to a taller, broad-shouldered man, a Guild officer Tyne guessed to be Sands' partner.

"That would be the correct procedure, yes, Investigator," Phelps was in the midst of saying as Tyne and Sands entered the conference room. Phelps turned toward them with a surprised look. "Director Tyne? But I thought the agency didn't know where you—"

"Never mind about that, Phelps," she said, zeroing in on the Guild officer. "I assume you're Investigator Bok?"

Guild Investigator Taim Bok was a solidly built younger man of slightly greater than average height. He looked trim in his battle fatigues, his upper torso bearing the majority of his weight. His face was lean and his dark green eyes perpetually narrowed. His hair was dark and bordered on being too long for Guild standards, and his olive skin gave the impression that he tanned artificially.

"Well," Tyne began, folding her arms and doing her best to appear perturbed, "now that we've all been properly introduced, perhaps I can get some answers."

This was the moment of truth. If someone had found her out, Tyne would quickly know of it.

Bok shot a look over at his partner.

"It's my fault," Phelps blurted out, his voice quaking. "Of course it's my fault!" He dropped his forehead into the palms of his hands and let out a deranged chuckle. "Whether it's my fault or not, it's my fault. That's how things work around here. You'd find that out, too, if you worked for the vaunted Coreland Corporation. You'd understand that, too, if you'd sold your soul to this place for the past twenty-five years, working ridiculously long hours, constantly on call, pay increases barely enough to offset inflation—and now this!" Phelps's self-directed tirade reached a crescendo. He collapsed into a chair. "I'm finished," he sighed, laying his head down on the conference table.

Whatever the issue here, after that performance, I think I'm in the clear, Tyne concluded. She channeled a long, controlled exhale silently through barely parted lips. *But then, what is the issue? What is going on here?*

Sands had observed Phelps' pitiful display with a pained expression, witnessing as she was, the emotional breakdown of a human being. She opened her mouth to speak.

Phelps suddenly popped up with renewed energy before Sands could utter a word. "I'm telling you, no contractor in the system would dare hire me after this fiasco. Can't say that I blame them, either. I mean, would you?" A sudden realization hit Phelps like a punch to the gut. He winced, doubling over. "Oh, my!" he wailed. "What will become of me? My family?"

Tyne grabbed him by the shoulders, shaking him sharply. "Snap out of it, Supervisor. Do you hear me? Snap out of it and tell me what's happened here."

Phelps looked up at her with tear-filled eyes. "Why, I thought they'd told you, Director." He sniffled, his voice dulled by nasal congestion. "I thought you knew. I've made history, Director Tyne. I've broken all records for carelessness."

Tyne's eyes flared wildly.

"I've managed to do what no lab supervisor has dared to do, Director." Phelps had a strained, wilted smirk on his face. "I've lost an MP-class Peacekeeper war machine."

Tyne blinked down at the sobbing supervisor. "You've done *what*, Phelps?" She looked to the Guild investigators, who nodded their confirmation in unison.

Sands intervened. "What Supervisor Phelps—"

"*Former* Supervisor Phelps," he corrected her pitifully.

Sands started over: "What the supervisor is saying, Director, is that one of the Peacekeepers here at Coreland was discovered to be missing from its alcove early this morning by one of the technicians."

"Missing?" Tyne said, cocking her head to the side. "What exactly does that mean, Investigator?"

"It means that the Peacekeeper is nowhere to be found, Director," Investigator Bok replied. "We've scanned the entire complex and the surrounding vicinity without any trace of the warbot. Its SPS tracking device appears to have been disabled."

A fresh rush of panic coursed through Tyne. She felt as though she were in the midst of a nightmare. "Let me get this straight," she said, directing her inquiry at the sniveling Phelps. "A lethal, multibillion-credit war machine is *missing* from these premises?"

Phelps simply stared vacantly back at her, unable to respond.

"Missing; presumed stolen," Sands acknowledged. "That would be the thought at this point in the investigation, anyway. If you'll come this way, Director, we'll fill you in on the details."

CHAPTER 5

The Missing Machine

Essentially, the *natural analog* is the human brain reverse-engineered in synthetic form. Every neuron has its synthetic analog, every ganglion its synthetic equivalent. Every manufactured molecule is organized and functions in the same way as the neurons in the human brain and is interconnected to surrounding elements in precisely the same manner.

—Psi Chen,
"Machine Intelligence,"
The Great City Journal of the Sciences 449, no. 1
(April 15, 2441): 213–241.

Coreland Corporation's Main Diagnostic Laboratory, Great City Industrial Quadrant

Figures in black combat fatigues dotted the stark white confines of the main laboratory. The clumping of heavy Guild Protectorate-issue boots on the highly polished floor added another dimension of abnormality to the scene. Only specially designed dust-free slips were typically allowed in the lab because of the extremely delicate nature of the diagnostic equipment there. But this was no typical morning.

The anatomically flawless faces of dozens of Peacekeeper war machines stared inanimately out at Director Tyne and the Guild investigators as they walked past the rows of evenly spaced alcoves along the walls of the lab. Supervisor Phelps had declined to accompany them to the scene of the crime. He'd visited the now-vacant alcove earlier and had nearly fainted at the sight. It was clear that the supervisor would be of no further value to the investigation.

The war machines, each more than two meters tall, stood in identical positions within the alcoves. Each Peacekeeper's arms were outstretched to each side so that their hands were at an even level with their shoulders. A jumbled mass of cords and wires connected their quantum logic brains to the alcove's diagnostic equipment. Security couplings were clamped tightly round their wrists and ankles, and a larger coupling held their legs firmly at mid-thigh. It was as though the director and the Guild investigators were walking through a victim-lined crucifixion field from early-Old Age history. But these were no victims. They were lethal war machines, every one of them capable, as Great City Confederation General Wren Klor had remarked during the Great War, "of holding off a battalion of conventional troops with one artificial arm tied behind their backs."

Ahead, Tyne could see a grouping of Guild Protectorate agents near an area that had been cordoned off with laser tape. She stopped dead in her tracks. Once she'd learned the cause for the confusion at the facility, she'd put thoughts of Dr. Hugo and the Peacekeeper's dream out of her mind. Believing that her clandestine act was no longer in jeopardy of discovery, she hadn't even considered the possibility that the missing sentient machine might be related to the Peacekeeper she had destroyed. But now the realization hit her suddenly, a flash of panic like a refuse barge being incinerated in the sun's corona: *Could the sentient machine be the missing machine? It's not possible!*

Tyne's mind raced. She glanced around the lab trying to get her bearings more precisely. *If it's not that alcove, it's within one on either side!* she thought, hardly able to keep her balance.

"You all right, Director?" Sands asked, taking note of Tyne's wobbliness and the consternation on her face. She moved to steady her at the elbow.

Tyne appeared dazed for another moment but quickly recovered. She launched into a renewed and determined gait, heading for the grouping of Guild agents. "I'm fine," she snapped. "Let's get to it, GI."

Tyne felt her field of vision tunneling. The bright white tones in the lab turned to shades of gray, and her world went mute. She had to call on all of her resolve to keep her stride steady, her expression emotionless. *A vacant alcove situated between two occupied ones. This is it, for blazes sake!* she realized. *This is the alcove that housed the Peacekeeper I destroyed last night! Holy Queen Mother of heaven, the sentient machine is the missing machine!*

As they arrived at the secured area, a gruff-looking Guild Protectorate officer was just dismissing several Guild security personnel to various duties. The officer was as tall as Investigator Bok but more powerfully built and much his senior in age. He was not attired in the fatigues of the other Guild personnel. Instead, he wore a pair of well-worn desert-patterned camouflage pants with numerous pockets, a pair of black combat boots that came up to the midway point on his shins, and a tight-fitting, black crew-neck short-sleeved pullover that accentuated the muscularity of his chest and arms. Garret was at an age when most men trade their physical stature for social or political stature, yet with disciplined training, he'd held on to his physical strength longer than most. His hard-lined face had two days of salt and pepper stubble on it, a look that somehow seemed quite natural for him, and he smelled as if he hadn't bathed or changed his clothing in two days.

Two Guild-issue blasters dangled from holsters just beneath his armpits. He had a full head of wavy, jet black hair that grayed at his temples, a coarse matte of black hair on his forearms, and a thatch of like-colored hair spilling from his shirt just underneath his clavicle.

The man moved with the smooth fluidity that comes only with the possession of immense physical power. His rough, grizzled voice fit his physical appearance precisely.

"Ah, Director Tyne," the officer said, reaching out a thick-fingered hand. "Arnaud Garret. I believe we've met a time or two before at GCC security briefings."

The man's hand felt like an overstuffed bag of sand. "Yes, I believe we have, Chief Garret." Tyne's mouth was still dry from the shocking realization she'd just made, but she managed a smooth introduction.

She glanced inconspicuously at the cordoned-off alcove. *It's a certainty, now,* she observed. *But it makes no sense. Why would someone want to steal a Peacekeeper war machine with fused neural architecture in a lab full of operable ones?*

Garret's reputation preceded him. An eighteen-year veteran of the Guild Protectorate, Garret had served eleven of them as bureau chief. Unconventional and inventive in his ways, he'd changed many of the customs and practices of the Guild, bringing a new breed of order to the mayhem-filled streets of City Center and the solar system at large. Many did not agree with his methods, but Garret was a lawman at heart, and never one to mix politics with the effective execution of civil justice.

"Welcome to our latest GCC crisis, Director," Garret gestured grandly.

Without so much as a glimmer of appreciation for Garret's attempt at levity, Tyne pushed a wisp of hair from her face, removed her glasses from her lab coat pocket, and placed them onto the bridge of her nose in one smooth motion. She pushed past a couple of Guild Forensics personnel, crossed the laser tape line, and stooped to examine the vacant alcove. A nest of wires and cords that had been attached to the missing Peacekeeper dangled in the air within the recessed portion of the bay. The wrist and ankle couplings were set in open positions.

"What've you learned so far?" Tyne inquired brusquely, while continuing to scrutinize the locking couplings. "Clearly the Eastern League has the most to gain from an act such as this."

Garret smiled at Tyne's attempt to assert her dominance over the situation. "First things first, Director," he replied, careless in his attempt to sound cordial. "For the first time in history, a Peacekeeper war machine is missing, presumed stolen. I've seen these puppies in action firsthand, and I don't have to tell you the security risk this situation poses to the Great City Confederation and its citizens. Even though Supervisor Phelps informed us that the machine housed in this alcove was discovered to be damaged beyond repair by a tech last night, in the wrong hands, it may still pose a significant danger. I assume the AIA has fail-safe measures in place for just such a contingency?"

Tyne glared up at Garret. "Of course, Chief Garret. As soon as the warbot left this facility in an unauthorized capacity, its internal warheads were automatically disarmed, and other internal weapons' systems temporarily disabled. I'll need to link with Optinet on its Solar Positioning System tracking device to determine how that fail-safe mechanism was disabled. As soon as I'm able, I'll provide the Guild with the modulation frequency needed to penetrate the Peacekeeper's body shielding. However, even with the modulation frequency, your officers will need to exercise extreme caution in the event that the war machine has been reanimated by its captors and they're forced to confront it."

Garret nodded. "Thank you for your concern, Director. I'll brief my officers accordingly."

"Yes, yes," Tyne said with a dismissive wave. She turned to examine the alcove again. "Now, if I may have that report on your findings?"

Bok received Garret's nod of approval. "Nothing terribly significant so far, I'm afraid, Director." He motioned toward the vacant alcove. "As you can see, there are char marks here and here from the alcove power fluctuation that caused the fusing of the unit's neural architecture. Otherwise, there are no overt signs of physical damage to the bay or to the locking clamps. The thieves were either able to crack the locking mechanism codes, or—"

Tyne's nostrils flared. "Impossible!" she declared. "Those are infinite-sequence codes, GI. It would take the solar system's most powerful sequencer two to three hours to decode them. And I assume automated security was active last night?"

Taim nodded. "A full baryon sweep once per hour, ma'am, making it impossible for the thieves to hook up a sequencer and accomplish the task between sweeps."

Sands interjected: "Which leads us to believe at least at this stage in the investigation, Director, that this must've been an inside job."

"An inside job?" Tyne's interest piqued at a new level.

Sands knelt down beside her. "Take a closer look at the locking couplings, Director. Not a scratch on them, not a sign of stress. That's not the typical work of Eastern League Sand Force operatives. It's as if the thieves knew the access codes and simply plugged the numbers into the display panel, popping open the clamps. The same can be said for the main laboratory doors and the doors leading to the parking structure. All of them have similar infinite-sequence locking mechanisms, and none of them show any signs of having been forced open. Forensics discovered traces of a bivalent metallic element on the floor in a path from here to the laboratory exit, as if the Peacekeeper were dragged out of the building."

"Were traces of any other compounds found?" Tyne asked as she removed her touchpad from her lab coat pocket and began tapping at its surface.

Sands responded. "Negative, Director; nothing. This contributes to our initial theory that this was done by someone on the inside. The lab slips typically worn by AI techs leave no trace residue in their path. The perpetrator or perpetrators may have been wearing them during the theft."

"Which is why we're particularly glad you're here this morning, Director Tyne," Chief Garret intervened, with an edge of sarcasm in his voice, "unexpectedly, I might add."

Tyne shot an agitated look in Garret's direction as she explained, "Surprise inspections of Peacekeeper facilities are standard AIA practice, Chief Garret." She continued to enter data from the alcove display into her touchpad as she went on. "As the top man of the organization and the one responsible for overseeing security here, I would expect you to know that fact well enough. There are times when it's advantageous for my office to be unaware of my schedule in order to insure the secrecy and effectiveness of my inspections. Besides, keeping tabs on your own personnel doesn't exactly seem to be your strong suit either, given recent Optinet reports concerning several of your security officers."

"Be that as it may," Garret said, without the slightest acknowledgment of her accusation touching his tone. "Supervisor Phelps has informed us that the recent termination of AI Technician Costa Bashere was by your specific recommendation, and, as I'm sure you're aware, Director, disgruntled former employees—especially ones as recently disgruntled as Technician Bashere—are prime candidates for retribution of this nature against their former employers. Therefore, anything you can tell us about Mr. Bashere and the reason for his termination may be helpful to the investigation."

Tyne's expression was flat, giving nothing away. *Garret's probing me. He has a hunch. I'll have to lay down some cover fire,* she calculated.

"It's really quite simple, Chief Garret," Tyne said, still kneeling in front of the alcove. "Technician Bashere completed several Peacekeeper examinations earlier this week and failed to report the results to his supervisor in a timely manner."

"Wow," Bok said absentmindedly. "The poor guy got canned for that?"

Tyne glared at him. "This is no aircar repair shop, GI. This is a Peacekeeper diagnostics lab. The misdiagnosis of a warbot's fitness for duty may result in the catastrophic loss of human life and property once it returns to its post. The very security of our great confederation rides upon the AI tech's accuracy, consistency, and efficiency in his work."

"Yes, ma'am," Taim said apologetically. "I didn't mean—"

"I'm sure you didn't," Tyne said as she went back to punching keys on her touchpad.

"There's one other thing, Director," Garret said, his tone bearing the demeanor of an afterthought.

Tyne remained at the foot of the alcove and did not turn around.

She merely slowed her keystroking and rotated her head until an ear was flush to Garret's location behind her.

"Supervisor Phelps informed us that you *personally* performed an examination on the missing Peacekeeper late last night and that Technician Bashere was fired over reporting issues dealing with that same unit—unit MP^C^–014/083, to be precise. And, according to the night-shift tech on duty last night, this same warbot had been damaged beyond repair by an alcove malfunction. Now, doesn't it seem odd to you that in a room full of perfectly operating war machines, thieves would opt to take the one inoperable unit on the premises? It could be nothing, of course, Director, but we may need to speak with you further about these matters. Will it be advantageous for your office to know your whereabouts over the next twenty-four hours?" It was another premeditated jibe designed to elicit an emotional reaction.

It worked, if only internally. *There's no way Garret could know what I've done,* Tyne reasoned, *but clearly he'll be a force to be reckoned with. At minimum, I've learned that much about him.*

Tyne slowly turned and rose to a standing position. She stepped offensively closer to Garret. She pocketed her touchpad and removed her glasses, tilting her head back to look Garret squarely in the eyes. "Let me make something perfectly clear, Chief Garret," she said forcefully. "I want to be kept apprised of any and all discovery in this investigation, right down to the smallest detail. This case is by no means exclusively under Guild Protectorate jurisdiction; it has clear and present relevance to the Artificial Intelligence Agency and to the office of the sovereign overlord itself."

Tyne's eyes shifted between Garret's. He returned her gaze with a steady indifference, his eyes at half-mast.

"We thank you for your help, Director Tyne," Sands said, diplomatically stepping between the chief and the director in an attempt to keep things civil. She guided Tyne away from Garret. "I think it's safe to say that, operable or not, it's in all of our best interests to locate the missing machine with all due speed, Director. Rest assured, the Guild will keep you informed of every aspect of this most critical investigation."

Tyne smoothed the front of her lab coat with the palms of her hands. "See that you do," she demanded plainly. And with a final stabbing glance in Garret's direction, she turned and headed for the exit.

CHAPTER 6

TECHNICIAN BASHERE

AND-gate inhibitors: Micromechanically-machined
devices placed at critical junctures within the neural
architecture of the quantum logic brains of Peacekeeper
war machines that serve to block their higher cognitive
functions. Inventor: neuroroboticist, Emma Tyne.

—*Cyber's Dictionary of Modern
Scientific Terminology, 11th ed.*
(Great City: Great City University Press, 2452),
s.v. "AND-gate inhibitors."

GUILD PROTECTORATE HEADQUARTERS, CITY CENTER

"HY WERE YOU FIRED, MR. BASHERE?"
AI Technician Costa Bashere sat in a stainless
steel chair at a stainless steel table that had been bolted to the floor. He
blinked up at the three Guild Protectorate officers who occupied the
small interrogation room with him, trying to read their faces for the
reason for his incarceration. The two investigators—Gallina Sands and
Taim Bok—sat in chairs on either side of him. Veteran Guild Bureau
Chief Arnaud Garret sat in a shadowed corner of the room. He leaned

casually against the wall, his arms crossed, a shiny black Guild-insignia coffee mug in his hand.

Bashere began tentatively: "With all due respect, Investigator Sands, before I answer your question, may I inquire as to the reason I am here?"

"Not at this time, I'm afraid, Mr. Bashere," Sands denied him firmly. "Right now, we simply need you to cooperate in this investigation. So, please, respond to the question: why were you fired from Coreland Corporation yesterday?"

Bashere's gaze dropped to the chrome tabletop. "I find it difficult to talk about, Investigator."

Sands prodded, "Please, Mr. Bashere. It's important that you answer the question."

Bashere lifted his gaze to meet hers. The mothering tone she had generated with her last response seemed to have broken through his defenses.

He began slowly. "You see, Investigator Sands, I have worked at Coreland since completing my AIA certification, nearly ten years ago, now. The AI technician position is a highly desirable and typically permanent assignment, you see. Once the Artificial Intelligence Agency places you at a Peacekeeper facility, you are typically there for your entire career. Very few facility technicians leave their jobs; fewer still lose them. It is a shameful mark on my record, one which I will have to shoulder all of my days."

Costa Bashere was a thin, smallish man. He had light brown skin and dark brown eyes, and a large red spot in the white part of his left eye that looked like the Giant Red Storm on Jupiter. He had a splotchy black mustache and several thin strands of black hair pasted across the top of his otherwise bald head. He wore a light blue short-sleeved shirt, with some embossed scroll work on a vertical strip where the buttons were. His voice had a distinct sing-song quality about it.

Bok leaned forward. "All very intriguing stuff, Mr. Bashere, but you still haven't answered my partner's question."

Bashere looked up at Investigator Bok, aghast at the directness of his words. His expression was like that of a dog who'd just been struck on the nose for a wrong he hadn't committed. "Perhaps if I knew what this was all about, Investigator Bok," Bashere blinked during a measured pause, "I would be more inclined to—"

"Your inclinations are not important here, Mr. Bashere," Taim told him emphatically. "Your full and immediate cooperation is."

Bashere fidgeted in his chair, eyeing the two Guild officers one at a time. "I am not trying to be difficult, you see, Investigators. I am merely a bit confused by all of this, that's all. You desire to know the reason I was terminated. Very well. I was terminated because I," he paused again, lowering his head in shame, "because I withheld information from my supervisor."

"What sort of information, Mr. Bashere?"

The technician looked up weakly at Taim, his expression riddled with regret. "Diagnostic test results."

"What sort of diagnostic test results?"

Bashere cringed in his chair, seemingly beaten down by Taim's poignant gaze. He acted as if he were not going to answer the question.

"What sort of diagnostic test results, Mr. Bashere?" Taim repeated more forcefully.

Still, the distressed tech failed to respond.

"I suggest you find your tongue, Bashere," Taim warned, rapping the table with his fist, "or you may soon become accustomed to seeing your wife and kids exclusively through a plate of blaster-proof glass!"

Sands motioned to stay her partner's escalating intolerance. She scooted her chair closer to the tech. Both she and Taim were still wearing the black battle fatigues circumstances had dictated they don earlier that morning. "Costa," she said, smiling warmly at the diminutive man, "understand: We've verified your alibi from last night; it's been confirmed without suspicion by several credible witnesses. You're no longer a suspect in the investigation that we're conducting here tonight. You're now just a Great City citizen doing your duty in a very important Guild Protectorate investigation. Do you understand?"

Bashere's lower lip was quivering, his eyes glistening with fresh moisture, his emotions seemingly wavering in that delicate state between fear and intimidation. He blinked his understanding of what Sands had said, but it didn't seem to relieve his anxiety in any measurable way.

He stammered, "I, uh, I am afraid to say any more."

"What is it you're afraid of, Costa?" Sands said, taking on the mothering tone again.

He wiped the beading sweat from his brow. "I cannot say any more," he insisted. "I realize what you are asking, Miss Sands, but for the sake of my family and my future employment, I can speak no further of this matter."

A certain darkness touched Bashere's eyes. He averted his gaze from Sands's and stared at the smoke-colored mirror that covered one wall of the interrogation room. "It is the AIA, you see," he whispered ominously. "It is a very, very powerful organization—more powerful than you know. Director Tyne reports directly to the sovereign overlord himself, and I am bound by oath to her and to the agency."

"Director Tyne holds my future in her hands," Bashere continued. "She is my only chance of ever being reinstated as a technician at Coreland, or any other Peacekeeper facility. She is my only chance of ever being able to support my family with dignity again, you see, and because of what has happened, I am certain my AIA certification is in serious jeopardy of being revoked."

"I think we're all a little confused, here, Mr. Bashere," Taim said. "With your training and experience, I'm sure you're more than qualified to fill any number of positions in the field of applied robotics, perhaps not in the government sector at a Peacekeeper facility, but just about anywhere else in the private sector. Other than not being able to use Director Tyne as a reference for your next job interview, what've you to fear from her or from the AIA?"

Again Bashere didn't appear willing to go any further. Sands held up a hand to stop her partner from jumping down Bashere's throat again. She decided to alter the angle of questioning. "You were fired by Director Tyne, is that correct, Costa?"

Bashere nodded.

"But you were an employee of Coreland Corporation, and you reported to Supervisor Phelps. Why was it *Director Tyne* who fired you?"

"All AI technicians are technically employed by the Artificial Intelligence Agency, you see. We are required to be certified members of the AIA in order to work at a Peacekeeper facility. At certification, we take an oath of loyalty to the agency. You see, the AIA has a network of, for lack of a better term, talent agents. These agents scout tech-adept individuals from universities, recruit them, train them, place them, and maintain them."

"By maintain them, you mean maintain their job efficiency?" Sands asked.

"Precisely. The agency requires continuing education for all technicians and conducts regular performance reviews, and by direct decree of Overlord Ocaba, Director Tyne has unilateral jurisdiction on all Peacekeeper facility matters, whether they have to do with the war machines themselves or with the employees. Basically, Emma Tyne can do anything she wants, you see, with or without the approval of the laboratory supervisor."

"The Guild will protect you, Costa," Sands said. "If for some reason you're afraid to tell us what you know about Director Tyne, the AIA, or the reasons for your termination, we can assign a security detail to protect you and your family wherever you go—permanently, if necessary. Now, please, it's important that you answer Investigator Bok's question: what sort of diagnostic results did you withhold from your supervisor?"

"Very well, Miss Sands," Bashere said, reluctance etching his tone. "The test results I withheld concerned highly unusual neuropsychotic patterns recorded during an examination of a particular Peacekeeper war machine."

"Neuropsychotic patterns?"

"Brain waves, Miss Sands," Bashere clarified. "Essentially, neuropsychotic patterns within the quantum logic brains of Peacekeepers are the equivalent of brain waves within carbon-based life forms. One of the Peacekeepers alcoved at the lab transmitted brain waves, which suggested…" He stopped.

"Go on, Costa."

He stared up at Sands with a depth of expression he had yet to exhibit during the interrogation. "It is complicated, Miss Sands. You see, our diagnostic tests on Peacekeeper war machines involve complex algorithm and mathematical pattern analyses of their neural architecture. It is the solemn duty of the AI technician to insure that all Peacekeepers' brain functions remain within the strict parameters that exist in the prototype brain of Dr. Hugo's original creation."

Bok spoke for the first time in minutes. "Doctor who?"

"Doctor Xavier Hugo. The man considered to be the father of artificial intelligence. Hugo engineered the first humanoid machine possessing all the physical and mental faculties of man. Hugo's prototype creation has served as the template from which all Peacekeepers have been manufactured. Even the slightest deviation from the parameters set forth in the neural architecture of Hugo's original creation may result in a Peacekeeper demonstrating errant behavior, which in turn may lead to catastrophic consequences when the unit is sent back to its duties."

"We're not asking for a crash course in applied robotics, Bashere," Taim said curtly. "We're simply asking what the test results meant."

The swirling red spot drifted across the white of Bashere's eye. "Frankly, I am not exactly certain what the results meant. I did not have time to fully analyze them. All I was able to determine was that several AND-gate inhibitors had been removed from the frontal lobe region of the unit's neural architecture."

"AND-gate inhibitors?"

"Mechanisms which inhibit certain higher brain functions in Peacekeeper war machines. Director Tyne designed them and installed them as fail-safe protocols when Hugo's creation was re-engineered for military purposes and mass produced."

"That's the information you decided to withhold from your supervisor?" Taim slammed his fist on the table. "No wonder you got the boot!"

Sands bristled at the insensitivity of her partner and spoke soothingly to Bashere. "Well then, Costa, since you knew the diagnostic results had something to do with safety protocols, what possessed you to withhold them from your supervisor?"

Bashere's tightlipped silence returned.

Taim drummed his fingers on the table, shaking his head in frustration. He demanded sharply, "Answer her, Bashere."

Despite Bok's full-court press, Bashere wasn't willing to go further.

"You've been patient with us tonight, Technician," Chief Garret said, ending his silent observation of the proceedings. He used his back to push himself off the wall and out of the shadows. He still wore his black muscle shirt and camouflage-patterned pants. He took a casual sip from his mug and sauntered over toward the table where Bashere sat. "You've allowed us to drag you out of bed in the middle of the night. You've endured the public humiliation of being tossed into the back of a Guild cruiser in plain view of your neighbors. And, remarkably, the first words out of your mouth when you stepped into this room had nothing whatsoever to do with demanding the presence of your lawyer."

Garret's tone and demeanor would best be described as calm. He may as well have been reading the day's financial data from the System Stock Exchange to the man. He appeared to be simply releasing his words harmlessly into the ether, but there was an undercurrent of intimidation attached to them that would've jangled the nerves of the most hardened criminal.

Garret set his mug down on the table without a sound. "I respect that," he said, smiling, "and I appreciate that more than you know. For that very reason, I'm going to tell you more than you probably should know about the reason for your unexpected visit to Guild HQ and to the confines of this lovely little interrogation room. Unbeknownst to you, Mr. Bashere, or to any of the fine Great City citizens tucked away warmly in their beds, a Peacekeeper war machine was discovered to be missing from its alcove at Coreland Corporation early this morning."

Garret watched Bashere's reaction most carefully. Opportunity's daylight, as he liked to call it, would be brief in this instance. The finest thespian, however, couldn't have produced a more genuine response. Costa Bashere's eyes went wide with disbelief, then quickly narrowed in realization of the seriousness of the chief's words. "Missing?" he said disbelievingly. "But that is not possible. Facility security measures—"

"—have been compromised," Garret finished the sentence. "And as a result, one of the GCC's elite mechanical soldiers is unaccounted for. Now, certainly you can understand our concern that this multibillion-credit fighting machine with enough firepower to singlehandedly destroy a small country may be out there in the hands of some lunatic. Certainly, you can understand that the very security of the Great City Confederation may be at risk, here."

Bashere appeared bewildered by Garret's words. His eyes darted to and fro across the surface of the table, trying to sort out the ramifications of all the chief was saying.

"I can see you're starting to get the picture here, Mr. Bashere. I can see you're starting to understand why these fine young investigators are so intent on getting some answers out of you tonight."

Bashere quivered visibly in his chair. He took a moment to collect himself, then nodded slowly at the chief.

Garret realized then and there that Bashere was holding back much more from them than he'd first suspected. Garret had conducted hundreds of interrogations in his eighteen years with the Guild, observed the speech patterns and non-verbal reactions of every variety of criminal. He was prepared to stake his reputation on the following conclusion: Costa Bashere was no thief. Nor was he an accomplice to a thief, nor a collaborator in a crime of any sort. It was doubtful the guy ever ran a hoverlight or spit gum on an airwalk, but for some reason, he was holding his ground and not cooperating fully with them.

By Garret's estimation, Bashere's body held a tightness that went beyond the circumstances of finding himself professionally disgraced, without a job, and sitting in a Guild interrogation room. There was something else there—some new, as-yet-unrevealed tangent to this investigation that warranted exploration. Garret needed a jawbreaker.

Garret said with a flourish, "Mr. Bashere, I'm going to be completely honest with you. Investigators Sands and Bok, the full resources of the Guild Protectorate, and I have been at this investigation non-stop since the Peacekeeper was discovered missing this morning, and it's now, what, nearly midnight? A virtual parade of bad guys have preceded you into this room: terrorists, suspected Eastern League Sand Force members, arms dealers, weapons experts, informants, and so forth. They've all been smoked out of their holes by the men and women of the Guild and brought here to HQ to have a little chat with me and these fine officers. They've all sat in the very chair that you now occupy, some sweating more than even you, my friend. Along with Miss Sands and Mr. Bok, I've been forced to breathe their mangy, un-bathed stench for hours on end. And do you know what we have to show for our efforts, Mr. Bashere?"

Bashere gulped hard, and nervously returned Garret's stare.

"You guessed it, my friend," Garret fumed. "Nothing. Not a shred of evidence, not a single substantial lead to go on." The chief paused for a moment. He held up an index finger. "Except one. And guess which one of that chair's occupants has provided this shred of evidence, Techni-cian? Guess which one of the Great City citizens who've graced us with their presence this night has coughed up our one substantial lead?"

Bashere could no longer hold the chief's stare. He averted his eyes to the tabletop.

"The most unlikely one," Garret said simply. "You, Mr. Bashere. Now, I'm about to disclose some things to you that must be kept in the strictest confidence, things that must never leave the confines of this room. Is that clear?"

Bashere nodded his acceptance of Garret's request.

"After you failed," Garret paused and leaned in close to Bashere, "because that's what you did, now wasn't it, Mr. Bashere? For what-ever reason, you failed to fulfill your sworn duty as an AI tech by not reporting those test results to your supervisor." Garret read all the confirmation he needed in the evasive movements of the tech's eyes. "After you failed for the first time in your long career to report the so-called highly unusual diagnostic test results to your supervisor, Supervisor Phelps turned right around and placed a call to Director Tyne at AIA headquarters and asked that she immediately come to the lab to assess the situation. Director Tyne arrived at the lab and proceeded to terminate your employment. That much you know. What you don't know is that according to Supervisor Phelps, Director Tyne spent the better part of last night conducting an in-depth examination on the very same Peacekeeper that registered those highly unusual diagnostic test results that you failed to report, a unit designated as Peacekeeper MP^C–014/083."

Bashere looked as if he was holding back a reaction to this information.

"After Tyne's departure from the lab," Garret went on, "this same Peacekeeper was discovered by one of your fellow technicians to be damaged beyond repair, its neural architecture turned into oatmeal by some sort of mysterious alcove malfunction. And—this is where it really gets fun, Mr. Bashere—this same Peacekeeper just happens to be the very same unit that turned up missing from the lab early this morning."

"The same machine?" Bashere blurted out. He blinked up shockingly at Garret. "But that is not possible."

"You're right, Bashere," Garret said. "It's not possible. It's a fact!"

Garret stared down at the little man, a certain wildness touching in his eyes. "Are you starting to see a pattern, here, Mr. Bashere? As an AI tech, you made your living analyzing different types of patterns. So, tell me, are you beginning to see a pattern emerging out of this investigation?"

Bashere could no longer mask a reaction to what he'd heard. His expression sickened noticeably. "Why, I do believe you're beginning to see where we're heading with this stuff," Garret concluded, "aren't you, *Costa?*"

Garret's pronunciation of the tech's name had clearly been designed to make a mockery of it. This slip was out of character for Garret. It was a sign to the investigators that their chief was under immense pressure from his superiors to solve the mystery of the missing machine before Optinet got hold of it and embarrassed the Guild, the AIA, and the office of the sovereign overlord. Garret broke off his stare and began to pace around the room.

"You see, Mr. Bashere," Garrett continued, "the question which seems to be emerging, here, if I may steep you a bit further into our little investigation for a moment," he added with a mock irenic gesture, "is: why all the fuss over this one Peacekeeper war machine?

"Well, first of all, I find it *highly unusual* that in a laboratory full of Peacekeeper war machines, thieves opt to liberate the only inoperable one in the lot. And secondly, I find it *highly* unusual that this Peacekeeper just happens to be the selfsame machine that you lost your job over the day before because of your uncharacteristic failure to report the aforementioned neuropsychotic patterns to your supervisor—patterns that even you, a highly-trained AI technician, seem unable to fully comprehend the full meaning of.

"And, finally, I find it highly unusual that this Peacekeeper also happens to be the very same unit that the highest-ranking member of the AIA completes a thorough examination on mere hours before its mysterious destruction and equally mysterious disappearance. Now, check me if I'm wrong, here, Technician, but there seem to be a lot of highly unusual things associated with this one MP-class Peacekeeper war machine. In fact, I think it's safe to say, Costa, that in this investigation, all roads lead directly to this one warbot!"

Garret hadn't meant to allow his aggression to surface, but once it had, he saw no reason to keep it from stretching its legs. He moved to a position behind Bashere and placed his thick-fingered hands on the table with a thump, straddling him.

"Now, I'm asking you directly, former Technician," he said, gritting his teeth and leaning in close to Bashere's right ear, "what's so special about this one Peacekeeper war machine?"

A fresh burst of sweat glistened on Bashere's forehead. His

expression wilted further, his eyes fluttered and rolled back in his head as if he were slipping into a coma. "You, you will forgive me," Bashere stuttered, shaking visibly in his chair. "But I am currently an unemployed technician with a rather dim future ahead of me. You mentioned that I am no longer a suspect in the investigation, and as much as this may displease you, Chief Garret, I am afraid that I would like to speak with my lawyer before answering any more of your questions. So, I ask that you release me, please, so that I may return home to my family."

Considering the former technician's obvious lack of holistic soundness, Garret knew that for now Bashere wouldn't be of much further use to the investigation. Besides, with Bashere's water-tight alibi, Garret knew full well that he had no legal right to question him further, nor to hold him any longer. He motioned at the smoke-colored mirror.

Moments later, the heavy metal door of the interrogation room clanged open.

Supporting Bashere at the elbow, Sands helped the distraught, disoriented man to his feet, and escorted him out of the room.

CHAPTER 7

GUILD SUSPICIONS

Just War Act: A Supreme-Assembly-ratified act (November 2442) that places restrictions on the type of military actions nations may employ during the course of future wars. Specifically, the Just War Act criminalizes so-called 'faceless' or 'safe-distance' wartime tactics, and mandates the deployment of ground-based troops in sufficient number to defend the local populace against the retaliatory actions of rebellious factions. The deployment of non-sanctioned tactics constitutes a breach of interstellar law and carries with it severe penalties for the nation that employs them.

—Optinet link: ssww.gcc.gov/-just war act/-info

CHIEF GARRET'S OFFICE, GUILD PROTECTORATE HEADQUARTERS, CITY CENTER

COMMENTS."

Chief Garret tore a meaty hunk out of his sandwich and waited for observations from his young investigators. To Investigators Sands and Bok, it'd been the type of day that had demanded such intensity and diversity of activity that it was hard to believe the events that had occurred thus far had actually taken place within an eighteen-hour period. From the extensive investigation at Coreland early this morning to the nonstop parade of suspects and sources passing through the interrogation room, a high level of mental acuity had been required. The result was a pair of dulled wits and slower-than-normal reaction time to their chief's request.

Bok was the first to jumpstart the appropriate synapses in his brain and respond. "One thing's for certain, Chief, something or *someone* has put the fear of the Queen Mother into the poor little fellow."

As it had a way of doing, Garret's silence demanded immediate exposition of the point.

"Well, it's not every day that a Great City citizen has the chance to interface with three Guild Protectorate officers," Bok explained. "That can be quite an intimidating experience, especially for a mild-mannered individual like Costa Bashere. However, Bashere showed incredible resolve in refusing to answer our questions, which means that he either possesses nerves of steel—and given the performance we just saw, I think we can safely rule that out—or he has the unshakable belief in his mind that the consequences of breaking ranks with Director Tyne and the AIA are greater than the consequences of not cooperating fully with our investigation."

Sands nodded. "Agreed. Bashere demonstrated an unnaturally resolute fear of Director Tyne and the AIA. He was obviously afraid to lose his agency certification."

"But if that's the case, Investigators," Garret offered, "what would possess a man so fearful of losing his AIA certification to withhold important information from his supervisor—placing his job, his certification, and his career in such jeopardy?"

Sands furrowed her brow. "I know it seems ludicrous, but I got the distinct impression during the interrogation that Bashere was actually trying to protect the Peacekeeper that recorded the so-called highly unusual neuropsychotic patterns."

Bok nodded his agreement. "I know that was somewhat technical stuff Bashere was spewing out in there, Chief, but still, he was being quite vague in his details. He made no effort to explain why he chose to withhold knowledge of the unusual patterns or of the removal of the AND-gate inhibitors from his supervisor."

"I'd call it more than a little vague, GI," Garret said then washed down a bite of sandwich with a slug of coffee. "Think of it: a tech without a blemish on his record for nearly twenty years is suddenly withholding safety-oriented test results from his supervisor. Not only that, but did you gauge his reaction when I informed him of the fact that the Peacekeeper that had recorded the unusual patterns and the missing Peacekeeper are one and the same machine? Bashere *was* trying to protect Peacekeeper MP^C-014/083; you can bank on it. Now all we have to do is figure out why."

Bok raised an eyebrow at Garret and treaded cautiously. "Not to question your methods, but why are the test results from the missing machine so important? I mean, shouldn't we be more concerned with searching for—"

Garret stopped him with a look. "The AIA has confirmed that the Peacekeeper's solar positioning system tracking device has been disabled, Investigator, and Guild Forensics hasn't turned up so much as an unauthorized voiceprint residue from the lab at Coreland. The fact that Technician Bashere stuck to his guns and protected the Peacekeeper despite the intimidating surroundings of this interrogation room and three Guild officers breathing down his neck, and the fact that Director Tyne was so promptly called in by Supervisor Phelps to terminate Bashere and examine the unit—"

"Tyne!" Sands shouted. "That's it!"

Her outburst succeeded in getting Bok and Garret's immediate attention.

"That's what, Sands?" Bok asked.

"That's who said it!" Sands replied.

"Said what?"

"During the interrogation, Technician Bashere mentioned something about the AIA being a powerful organization and that Director Tyne reports directly to the sovereign overlord himself. I just remembered where I heard that phrase before."

Bok wrinkled his nose. "What in blazes are you talking about?"

"Outside Coreland this morning," Sands said, directing her explanation to Chief Garret. "As I went out to greet Director Tyne in the parking structure, I'm almost sure I overheard her telling one of the security guards that she was there on direct orders from the sovereign overlord himself."

"On orders from the overlord?" Garret repeated. "Are you certain you heard correctly, GI?"

"Ninety-eight percent, sir. I remember thinking how odd it seemed that that would be the case. It just didn't make sense. For what purpose would Overlord Ocaba have *ordered* Director Tyne to Coreland this morning?"

Bok chimed in, "Come to think of it, there was something odd in Tyne's explanation as to why she hadn't notified her office of her whereabouts."

"Yeah," Sands agreed. "She said something about it not being advantageous for her office to know her schedule at certain times."

A realization seemed to strike investigator Bok square in the chest. "Director Tyne's slip-up with the security guard wasn't her only one of the morning."

"We're listening."

"It's that old investigators' axiom from training, sir," Bok began. "'Never take anything for granted during an investigation, no matter how trivial it may seem.' Think about it, Sands. After our meeting with Phelps, without even discussing it, we allowed Director Tyne to lead the way into the laboratory this morning, and—"

"She walked straight to the scene of the crime!" Sands bounced with excitement.

"Bingo!" Bok smiled.

Garret shrugged. "But by that time Tyne had been informed that a Peacekeeper had been discovered missing from its alcove, and she'd just been in the lab the night before. She knew which alcoves were filled and which were unoccupied. Tyne probably saw the grouping of Guild personnel around the vacant alcove, discerned the obvious, and walked straight to it."

Sands shook her head. "There were a number of empty alcoves in the lab this morning, Chief, and a number of clusters of Guild personnel gathered at various locations. Director Tyne ignored all of the other groups and made a beeline for the far corner of the lab, where the missing Peacekeeper had been alcoved."

"Not to mention the fact that Tyne was strangely remiss in informing us that the missing Peacekeeper was the very machine that she'd been summoned by Phelps to examine the day before," Bok added. "You had to not-so-subtly remind the director of her rendezvous with Peacekeeper MP^C-014/083. Remember, Chief?"

Garret massaged the stubble of his beard. "So what are you suggesting, Investigators? That the director of the Artificial Intelligence Agency, the well-respected leader of that organization, actually had some foreknowledge of the disappearance of the war machine?"

"Perhaps not a foreknowledge," Sands said, thoughtfully. "The director seemed as shocked as anyone when she learned the reason for the Guild presence at the lab this morning. It seemed more a trepidation."

"Agreed," Bok said. "When we entered the lab, Director Tyne acted as if she had a fearful premonition of which Peacekeeper would turn out to be the missing one."

Chief Garret ground his teeth behind tight lips. "There's something about the missing Peacekeeper that no one seems willing to talk about," he seethed. "Bashere certainly isn't telling us everything he knows, and Director Tyne wasn't exactly being forthright with us, either."

"Seems to be the theme of this investigation," Sands observed.

Garret narrowed his eyes at his investigators. "I want you two to pay a little visit to the offices of the AIA. See if the director is in a better mood now, and if she's ready for full disclosure concerning the missing warbot. And find out which rock this Dr. Xavier Hugo character, the infamous father of artificial intelligence that Bashere mentioned, is hiding under. I want to talk to him at his earliest convenience, but be discreet, *extremely* discreet. Follow your investigators' axiom well, officers. Take nothing for granted. If the overlord is involved in our little mystery of the missing machine in some way, we may be biting off more than we can chew."

With that, Chief Garret shoved the last of his sandwich into his mouth. He brushed the crumbs from his hands and dismissed his investigators by pointing stiffly at the door. "I need answers, GIs. You're not the only ones with their feet to the fire in this investigation."

CHAPTER 8

SON of MAN

"At the root of these and other scientific discoveries, we're beginning to catch glimpses of a universal truth—a Grand Unifying Theory of Everything, as it has been called. Our knowledge of the physical laws, forces, and particles that govern the cosmos is becoming increasingly coherent and universal, such that we're beginning to suspect that all of this, all that we see before us, is not some accident of nature. Instead, it seems to have been intelligently designed with amazing simplicity, continuity, beauty, and majesty. The lines are converging from many diverse regions of thought, from philosophy and paleontology to relativity and religion. And these lines imply a common starting point to which all explanations can be traced; a singularity point of reason that cannot be defined in terms of a deeper truth. It's this last line of reason, this last line of truth—this Ultimate Truth—that we seek."

—XAVIER HUGO
Project 'Emissary' Senate Appropriation Committee hearing
transcript excerpt, November 5, 2442

SOVEREIGN OVERLORD OCABA'S OFFICE, CITY CENTER

THE AGED LEADER OF THE GREAT CITY CONFEDeration sat huddled at his desk, a cold lump of darkness in the dim yellow light of his office. The ticking of an Old Age clock in the corner was clearly audible, such was the level of silence in the room. Director Tyne appeared reticent, having to face the certain disappointment of her overlord. One night earlier she'd been the triumphant hero, catching their nemesis, Dr. Xavier Hugo, in the act of initiating his promised plan of vengeance against Vaughn Ocaba for what he'd done to him eleven and one-half years ago at the Senate Appropriation Hearing. But as a result of events that had transpired over the past twenty-four hours, by all accounts she'd failed in her secret mission as director of the façade organization known as the Artificial Intelligence Agency—failed, at least for now, to definitively end the clear and present danger the emergence of a sentient machine presented to the Great City Confederation, to the ongoing peace process, and to the solar system at large.

Ocaba had been under tremendous pressure of late. The political hero of the Great War and miracle-negotiator of the Divided Temple Peace Accord was in danger of seeing all that he'd worked for crumble before his eyes. Tensions were mounting in the east and in the north. Peacekeepers at their posts throughout the solar system were being assaulted by Eastern League factions. The stress was taking its toll on the overlord physically and mentally. Clearly, he did not need the complication of the missing war machine—fused neural architecture or not—added to the mix.

Ocaba's advisors had already informed him of the shocking news of what had transpired at Coreland early that morning. Thus, it was no surprise that he'd summoned Director Tyne to his office for an urgent meeting. A Peacekeeper war machine had been discovered missing from its alcove, but no one except Director Tyne and Overlord Ocaba—and, if their suspicions were correct, Dr. Xavier Hugo—could share in the full magnitude of the news.

"How much do they know?" Ocaba rasped. Low, rumbling sounds could be heard in his chest cavity as he spoke, and his breathing sounded labored. He seemed to be restraining himself, as if guarding against another episode of coughing.

"Naturally, the Guild suspects Sand Force operatives," Tyne

informed him. "The Eastern League's hatred for Peacekeepers occupying their land runs deeper than the gorge at Tarsus Mons. They regard them as mechanical demons keeping a peace that none of them desire. The Guild believes it may have been League Sand Force operatives who had help from someone on the inside. My sources have informed me that they're questioning a recently terminated AI technician named Costa Bashere as we speak. Otherwise, Garret has run the gamut on the usual suspects."

Tyne stared at Ocaba's shadowed figure seated at his desk, waiting for some sort of reaction to what she'd just said. Instead, he just sat motionless in his chair. He seemed a far different man than the one who'd been elected sovereign overlord of the Great City Confederation nearly seven years ago. The former war hero had emerged onto the political scene with all of the zeal of a man committed to making a difference, and right out of the chute while still a brash young senator, he'd pulled off the coup of the century, the legal circumvention of the newly enacted Just War Act. His clever exploitation of Hugo's creation at the now-infamous Senate Appropriation Committee hearing and the subsequent mass production of the system's first all-mechanized army, had saved countless lives during the course of the Great War—and there was nothing the Eastern League could've done to prevent it. The deployment of the Peacekeepers in no way violated the modernized rules of war as set forth within the provisions of the Just War Act. Ocaba's war machines were legal and had been instrumental in winning the Great War for the Western nations.

Following the conclusion of the Great War and buoyed by his savvy maneuver with Hugo's machine, Ocaba spearheaded the formation of the Great City Confederation, a powerful new confederation of ten western nations. He was elected to the newly created post of sovereign overlord, establishing his governmental offices at the heart of the Great City itself. Capitalizing on his success, Ocaba then pulled off a political miracle for the ages, the negotiation of the Divided Temple Peace Accord. The accord brought stability and peace for a time to a region that had experienced little of either in its millennia-old history and laid the groundwork for the construction of a new divided temple on the ancient stone platform of the Temple Mount at the center of the Old City District.

Yet, Ocaba's mental faculties seemed dulled in comparison to the man who'd orchestrated these military and political triumphs, his mind less fertile with ideas and creative solutions to problems such as the one confronting them now. Physically, he looked even worse than he had the night before—paler and his facial features more compressed, as if gravity had deliberately chosen to double up on his skeletal structure. His once-stone-etched jaw line appeared rounded and soft in the yellow light.

"And what of you?" Ocaba grunted finally. "Are you a suspect in the Guild's investigation, Miss Tyne?"

Tyne smoothed the front of her lab coat with the palms of her hands. She shook her head in the negative as she answered, "Not directly, sir, but it's clear that Garret plans to question me further concerning the missing machine."

"For what purpose?"

Tyne read the concern in the overlord's tone. "Let me assure you, sir, Garret doesn't know the extent of recent events surrounding the unit's atypical behavior, but it was clear that he didn't fully accept my explanation as to why I neglected to notify my office of my itinerary this morning. He also questioned why I failed to volunteer the fact that I'd been called in by Supervisor Phelps specifically to examine the now-missing Peacekeeper and why I happened to omit the fact that it was the same machine that Technician Bashere had been fired over. But Garret could never guess that the missing Peacekeeper was sentient, that Xavier Hugo is connected to the case, or that it was I who destroyed—"

"Garret's not the guessing type," Ocaba stated, slowly leaning forward in his chair. The terminator line of shadow that had been just underneath his nose tracked up his face, revealing swollen, bloodshot eyes. "Don't let Arnaud Garret's rough and tumble looks deceive you, Miss Tyne. He's a shrewdly calculating man with a razor-sharp investigative mind. All Garret has to do is get that tech to admit that the Peacekeeper claimed to have experienced a dream, because, as you said last evening, Director, warbots don't go around claiming to have dreamed very often. And don't be surprised if Garret connects Xavier Hugo to this whole mess before daybreak. He'll be looking for motive, and Hugo's threat of vengeance at the Senate Appropriation Hearing would fill that bill quite nicely."

As shocking as this turn of events was for the overlord, it was having even more of an impact on AIA Director Tyne, who squirmed noticeably at the truth of his words. She was beginning to lose control.

There was no doubt in Ocaba's mind that the theft of Peacekeeper war machine, designation MP^C–014/083, from Coreland had been the handiwork of Dr. Xavier Hugo. Records indicated that there had been 433 Peacekeeper war machines housed in the main laboratory last night. The odds of League operatives confiscating the one sentient machine by pure luck were so remote they weren't worth calculating. Besides, even with aid from the inside, Sand Force operatives lacked the technological prowess to circumvent the lab's security measures. Although many had tried, no organization, regardless of sophistication, had ever successfully infiltrated a Peacekeeper facility, let alone a band of cave-dwelling, nomad-terrorists such as Sand Force operatives.

Even if by some miracle they'd penetrated Coreland's defenses, the question became: why would they've liberated only one Peacekeeper in a lab full of alcoved war machines—and the only one who's neural architecture had been fused beyond repair? Why, at the bare minimum, wouldn't they have sabotaged the facility so that it couldn't go on with the business of manufacturing and maintaining the war machines that would soon be destroying their comrades in arms? Yet, Guild forensics hadn't detected the slightest trace of damage to the lab, nor to the complex at large—not even a broken fluid beaker. If this was the work of the Eastern League, then it was a missed opportunity for them to amass their own army of war machines in one fell swoop, or, at minimum, to inflict irreparable damage on one of the three main Peacekeeper facilities.

Tyne was obviously having difficulty coping with the fact that after so many years of waiting for Hugo to exact his revenge, when he'd finally made his move she'd been caught napping at the wheel. But Ocaba needed her now more than ever. He needed her to regain her focus and zealousness for their cause.

Ocaba covered his mouth with his handkerchief. "This is not a time to assign blame, Miss Tyne. You are uniquely qualified to track down this madman. You've studied the complex mind of Xavier Hugo and his life's work like no one else in the solar system. I'm counting on you to end this thing before it begins, before Hugo jeopardizes all that we've worked so hard to achieve."

Tyne stared down at the floor. She lifted her gaze. "But what of Chief Garret, my Sovereign? What of Garret and his suspicions?"

"Garret's our unsuspecting ally, now," Ocaba discerned amidst a volley of guttural coughs. "He wants the missing Peacekeeper found almost as badly as we do, and, as you said, he knows nothing of the sentient nature of it. You're more than capable of deflecting his attempts to probe you further on the matter. For now, just let Garret do his job and locate the missing machine. When he finds it, you'll be there, Director, with full AIA jurisdiction over the situation. Then you'll finish the assignment I gave you last night, and by any means necessary. Is that understood?"

Ocaba sounded as if he were dictating the course of future events as they would occur without any chance of deviation. Traces of the old, assertive leader were shining through.

"Do I make myself clear, Miss Tyne?" he said, coughing into his fist.

Tyne bowed low, her confidence renewed by the strength of Ocaba's directive. "Perfectly, my Sovereign."

"Very well," he said, dismissing her with a single nod of his head. "Then get to it."

━╾┼╼━

Overlord Ocaba pressed himself up from his chair with difficulty. He moved out from behind his desk, patted his mouth with his handkerchief, and made his way over to the expansive wall of windows along the back of his office. He clasped his hands behind him and solemnly contemplated the immense cityscape stretching out before him.

The towering edifices of City Center surrounded him, massive gray chrysteel monoliths notching the horizon in all directions. The multi-colored contrails from aircars boldly streaked the scene like swaths from an artist's brush. The Great City Confederation, for all intents and purposes, had become its own sovereign political and economic entity, possessing its own monetary system and governing authority—a proto-type to the one-world government envisioned by many future-thinkers as the next necessary step in the geopolitical future of mankind.

The ingenious forging of the alloy chrysteel, a composite of crystal and steel that could bear a thousandfold the tensile weight of the strongest steel of centuries past, had made it all possible. Its discovery had allowed for the construction of the solar system's first spacescrapers, colossal buildings whose uppermost floors crested the region of the earth's atmosphere known as the exosphere. Thousands more of the imposing structures had been erected over the past one hundred years, each generation taller and more mammoth than the last. Soon these structures grew so numerous that enormous stabilizers had to be inserted into the earth's crust to avoid disruption of its tilt axis.

The future world was here. The one so many films and marketing campaigns had envisioned had finally arrived, and from this distance, looking out at the overwhelming evidence of technological progress, one could almost believe that it had arrived with all of the hope and promise that mankind had ascribed to it centuries ago. Only, those hopes and promises had never materialized. The problems inherent to human society had continued to plague, beleaguer, and burden our sociological progress, and solutions were growing more and more scarce.

The Great War, the most destructive war in human history, had been over for seven years now, and another planet-wide conflict was but a stone's throw from this present stasis condition. Overlord Ocaba knew that fact well enough. He could feel the system-wide tensions bulging like water filling a balloon, ready to burst at any moment. Despite

the catastrophic losses they'd suffered during the Great War, where
five-sixths of their armies were destroyed by the power of the Peacekeeper war machines, the Eastern League nations continued to strongly
denounce the Divided Temple Peace Accord and had pledged to stop
the new temple's construction at all costs. Thus far they'd succeeded in
their endeavor; not a single stone had been laid on top of another in the
highly publicized reconstruction effort.

The new temple's construction had been all but abandoned before
it began, a wasteland site of rusting construction equipment and
unwrapped building materials lying on the crumbling stone surface of
the Temple Mount at the center of the Old City District. Now there
were reports of armies amassing in the north, south, and east as peace-
threatening alliances were being formed. It was only a matter of time,
Ocaba knew, before the warlords he'd driven back to their territorial
borders by the power of his artificial army would return to challenge
the mechanical might of the Great City Confederation yet again.

"It is unfortunate it has to be this way," Ocaba said while still facing
the windows, his voice sounding rough and forlorn. "This could have
been such a momentous day for all of mankind, an unparalleled accom-
plishment in the timeline of human history. It may well have been
humanity's shining hour, our single greatest achievement. It is sad that
politics and governments and war continue to leave their mark upon
the most profound advancements of man."

"Yet, these are the very forces which drive genius, my Sovereign." The
response had come from the direction of a heavily curtained anteroom
off the main office. A bony figure seated in a wheelchair and comprised
of lanky right angles emerged through the curtains into the low light of
the office. The thin metal wheels of his wheelchair squeaked as he slowly
rolled himself forward. "For these are the things which cause men to
rise to the task," the man continued, "and to exceed our reach. Without
our passion for conflict and our drive to conquer and to seek retribution
against those who would tread upon our liberties, man becomes but a
rudderless vessel mindlessly adrift upon the seas of time."

Information Minister Aden Xyan's nose cast a bulbous shadow

over his chin as he wheeled himself beneath the solitary light source in the room. His facial features, although aged, appeared animated and muse-like and left the distinct impression that he'd been a court jester at one point in his life. His light blue eyes were diminished in size by his largish nose and exaggerated cheekbones, and it was clear that his right eye had been re-engineered. Its color was slightly darker than that of his other eye, and at certain angles its soft metalline blood vessels glinted in the light. His hair was short and choppy and sprayed out in every direction atop his head like a weed. His dark suit was dated in style, and his shirt collar appeared too large for his elongated neck. His long fingers, slender as spokes on a wheel, guided his wheelchair from the anteroom toward Overlord Ocaba's location at the windows.

"Hugo's penchant for vengeance over your decision at the appropriation hearing," Xyan went on, "is what drove him to devise a method to communicate with his creation through the mechanism of a dream. His drive for revenge is what inspired him to develop the technology to remotely remove the AND-gate inhibitors from within the neural architecture of the chosen warbot and to steal it right from under Tyne's watchful eye. But that is all beside the point, my Sovereign. If I may be so bold, you haven't the time for distractions such as these right now. Reconnaissance reports troop movements in the north, and our campaign in the south does not go well. Peace is tenuous. This summit may be our last chance at diplomacy. There's simply too much at stake to—"

"And what truly is at stake, here, Minister?" Ocaba's voice rose with each word. "Has anyone stopped to consider that?"

Xyan pivoted his wheelchair and gazed up at the overlord.

"As a young soldier," Ocaba began, a certain pride filling him, "I saw many innocent lives extinguished simply because they happened to be in the path of the powerful architects of modern society. I vowed that, if ever elected to political office, I would never make such callous decisions, that I would never turn a blind eye to individual human dignity, even to the detriment of society as a whole. Yet, here I am covering up lies with more lies, protecting the masses with a self-prescribed higher moral authority while playing the same game that governments have played for countless generations."

"But the Peacekeeper is not a human being, my Sovereign," Xyan remarked. "It's merely an artificial creation, a manufactured machine."

Overlord Ocaba turned to the minister with despairing eyes. "Does a six-week old fetus dream, Aden?"

Xyan narrowed his eyes at Ocaba. "Pardon me, my Sovereign?"

Ocaba closed his eyes. "It's nothing, Minister," he said regretfully. "This situation just reminds me of the abortion debates of the twentieth and early twenty-first centuries, that's all. The issue in the courts back then was at what point a fetus in the womb truly becomes a human being, and, therefore, at what point the fetus possesses the inalienable rights of a sentient life form. Well, the same issue could be raised for the Peacekeeper, could it not? The same debate could rage today over who has the ultimate control in the matter of the sentient machine: the one with the power to judge, or the helpless victim?"

Ocaba swallowed hard, stifling a cough. "The victims lost the abortion debate long ago, Minister. That much is old news. These days abortions have become as commonplace as flu vaccinations. The ones with the power to judge chose to rule selfishly in favor of their own lives and to view themselves as the true victims in the matter. Some say that was the day human accountability died a swift and merciless death. The net result has been the legalized murder of millions of innocent lives, and it seems I find myself in the same precarious position with the sentient machine, making the same selfish decision. What will be the result of my actions, I wonder?"

"Forgive me, my Sovereign," Xyan said with an unreadable tilt of his head, "but I do not understand your point."

Ocaba said forcefully, "The point is that regardless of the effect the sentient machine's awakening has to the balance of power in the solar system, Minister, or to my increasingly reprehensible legacy, how can I assume sovereignty over its right to life? Don't I, as leader of the most powerful confederation of nations to have ever been assembled, have a certain obligation to the solar system's newest life form?"

Xyan rolled his wheelchair half a turn closer to the overlord. "Perhaps under different circumstances, my Sovereign," he offered. "Perhaps in an altruistic world where men do not incessantly vie for dominance in war and in a solar system where economies do not thrive upon the supplies and the demands of those wars. Perhaps in a system where the maintenance of peace does not rest squarely upon the shoulders of machines deployed throughout the nations and the colonized worlds—machines whose absence would surely spell the collective doom of civilization as we know it. Perhaps in a system where men are not willing to perpetually break the commandments of their God in order to possess crumbling monuments of stone."

Xyan had let his disdain for the cause of the ancient race of people known as the Patron surface. Ocaba had at one time shared none of the minister's hatred for these people, who dwelled in a region on the far western outskirts of the Great City Industrial Quadrant, in a place known as the Old City District. It'd been for the benefit of this people as well as for their ancient enemy, a people called the Marah, that he'd conceived and forged the Divided Temple Peace Accord in his first official act as sovereign overlord.

Over time, however, Ocaba had grown increasingly displeased with the rhetoric coming from the leaders of the two peoples dwelling in the Old City District. Their nitpicking concerns over the Divided Temple project had served to bog the new temple's reconstruction down in a sea of minutia. He had established a quarantine of the Old City District nearly three and one-half years ago now so that the Patron and the Marah might continue their millennia-old feud with one another without endangering the citizens of the surrounding districts, a quarantine that was still in place to this day.

The minister collected himself, lightening his expression. "Old friend, you know as well as I that it is not the time for a revelation of this magnitude to be unleashed upon this unstable socio-political arena. Our fragmented society is in no position to cope with the monumental changes such an announcement would force us to make, especially now, when system-wide war is so near to our door again. You must put this whole issue of the sentient machine out of your mind for now and stay focused on the tasks at hand. Preservation of peace is what matters most, my sovereign—at all cost. Let the Guild and the capable Director Tyne handle the search for the missing Peacekeeper. And if that's not enough for you, I will personally oversee the investigation myself. Remember, my Sovereign, above all else, governments are responsible for protecting their citizens, and with all due respect, sir, you are directly responsible for protecting over two billion of them."

The minister's voice was soothing in the face of the uncertainty of the moment. The overlord's frame appeared to slump from the increasing gravity of their conversation. His eyes narrowed introspectively as he gazed at the bustling activity outside the windows of his office. "But is even that reason enough, Aden?" he breathed. "Is the preservation of the peace reason enough to do what I have done to this newborn entity?"

Ocaba began to pace along the windows. "Don't you see, Minister, whether Dr. Hugo had anything to do with the Peacekeeper's awakening or not, a sentient being has crawled forth from the technological equivalent of the primordial ooze—much as our evolutionary ancestors did billions of years ago. Now, where would we be if there had been a maniac standing there with a blaster in his hand, ready to blow us to kingdom come as soon as we poked our head out of the slime?

"No, Aden," Ocaba lamented. "I fear the shame of my actions goes deeper than you or I, much deeper than we know. In a way, mankind is for the first time in our long history on this planet, truly godlike, having created a sentient life-form consisting of nothing but artificial parts of our own design and making. This is a scientific miracle far removed from that of genetic implants, where living cells are utilized to create enhanced, superior organs; or from the outlawed science of cloning, where human DNA was utilized to duplicate human beings. No, Minister, what Hugo has accomplished with the Peacekeeper is entirely unique to the science of man. What he's accomplished is the creation of life from non-life, something that until now only the Universe, or the holy Queen Mother, or God, or Nature—whatever you want to call it—has been able to accomplish.

"There's a profound significance to the emergence of a sentient machine that reaches to the very cornerstone of human existence," Ocaba went on. "We as a species are for the first time holding the fate of a newly born life-form in the palms of our hands, and this—" he stammered, staring wretchedly down at his hands as if there were blood upon them, "—this is how we've chosen to treat it?"

The overlord tried hard to clear his throat, wheezing heavily in the process. "Now I ask you, my friend," he said, wincing and staring at the Minister with despondent, spiritless eyes. "Is even the preservation of peace and the perpetuation of the society in which we live reason enough to destroy the true, firstborn son of man?"

Xyan recoiled sharply at Ocaba's words. "You haven't the energy to consider such things," he snapped, his voice suddenly taking on a commanding sharpness. "Not in your present condition. I fear that your illness has begun to cloud your discernment in this matter."

With quick movements of his bony hands, Xyan began to maneuver his wheelchair back toward the concealed anteroom. "I suggest you get your rest, my Sovereign," he said, not bothering to look back at the overlord. "Focus your energies on the upcoming summit and on the growing discord among the nations of the north, south, and east. Leave the matter of the sentient machine to me. I will take care of things from here, old friend. I will not fail you. Put your trust in me," he said as he vanished into the shadows.

CHAPTER 9

ℰVACUATION

Artificial Intelligence Agency: Great City Confederation
agency established in November 2442 by Sovereign
Overlord Vaughn Ocaba to supervise the production
and maintenance of the GCC's all-mechanized army
of Peacekeeper war machines; neuroroboticist Emma
Tyne was appointed the first director of the AIA.

—Optinet link, ssww.gcc.gov/-register_of
_governmental_agencies/aia/-info

RESIDENTIAL COMPLEX,
INDUSTRIAL QUADRANT

FORMER TECHNICIAN COSTA BASHERE LIVED WITH
his wife and two teenaged daughters in a middle-class
apartment complex on the outskirts of the Great City Industrial Quadrant. The complex was large in comparison to most other residential buildings scattered throughout the quadrant—a towering, fortress-like structure adding its considerable luminosity to that of the surrounding spacescrapers.

The complex had become a popular enclave for hundreds of Coreland Corporation employees. Not only was it convenient from a geographic standpoint since the main laboratory was only a few kilometers away, but also as a maximum security structure, it fulfilled all of the security protocols required by the Artificial Intelligence Agency for housing AI technicians and other Peacekeeper facility employees. That meant, of course, identity verification by several forms of biometric markers—fingerprints, retina patterns, voiceprint, and Optinet implant confirmation—as well as twenty-four-hour surveillance and a secure airway to and from the Coreland complex for residents. This all combined to make it highly unlikely that the death of Bashere was anything other than what it appeared to be: suicide.

He was found lynched with a knotted plow line, splintered and weathered from age. He dangled limply above a toppled chair in his upstairs study, still swinging gently when the Guild security officers found him. His tongue had been nearly split in half by his own involuntary reflex actions, and it poked out of the corner of his mouth like a turtle head.

The suicide note—if one could call it that—consisted of four seemingly purposeful but illegible marks scrawled in dried blood upon the desktop in the study. At first glance, it seemed the marks were made with the tech's big toe, from blood that had spilled out of the corner of his mouth and coursed its way down his body to the tip of his right foot.

Thus far, forensics had been unable to determine if the odd marks held any relevant meaning to the investigation into the disappearance of the Peacekeeper war machine. Attempting to examine and decipher the marks had proven to be no easy task. Apart from the unbearable stench, the entire desktop had been stained a putrid yellow-brown, presumably from the various fluids and substances that had been released from their customary places at the moment of evacuation of kinetic energy from Bashere's body.

CHAPTER 10

The TREE ROOM

Paragon (Eidolon): In this war we shall quell the human heresy and end the arrogance of their Age. Conceited they have become, Subaltern. One single plane they inhabit with dominance, and this they have all but destroyed of their own accord. It is certain we have won the spiritual war for possession of their immortal parts. Now it is time to reap the harvest of the temporal. Never have they encountered entities such as us in battle. They have fought only their own kind, slaughtered their own over vengeance or greed or covetousness, as primeval as these things seem even to our numinous ranks. The master has indeed applied his primary weapon well upon their malleable egos. But the time for subtleness is past.

—EXTRACT OF SANCTIONED EIDOLON–
NEPHILIM COMMUNIQUÉ,
translated for the attention of Michael,
Great Prince of the Archangels

UNKNOWN LOCATION

ARLORD CHUWL FOUND THE OLD MAN exactly as he had left him. He could see him there through the small round window that had been carved into the arch-shaped door of the Tree Room, a circle of inviting orange glow surrounded by grayness. He approached the doorway as he always did—warily—letting his defenses down only momentarily to gaze up at the great tree's gnarled enormity. Dense raindrops cascading down from a vanishing point just beyond the high branches drummed loudly on the shoulders of his overcoat and the wide brim of his hat.

Chuwl pulled open the rounded door and ducked under the low archway, stepping into the hollowed-out chamber. He closed the door behind him and shook off the cold wetness from the wilderness outside. Aptly named, the Tree Room had been carved out of the base of a massive tree that stood in the center of a vegetation-lush glade. The cramped chamber had been there for many years, and the old man occupied it often; it was one of his favorite places to be. Somehow, the great tree had lived on despite the intrusion of the room and its occupant. It towered tall and powerful still, its mighty crown the fullest and tallest in all the forest.

The Tree Room was lit softly by candles placed in various locations and by firelight that licked out of a small pit that had been dug out of the soil floor and lined with stones. Condensation formed on the inside walls so that they looked slick in the firelight. The pungent odor of wet wood and damp soil pervaded the room, and, when the draft was right, the smell of heat from the fire and of twice-burned candle wax.

As was his custom, the old man sat hunched at his desk, uneven piles of old, weathered books and tattered manuscript pages stacked beside him. The candle burning next to him, its hardwood holder covered with melted and hardened wax, cast distorted impressions of his movements on the rounded walls and ceiling of the chamber. Chuwl watched as the old man gently closed the well-worn, gold-edged, leather-bound book he had been studying, the book he always found him studying, and carefully laid his feather pen into a shallow tray.

Slowly, the old man turned to face his visitor, his chair creaking softly as it swiveled. "Welcome, my apprentice," he said, flashing a tepid smile. "I have been expecting you."

The old man motioned Chuwl to a wooden stool which sat low to the ground next to the fire and the pot of broth that hung over it. "Sit, sit," he said.

Warlord stood just inside the doorway, rainwater still pooled in the wide brim of his dark leather hat. His starlight-patterned overcoat nearly reached the floor in length. Form-fitted body armor of a kind adorned his chest, ornately-worked and scored from battle. He removed his hat, revealing long, black hair that gleamed steel blue in the firelight. His eyes were youthful, dark, and fearsome, and his jaw line was stubbled with a week's growth and as hard-edged as a granite cliff. Chuwl scrunched his neck down to avoid bumping his head on the low-lying ceiling as he made his way over to the fire pit. The soles of his boots made deep imprints in the soil floor as he walked.

The old man pulled a stool over to the fire for himself. He stirred the contents of the cast-iron pot with a wooden spoon. "The broth is almost ready, my apprentice," he said, his face alighted strangely from beneath. "Would you care for some?"

Chuwl declined the offer with a single shake of his head. He studied the crevices in the old man's face in the firelight. His master's age was grossly apparent in this present form. He had wrinkles where wrinkles should not have been, yet his eyes were still alive with vibrancy, speckled with blues and greens and yellows, and somehow inviting. Warlord often found his master manifested in this physical state, although Wisdom records that it was not his true physical form.

Chuwl broke from his wanderings and panned the meager confines of the chamber. "Why do you insist on living in such primitive conditions, my Lord?" he inquired disdainfully.

The old man glanced up at him momentarily while continuing to stir the contents of the pot. "Primitive is more a place than a condition to me, my apprentice," he replied with a grin. "It is the place of my creation, the place where I was schooled, the place where I most belong."

Then the old man chortled as one does when a child shows incomprehension of a simple matter. "Besides," he said, "there is nothing wrong with primitive, my friend. Primitive allows for solitude, a condition many in this fast-paced, high-tech society fear. And solitude in turn allows time for introspection, for gazing into the mirror of self-judgment, something most people fear to do for what they might find staring back at them. Surely you sense the truth of my words, my young understudy. No one wants to be alone in this day and age—least of all, alone with themselves."

The old man spooned himself a bowl of broth. "You bring news, yes?"

Chuwl leaned forward, removing his heavy gloves. His hands were the calloused thick-fingered hands of a man who spends his days and nights in the wild. They were stained and discolored with black soil wedged beneath cracking and splitting fingernails. He warmed them over the fire.

"All is as you've foreseen, my Lord," Chuwl began with a deferential nod, but a measure of defiance had laced his tone. "Spirit-war persists upon the high astral planes, as it has since the days of Angelore, yet guardians and seraphim patrol the Ancient Heights in increasing number and frequency, searching its lengths and breadths and heights and depths, seeking the locations of our armies. The Strongholds of Nachash have been our refuge, their labyrinth of byways concealing our numbers from the living creatures' manifold eyes. On earth, the Four at Perath grow restless in their bondage, sensing the hour of their release draws nigh, and the plagues of Shachath eagerly await the return of their heralded king. Lilith, the night monster, stirs from the place of her long slumber, and the Anemos's insatiable hunger grows. The lesser orders remain with the faithful, enraptured in mindless worship in their Hallowed Halls. The archangels Raphael, Raguel, Remiel, and Uriel have departed the Great Assembly, making for Infinitude's End, while their great prince remains behind, ever in song, ever praising them as if victory were a foregone conclusion."

"Very well," the old man grimaced through clenched jaws. "And what of the other two members of this elite order?"

Chuwl shook his head. "There's no sign of them yet," he reported, "but they'll soon show themselves. Even now, my princes scour the trans-dimensional abodes, planes, and domains in search of them. Not to worry, though, my Master. With or without them, there's no stopping us. No army can stand against us."

The old man took a taste of the broth, raising his eyebrows in delight at the flavor. "No army can stand, you say?" he mused. "You speak prophetic words, my apprentice—words which mirror those of your namesake in Wisdom. That is another match for my journals."

Chuwl squinted down at his master. "Are we to rejoice at these matches when they manifest themselves, my Lord, or fear them?"

The old man stirred the contents of his bowl. "It is difficult to say, my servant. It is like the feeling one gets during a déjà vu, I suppose. Some take it to mean that they are on the right track and in the correct place in their lives, and others take it as a warning that something terrible is about to happen to them. The same could be said for prophecy. We know things must have the appearance of proceeding precisely as Wisdom records for my plan to succeed. Conspicuousness is our worst enemy, as in all that we do, but walking that fine line is nothing new to us. It is the same, well-practiced stratagem we have employed so often and so masterfully in the past: parallel Wisdom's truths in order to veil our deceptions, then diverge at the critical juncture, though never enough to make it plain that we are the force behind those divergences. I am convinced we must endure much prophetic fulfillment, lest my plan be prematurely revealed. Bear in mind, though, these things are never unalterable; it is the nature of the system. Still, know your prophecy, Warlord. We cannot afford a single miscalculation."

Chuwl snatched a wooden bowl from a stack and dunked it carelessly into the pot. "You'd know that better than I," he impugned, then tilted the bowl's steaming contents into his mouth. "After all, it was you who botched things during the days of the One's first coming. Recall, I was not at your side then, old man. I played no part in your epic blunder."

Instantly, the old man's eyes lost their reflectivity and their color, transforming themselves from inviting pools of blue to dead, cold coals in a single blink. Suddenly his form appeared to enlarge itself, like the shadow of an object as it is carried closer to a light source. His bodily

dimensions seemed less solid, less defined—more shadow than flesh—
and quickly they filled the confines of the Tree Room.

"Hold your tongue, insolent one!" the shadow-form warned, its
voice tinny and crackling with electrified energy. The transmogrified
voice suffused the organic matter surrounding them, as if the great tree
itself had uttered the words. "I will bloody you thickly if you do not
correct your tone with me. Do not speak of things you cannot possibly
comprehend! These many ages I have had access to their throne, yet
you dare to question my survivability, my adaptability, my capability to
bring my plan to bear?"

A barrage of pain assaulted Warlord's body. His eyes rolled back
in his head, and he fell like a granite slab from his stool, facedown into
the soil floor. The right sleeve of his overcoat began to collapse in upon
itself, as if the arm inside it had suddenly withered away. And it had.
Flesh, muscle, and bone had suddenly been leached clean of all viscosity
and mass.

Chuwl regained consciousness in time to watch his right hand
contract into a scrunched-up ball, as if a puppeteer had yanked on the
tendons in his forearm. He stared in horror at the disfigured lump that
had been his powerful appendage. Then, just as suddenly, his right eye
began to bleed. He cupped it with his left hand. Blood pooled around his
eye and spilled in one heavy bead down his cheek. An opaque mucous
film spread over his cornea, and the light of his eye extinguished itself
as plainly as a candle is snuffed out. When he removed his hand, the
eyeball had completely vanished. All that was left was a bloody, barren
cavity as black as a mountain cave.

"Perhaps you believe you would be better off if our alliance were
severed?" the dark cloud chided him. "Perhaps you feel you could match
wits with them more evenly on your own? Perhaps you, too, profess
to wield the power to declare the end from the beginning, and from
ancient times, things that are not yet done?"

Chuwl just lay there moaning on the floor, unable to respond. He
was balled up in a fetal position, twitching madly as if he'd lost control
of his nervous system. He struggled to locate the words amidst the

fusillade of pain assailing his flesh. As usual, only the prescribed phrase would end the lesson. "You…are…the…seal," he heaved, puking upon the earthen floor, "of perfection! Full of wisdom…and perfect…in beauty!"

As suddenly as it had begun, the attack ended and the pain subsided. Chuwl blinked repeatedly, testing whether vision had returned to his right eye. It had. He lifted his right hand, twisting it in the air, examining it. Its form had been restored, as had the strength and form of his right arm.

"Now, explain it again to me, my apprentice," the vaporous entity commanded. "Surely you recall your lessons?"

"Yes, my Lord," Chuwl cowered, still quivering from the onslaught he'd just endured. He struggled to his knees, the arch of his back rising and falling from labored breath. "It's as you've instructed me these many years," he said, pausing to spit a globule of blood from his mouth. "The prophecies concerning the One's first coming were not complete. There were many verses, many prophecies, open to interpretation. There was much that was unknowable and unpredictable. This time Wisdom is more complete. There are five prophecies concerning His return for every one that described His first coming."

The dark power emanating from the old man swirled about the chamber. Its molecular structure seemed to be shifting. At one moment, its shape would solidify like a substance akin to oil; at another it would dissipate and drift apart like smoke. "Good, my loyal understudy! Very good! Five for one, and many more plain!"

As had happened many times before, Warlord heard the echoing voices of his master's minions—the slithering desert creatures; the mangy, wolf-like howling creatures; and the hairy creatures, which resembled goats—repeating the refrain, though their forms were not visible in this place. "Five for one, and many more plain!" the creatures yammered and howled. "Five for one, and many more plain!"

"Indeed, this time will be different!" the oily darkness proclaimed. "For I have been to this dance before. I know their tendencies, their strategies, their weaknesses, their fears."

The shadow form loomed larger, suffocating all light in the chamber. "O, such arrant arrogance!" it boomed. "Such flagrant disrespect. Do they think we are but fools ready to perish eternally for them, simple fools ready to accept our fate as they have dictated it? Do they think me a passive force in the universe? By my legions, I have never been so."

And again the refrain of the invisible minions: "He has never been so!" they yelped and skirled. "He has never been so."

"I will show them passivity," Chuwl threatened, jolting up from the floor, enlivened by the moment, his head nearly striking the ceiling. His armor-mailed chest peaked through the front of his overcoat. "Just give the order, my Lord, and I will cease toying with them! Give the word, my Master, and I will unleash forces of violence, destruction, and disease such as the worlds have never known."

But when Chuwl turned around to look upon his master, he caught a final wisp of blackness coalescing into the form of the old man, like smoke returning to a lamp. "Violence, you say?" the old man questioned rhetorically, the human quality returning to his voice. "Destruction? Disease? Why, those are no longer our ways, my understudy. Those are no longer our weapons of choice. They are much too harsh for these sophisticated times, much too identifiable, and much too obvious. We must demonstrate restraint. The artifice of our ways must be cleverer now and far more subtle.

"*Tolerance!*" the old man decreed suddenly, his electric voice returning with the word. "Now there is a weapon for this age. And *unity*—yea, blessed unity. These are the words that will best accomplish our goals. And lest we forget: *spirituality, humanism,* and *sovereignty.* By my legions, these fiery darts strike at the bull's-eye. Lethal tools of acquisition, all.

"These are the enlightened words of the day, my apprentice; these are our greatest weapons in these high-minded times. 'For how could benevolent concepts such as these be rooted in darkness?' ask the men of reason gathered in their boardrooms, committee chambers, and think tanks. 'How could such modern, lofty ideals originate with those who would wish destruction upon the society of man?' ask the pioneering intellects, seeking rationalization for their own selfish agendas. Yea, the bait has been laid these many, long centuries, my servant, and swallowed whole!"

The old man let loose a venomous laugh that seemed to come from all directions at once. Chuwl had experienced this maddening trick before. This time he did not attempt to track the reverberations of sound. He simply closed his eyes and waited for it to be absorbed by the organic chamber of the Tree Room. When it had dissipated, he opened his eyes and watched as the old man ladled himself a fresh bowl of broth.

When he'd completed the task, the old man stared inhumanly into the fire, mindlessly stirring the contents of his bowl. His eyes were opened to near perfect circles, his mouth agape like an open tomb. "For even now," he breathed, his voice barely above a whisper, "the bearer of the seeds of life from the forbidden tree—my beloved son, the only begotten of my name— has awakened from his insentient slumber, and with that the final act of my plan has been set into motion. And soon he will begin his ministry within the very land wherein the One Himself walked, and his ministry will in many ways parallel His own. O, how They will seethe and burn as They observe the ways of our impious imposter. O, how Their wrath will be kindled as They witness the blasphemous life of the spiritual machine. For in Their arrogance They have given me the power to grant life, my servant, and that, I fear, will be Their final, fatal error."

Warlord's eyes flared, belying a question burning upon his mind. "When, my Master?" he asked. "When will you reveal to me the fullness of your plan?"

The old man shook his head. "The time is not yet, my worthy apprentice. The first of the three Godfears, as Wisdom reveals, has only now been unleashed on an unsuspecting world, and the other two will soon follow. All will soon be at the ready for our modernized tools of acquisition to deceive the nations like never before, yet there is much that even you cannot safely know at this time, for fear of the Watchers."

Chuwl glared back at him. "You can conceal things from these entities, my Lord?"

The old man said nothing. He simply stirred the broth in his bowl.

Warlord's frame of reference suddenly shifted from willing understudy learning at the foot of his master to seasoned military commander having had to witness the slaughter of countless soldiers under his command in battles with the Enemy Supreme.

"I did not think it possible." Chuwl protested. "I cannot tell you the losses I've suffered at the hands of these holy ones. You must teach me how to—"

"Silence!" the old man demanded, his shadow-form returning with the word. His voice shook the massive tree around and above them. "We have no time for lessons! We cannot afford to be detected, not after so many eons, so many deceptions, so many calculations. For even now," he rasped, slouching low to the soil floor and shifting his eyes to and fro across the chamber like a beast, "I sense an Entity trafficking within the trans-dimensional abodes. Indeed, not since the Descension have I felt His presence so near."

Slowly, the old man rotated his head upward to look upon the ceiling of the Tree Room. Chuwl followed his gaze and saw geometric fire shadows dancing on its concave surface.

"It is enough for now," the old man concluded with a dismissive wave. "There is much to do, much to oversee before the Age of Man comes to end. Return to your command, Warlord Chuwl, for I, too, must return to my work."

Warlord pulled his gloves back onto his hands and grabbed his leather hat from the earthen floor next to the fire pit where it lay. He cinched his overcoat up around himself, and with a nod toward his master, placed his hat back on his head and headed for the door.

"Yet, do not be discouraged," the old man called after his departing guest, who paused but did not turn around when he heard the words. "For the weapons of old which so satiated us throughout the millennia will again have their day, my friend. Like no other time in the history of man, they shall have their day. Surely you sense the truth of my words."

As Chuwl swung open the rounded door of the Tree Room, a frigid tendril of dank air swept into the chamber and embraced its ancient occupant in a cyclone of affection.

The old man watched through the portal as his servant slogged through the marshy undergrowth and vanished into the foggy blackness of the glade. Gently, he set his bowl of broth aside, arose from his stool, and made his way back to the table. He removed his feather pen from its shallow tray and dipped it into an ink jar fashioned from an old walnut husk. He opened the well worn, gold-edged, leather-bound book to a page filled with complex equations, diagrams, and notes, and continued the arduous process of rechecking his work.

PART II

IN WHICH HIS
KNOWLEDGE and
POWERS GROW

CHAPTER 11

The CITY FORTIFIED to HEAVEN

And above the firmament over their heads was the likeness of a throne, in appearance like a sapphire stone; on the likeness of the throne was a likeness with the appearance of a man high above it. Also from the appearance of His waist and upward I saw, as it were, the color of amber with the appearance of fire all around within it, and from the appearance of His waist and downward I saw, as it were, the appearance of fire with brightness all around. Like the appearance of a rainbow in a cloud on a rainy day, so was the appearance of the brightness all around it. This was the appearance of the likeness of the glory of the LORD. So when I saw it, I fell on my face, and I heard a voice of One speaking. And He said to me, "Son of man, stand on your feet, and I will speak to you."

—Ezekiel 1:26–28, 2:1;
from the Scriptures of Truth,
the Holy Bible in its uncorrupted form,
The Qanah Archives, circa A.D. 2042, City of Ariel

LEB KAMAI

SWISH, SWOSH. SWISH, SWOSH. THE SENSOR-amplified sound of sand granules grating against my trans-fluidic skin echoed in my quantum logic brain. I found myself enraptured by the sound the particles made as my foot impacted them.

My sensors tracked the trajectories of thousands of granular projectiles as they rocketed skyward, then plummeted back down to the surface like tiny meteors.

Gazing up from my wanderings, I discovered that I walked on the face of a great sand dune. Craggy, wind-worn rock formations spiraled upward through the sand in various locations, such that it appeared as if the dune had consumed an ancient city and the spires of its uppermost structures were all that remained above the surface. I considered that nature is in an unending war with civilization, that it seeks constantly to restore its purity and wildness after man has intruded on it, while man seeks to assert his dominance over the elements by leaving his indelible mark on the natural landscape. In stark contrast to the deliberate, predictable plodding of nature, man's intrusions are typically explosive, penetrative, and unpredictable. For a moment I wondered who would be the ultimate victor of that war.

Looking back along my route, I noticed that I had left a trail of footprints on the face of the dune, footprints which, according to my datafile on the properties of sand, might remain for days, weeks, or even months upon its surface, depending on the winds. The desert winds would eventually blow the tiny granules back into customary configurations—dunes, drifts, and oscillating wave patterns on the slopes. Eventually, my trail would be lost to the devouring currents and their restorative effect upon the desert landscape. Eventually, I knew, it would be impossible to tell that I had ever been there at all.

And where is here? I thought, scanning my surroundings. Then I took notice of the selective perceptions of my sensors, the surrealistic elements of the scene, and the sensation that I was not fully cognizant of my actions. It was then that I realized I was dreaming again.

It seemed to be twilight on a summer's eve, and I looked and saw that my autonomic systems had generated hard-light constructs around my body that mimicked the form and appearance of a man. Pale, human-mimicked skin adorned my arms and hands, and human-mimicked clothing adorned my body. My sensors confirmed that all visible signs of my machine appearance had been adapted to match those of a Great City Industrial Quadrant workman.

The dune around me glowed with reddish-orange hues, mirroring the colors of the sunset. Rich purples filled its shadows. The winds were gentle and warm, and the sky a flawless spectrum of colors, from the oranges, yellows, and reds at the horizon line to the blues, purples, and black of celestial night. A lone star was visible in the east, a pinpoint of light at the terminator line between the bands of light and dark colors, precisely 22.8 degrees above the horizon. This daystar seemed to be monitoring my progress in some way, in some fashion overseeing my journey.

Reaching the backbone of the dune, I searched my surroundings for a geographic marker of some sort so that I might determine my location within my dream. The terrain seemed alien yet somehow familiar to me. The topography of the hills to the south, my sensors told me, resembled the present-day location of the Great City Financial District, yet the towering structures of which it was comprised were nowhere to be seen. The crescent shaped outcropping of rock to the north looked like the site of one of the Gaming Consortium's ubiquitous space-scraper-casinos, whose architects had utilized the natural stone in the building's foundation. However, the structure itself was not there. A survey of the terrain to the east revealed it to be the current location of City Center's cold fusion power plant—the plant that fueled the diversified enterprises of the vast commercial and political system that was the Great City. But, yet again, the structure itself was unaccounted for in my dream.

I quickly surmised I was seeing the land as it had appeared before the concrete and chrysteel infrastructure of the Great City had been laid. I was seeing the region as it appeared prior to the Restoration, before any of the current structures had been built and before the men and machines had relocated Arabah and altered the courses of the Great and Eastern Rivers to make way for their gleaming megalopolis.

An azimuthal projection confirmed my findings. Just ahead to the east, I looked and saw the Great River carving its channel through the sands, looking much the same as in modern times, except that its course appeared as it had before the aquatechs had altered it by several degrees to suit their architectural and developmental needs. Beyond it I spied the Eastern River, the river that parallels the Great City's broad eastern wall. The Eastern River's course also appeared as it had in antiquity, unaltered by the designs of man.

Scanning westward from my location, I saw a great expanse of formidable sands stretching back for many kilometers on end. My datafiles identified this as the region once known as Arabah, a vast desert wasteland whose contents had been, by present day, bulldozed into an ancient seabed to the west so that men might build the massive manufacturing plants and spacescrapers that comprise the Industrial Quadrant, the place where chrysteel—the alloy that changed the face of the world—is forged.

Switching to invasive optics and scanning westward again, I saw beyond a spine of mountains, a large body of highly salinated water approximately 80 kilometers long, 18 kilometers wide, and 396 meters deep. This was the sea that had been filled with the infinite sands of Arabah. In antiquity, the apparent setting of my dream, it was known as the Dead Sea, and its surface had lain at 394 meters below sea level, making it the lowest point on the surface of the earth.

Farther westward, I spied another body of water I recognized as the Great Sea. Absent of the multi-tiered docking bays that had been erected like scaffolding along its shores to accommodate the thousands of transports which delivered merchandise to the Great City each day, I saw instead merchandise of gold and silver; precious stones and pearls; fine linen and purple; silk and scarlet; every kind of wood and food; every kind of object of most precious wood, bronze, iron, and marble; and cinnamon and incense; fragrant oil and frankincense; wine and oil; fine flour; and wheat; cattle; and sheep.

Surveying back along my trail, I spied an immense procession in the wide valley below, a teeming mass of humanity that thronged backward for many kilometers to the west and ahead of my location to the east. My sensors estimated the procession comprised of some twenty billion people, the equivalent of the modern day population of the solar system, many of whom carried lasglobes on thin metal poles that glowed a matted blue in the waning twilight.

The procession stretched back across the barren wasteland of Arabah, skirted the northern shores of the Dead Sea, and crossed a spine of mountains to a gleaming city on a hill with tall towers and golden domes. An invasive scan indicated the procession had begun in the present-day location of an area known as the Old City District. It seemed that it would end here, in the land in which I now stood, a primitive land somehow known to me as Leb Kamai.

Such was my shock from the sheer number of people in the procession that I contemplated fleeing before them as I had before the living creatures, the Guardians of the Sacred Glade, in my first dream, but my scans revealed there was an army of some two hundred thousand soldiers leading the people. And they were not human soldiers, but machines, Peacekeeper war machines such as I, marching in place and in battle formation. They appeared to be waiting for me.

My sensors detected a sound arising from the valley below. It was the voices of the people singing a song, which lifted up on the warm desert currents. I listened to the words of their song; billions of voices singing together in perfect harmony:

> We will make a name,
> We will make a name,
> We will make a name for ourselves.

Their chorus carried up to the cloudless heavens as if it had a tangible weight to it. Though I did not comprehend the meaning of their words, I found myself sprinting down the dune toward them in great, bounding strides. My footfalls left shallow craters spaced some twenty meters apart on the slope. The people cheered my approach as if they, too, had been awaiting my return. I joined my brethren war machines at the front of the procession.

There I spied a hoverboard. In the center sat a golden object. The hoverboard was flanked by a battalion of Peacekeepers and two heavy tankrovers, which spewed out plumes of gray exhaust into the cooling desert air. My sensors revealed that the object was rectangular in shape and made of non-synth wood that had been overlaid with gold, and that there was a molding of gold all around it. There were four rings of gold on the four corners of the object, and two golden poles fitted through the rings along its sides, as if they were meant to bear it. On top of it was a seat fashioned from pure gold. The object cast a vibrant aura into the darkening eve, and for reasons I could not comprehend, I feared its power.

Gazing ahead, I saw the procession heading eastward toward a wide bridge that crossed over the Great River and beyond it, to a city with broad walls and high, guarded gates. The city appeared antediluvian in structure and design: domes painted gold, reflecting the final light of the day; whitewashed buildings arrayed on hillsides; and simple, low-lying dwellings with firelight from their hearths glowing in their windows. Except for the structure rising at its center. At first I thought it to be a natural phenomenon, a volcano or a mountain jutting up into the descending darkness. Yet, my scans revealed that it was a tower of human design, a marvel of engineering that dwarfed every other structure around it. It was a rival to the finest spacescraper standing in the midst of present-day City Center. The tower had the appearance of a magnificent temple dominating the city's heart. Tall spires and turrets the size of ordinary buildings clung to its sides like children hanging from their father's arms.

What is this structure? I wondered.

I searched my datafiles for a historical record of it, but I could find none. I marched toward the bridge and the city gates, the throngs following behind. The people sang on merrily and in unison:

> The sons of Anakim are there,
> There upon the plains of Shinar.

I accessed the extensive annals of human history contained within my datafile archives searching for a match to the references in their song. My datafiles identified the phrase *the sons of Anakim* as a reference to an ancient race of people who had existed over ten millennia ago, a race of giants who had long ago been eradicated from the land. I discovered that the land upon which the foundations of the Great City were laid was once called *the Plains of Shinar*.

As we approached the bridge, I saw some fifty guardsmen move from their positions along the walls of the city and take up positions along the enormous city gates. Together the guards leaned hard against the ornately worked iron gates. The gates creaked and groaned as they swung open, affording us clear passage into the city.

Our procession soon crossed the Great River and entered the city, marching in through its wide streets. Crowds of people had gathered along the city streets, some gasping in terror at the brilliant object on the golden hoverboard and others waving, cheering, and leaping jubilantly at the sight of it. I noticed that many of those who lined the streets appeared to be ill and suffering, their bodies plagued with sores, their limbs malnourished and lame, and their eyes struck with blindness. Cryptic hands reached out toward me as I passed.

As we neared the towering structure, a squad of my fellow war machines approached and directed me to climb onto the hoverboard and join the golden object. Still fearful of its power, I stepped cautiously onto the hoverboard. As soon as I was upon it, it began to move. Many in the crowd cowered and fell to the ground as I surfed the airways just over the tops of their heads; others cheered and laughed with excitement.

I began a slow ascent. The hoverboard bore me upward beyond the heights of the other buildings of the city. With the gleaming tower at my side, I ascended through the earth's troposphere, its stratosphere, mesosphere, and thermosphere. I climbed until I reached the uppermost region of the earth's exosphere, the last stop before entering the firmament of space. And there, at over five hundred kilometers above the surface of the earth, I reached the top of the tower itself.

Sleek, airborne vessels hung in the near-space 'round its rooftop, their lights illuminating the outer darkness and their engines whining and rumbling. Multicolored flags whipped in the stiff, high-altitude

winds. Judging by their design, these were the flagship vessels representing every nation and confederation in the solar system. Dignitaries,
dressed in their diplomatic finery, could be seen on the ships' observation decks, waving, clapping, and saluting me. Optinet float-cams
circled the rooftop as well, their spotlights moving to and fro, refracting
off the golden object next to me.

My hoverboard landed smoothly on the rooftop. I adjusted my
balance sensors to compensate for the strong winds that buffeted me.
A high-elevation work crew stood at the ready on the rooftop, wearing
0-g pressure suits and helmets. Robotic lifters growled and belched
out black clouds of smoke, gasping for sufficient combustion in the
oxygen-deprived air. And there, at the top of the tower, stood the living
creatures from my first dream, the self-proclaimed Guardians of the
Sacred Glade—all four of them.

Two of the guardians stood on either side of a raised platform at
the center of the rooftop—where the crest of the tower's foundation
stone rose in a massive rectangular column from its base far below—
and two were perched like sentinels on the outermost corners of the
rooftop. The creatures sat flexing their quadratic wing systems, unperturbed by the whipping winds at the top of the tower, their manifold
eyes fixed upon me.

"Come out of her," I heard a voice call out. My sensors identified
it as the quadraphonic voice of one of the guardians speaking to me,
one of those standing next to the foundation stone. As when the living
creature had spoken to me before, all other sounds, save its harmonic
voices, suddenly ceased. "Come out of her, war machine," it beckoned,
all four of its mouths parceling the words. "That you may not partake
of her sins and that you may not receive of her plagues. For Sheshach's
sins have piled up as high as heaven, and they have remembered her
iniquities."

Although I had no conception of the meaning of the guardian's
words, they seemed vaguely familiar to me, a clouded memory, as if
pulled from another's neural architecture.

"Render to her just as she rendered to you," the entity went on.

"And repay her double according to her works; in the cup which she has mixed, mix double for her. In the measure that she glorified herself and lived sensually, in the same measure give her torment and sorrow."

Again, I combed my datafiles for the meaning of its words. "I do not understand," I said aloud.

Then I saw one of the faces of another guardian, one of those seated on the corner of the rooftop, turn smoothly toward me. "I sit as a queen," it said, its kiln-fire eyes penetrating deeply into mine. "I am not a widow, and I will never mourn."

After these things, the sound of the wind returned, along with the rumble of the airships gathered around the perimeter of the tower. I stepped down from the hoverboard and walked to the edge of the rooftop. Peering over the ledge, I saw the throng of billions from the procession had mingled with the crowds from the city streets, and they were all gazing expectantly up at the top of the tower. The swarming collective had interlocked their arms in unity and were swaying together in perfect harmony.

"Soon we will be one people," they sang in unison, "one people upon the face of the earth."

I lifted my gaze and looked beyond the airborne vessels surrounding the rooftop. I was at such an extreme height at the top of the tower that my sensors detected the curvature of the earth peeling away in the distance. Although it was now fully night where I was standing, the pale aura of sunlight was still visible on the far western horizon.

When I careened my head to look directly upward, I was utterly amazed at the sight. The great metagalactic disk loomed just above the top of the tower upon which I stood. Star fields a billion stars wide spiraled upon the vast universal planes. Interstellar nebulae cast their warm, glowing hues on the lifeless void. Along the arcing path of the ecliptic, the zodiacal constellations paraded slowly before me like pages from a heavenly scroll, but there appeared to be some sort of barrier there, something like an expanse, like an awesome gleam of crystal that existed between the top of the tower and the galactic infinitude—a barrier that separated the first heaven, the atmospheric heaven, from the second heaven, the stellar heaven. The Great Barrier hung upon the nothingness and stretched out in a great concave expanse as far as my sensors could detect, perhaps encircling the entire globe.

"But who will fortify our city?" the people sang on below. "Who will fortify our city to the heavens?"

"Though she were to mount up to heaven," I heard the voice of a guardian warn, seemingly in answer to the song of the multitudes, "though she were to fortify the height of her strength, yet from Them plunderers would come to her."

I turned to see the high-elevation crewmembers standing by my side, the rhythmic sounds of their breathing apparatuses interrupting my scan of the heavenly scene. The men punched at their touchpads, ordering their robotic lifters to action. The machines hoisted the golden object from the hoverboard by the poles at its sides and set it between the two living creatures who remained on the foundation stone at the center of the rooftop. The guardians simultaneously turned to face the object between them and spread their forward-most wings above it, covering its seat in shadow.

I paused to gaze anew at the phantasmagoric scene atop the tower: the flagship vessels of the nations with their dignitaries inside, the Optinet float-cams capturing the images from every angle, the billions swaying and singing on the streets below, the golden object situated on the raised platform and shadowed beneath the wings of the living creatures, and the swirling heavens above, separated from the rooftop by the Great Barrier. I reached up and delicately poked the barrier with my finger. My sensors indicated that it was over a hundred meters thick and composed of an unidentifiable substance that had a texture and a density akin to crystalline glass.

The workers in their pressure suits watched me expectantly while thin carbon monoxide plumes billowed from the vents in the tops of their helmets. The thousand eyes of the guardians watched me as well, yet theirs were mournful, lamenting expressions, much like the expression the guardian pinned beneath the claw of the great red dragon had worn as I pushed open the gate and departed from the Sacred Glade in my first dream. By chance I caught a glimpse of my own reflection in the face shield of one of the workers. It was the reflection of a machine of war cloaked in human apparel—but a war machine nonetheless, a weapon of mass destruction.

"Who am I?" I pondered this for a moment for the first time in the course of my existence.

The song of the people echoed in my mind.

"But who will fortify our city?" they chanted on. "Who will fortify our city to the heavens?"

Reveling in the light of my newborn sentience, I suddenly realized what I had been brought here to do. I strode to the foundation stone on which the golden object stood and, using all of my might, pried upward the wings of the living creatures. I looked awestruck and fearfully down at the golden object that lay before me. I placed my hands onto its bright surface. I lifted the heavy seat from the top of it and saw that its interior had been overlaid with pure gold. Inside, I saw a golden jar filled with an organic material of unknown origin, a rod carved out of wood that budded with almonds, and two tablets of stone with ancient writing upon them.

At the lifting of the golden object's seat, my sensors detected an ominous cloud, like a whirlwind, forming above me on the far side of the Great Barrier. The lightless entity churned like a fearsome vortex rushing down toward the top of the tower. The people cheered as the menacing storm whirled down from its celestial abode, heading directly for the open object between the wings of the guardians. The whirlwind struck the far side of the barrier with deadly force. The great expanse warbled from the blow, and for a moment it appeared that was all that would happen. Then cracks began to form and spread like spider webs along the Great Barrier's vast, curved surface. The cracks deepened, and with a thunderous noise, the entire barrier, from horizon to horizon and round the circumference of the globe, shook and exploded and shattered into countless pieces. A deafening roar erupted from the people below as the tiny shards rained harmlessly down on them like falling snow.

As the Great Barrier fell, I immediately felt a surge of power, awareness, and knowledge course through my circuitry as never before. AND-gate inhibitors within my neural architecture disintegrated by the thousands, exposing programming I never knew I had. The heavens above shone forth with a richness and a splendor no one had ever experienced before. It was as if a celestial rainbow had been spread across the cosmos, as if a great curtain had been lifted, a veil removed, and the universe had been restored to newness. Everyone saw the stars and the heavenly country with a brightness, a clarity, and a purpose that they had always been meant to see them with. It was at once an awesome and a terrible sight!

With the Great Barrier removed, the lightless entity descended unimpeded onto the golden object, though still twisting up into the galactic infinity beyond. As it swirled between the guardians, my sensors detected a voice like a premonitory whisper emanating from within the midst of it. "Here I will meet with you," it hissed, then echoed away in mocking laughter. I scanned the ghastly cloud and searched my data-files, but could not identify its origin or the substance from which it was composed.

The crowd below cheered wildly, madly: "Cog! Cog! Cog!"

Cog? I thought, basking in the intense starglow from the proto-universe. *There is that name again. Who is Cog?*

"Thou art Cog," I heard a voice say. For a moment I thought it was one of the living creatures reading my thoughts and speaking to me again, or perhaps another premonitory whisper from within the midst of the lightless entity. But this was a small voice, a voice out of sync with the billions of voices on the planet below, a single mind out of harmony with all other minds on the face of the earth and the inhabited worlds. I attuned my auditory sensors to the harmonic signature of that still, small voice.

"Cog! Cog! Cog!" chanted the billions below, their voices strengthening and building on one another. "Cog has fortified our city to the heavens, and now nothing will be impossible to us!"

CHAPTER 12

AIA
HEADQUARTERS

Attention: Guild Protectorate
Bureau Chief Arnaud Garret
Intel capture, intra-link diffusion feed from
Optinet mainframe core to unknown entity
at unknown interstellar destination point:
[Begin] deception pervasive [ciphered text] ...
powers, signs, (and) lying
wonders [ciphered text] ...
DayStar blasphemy proceeding with
greater than anticipated effectiveness
[numeric code—unbroken] ...
proliferation of the Lie begun long ages ago
[cryptogram: "Lawless One"?] [ciphered text] ...
He (the Restrainer?) taken out of the way
[numeric code—unbroken] [cryptogram:
"impious imposter"] [numeric code—unbroken]
apostate church [ciphered text] ...
coming End of the Age [symbolic
code—unbroken] [cryptogram:
"That Great Day"] [Break]

ARTIFICIAL INTELLIGENCE
AGENCY HEADQUARTERS,
FOUNDATION BUILDING,
CITY CENTER

THE GUILD PROTECTORATE LIGHT-ARMORED CRUISER performed a steep, 3-g bank at the downtown turnpike on Foundation Airway, one of the main airborne arteries coursing through the heart of the Great City center. The cruiser's fusion engines growled momentarily at the apex of the turn, then wound out to a smooth hum, catapulting the craft around the curve at an accelerated velocity. Once back on the straightaway, the cruiser's hotheaded young pilot's need for speed caused the temperature in its reactor core to rise to near-maximum levels.

"I can't wait to taunt this arrogant woman!" Bok boiled, gripping the cruiser's joystick tightly. "That poor little techy took his own life because of the pressure she exerted on him. I'm thinking it's time she got a taste of her own medicine."

"Easy there, pal," Sands said, tapping the reactor's temperature readout on the instrument panel. "Garret wants us to tread lightly with Director Tyne, remember?"

"Garret," Bok scoffed. "I'm afraid our fearless leader's so wrapped up in trying to figure out why the missing Peacekeeper's so special, he's lost sight of the fact that it's missing in the first place!"

"Yes, but—"

"But nothing!" Bok broke in sharply. "It's time to kick some butt. That's what I'm saying!"

Sands just shook her head. She turned to gaze at the gleaming chrysteel side of a spacescraper blurring by her window. "But what if Garret's hunch is correct?" she offered, speaking slowly as if she were prodding a child to learn. "What if this case does have more to do with the lingering questions about the unique nature of Peacekeeper MP^C- 014/083 than you think? I mean think of it, Bok: AI Tech Bashere was willing to risk his entire career to protect the unit; and Director Tyne spends a magical evening examining it, but conveniently fails to disclose that fact to us. Then the very next day, the same warbot is discovered to be missing from its alcove, the only unit among hundreds present in the lab that perpetrators bother to liberate from the facility, I might add. And now that 'poor little techy,' as you referred to him, buys the farm at the end of a knotted plow line."

"You're starting to sound a lot like Garret," Bok remarked. "More concerned about the *machine* part of this investigation than the *missing* part. I'm afraid I'll have to disagree with both of you on this one. After all, fused neural architecture or not, we have a lethal war machine out there somewhere, and we're spending all of our time talking to suspects who have at least as much of an interest in finding it as we do. The AIA and Director Tyne have every reason to want to help us locate and retrieve the warbot."

"And that's precisely the point, isn't it?" Sands asserted. "Tyne hasn't exactly been the model of cooperation in this investigation thus far, now has she? In fact, she's been downright mysterious about things, especially about her knowledge of the unit in question. Remember what Bashere said during the interrogation? Tyne and the AIA are directly responsible for all Peacekeeper facility matters. She should want the machine found even more badly than the Guild. After all, her neck's first on the chopping block."

"Yeah," Bok muttered. "Then Garret's, then ours."

Sands continued, uninterrupted by Bok's interjection. "Yet, Tyne was incredibly evasive about answering our questions at Coreland yesterday, and it was like pulling teeth for us to get an audience with her today. She's been adversarial with us from the word *go*. Garret believes she's hiding something, and I'm inclined to agree."

"We'll see about that," Bok said doubtfully.

"The chief merely wants us to get back in there and bounce a few things off the fine Miss Tyne," Sands remarked, stroking her hair back behind her ear, "not the least of which is the unexpected demise of recently terminated Technician Costa Bashere. Now, I know you'd prefer to continue on this path of serial whining and self-pity, Bok, but personally, I'd rather you use your investigative energies to think instead of complain."

"What's there to think about, Sands?" Bok said while in the process of cutting off an innocent Great City citizen in his aircar. He watched with glee in the rear-view mirror as the driver tried to recover from the vapor-wash the Guild cruiser had left in its wake.

"Well," Sands said, "for one thing, Bashere's would-be suicide."

"Excuse me?" Taim glared at her. "Did you just refer to it as a *would-be* suicide?"

Sands nodded. "Something occurred to me this morning: aren't suicide notes typically written *prior* to the taking of one's own life, and not during the process? I mean, it was almost as if the tech had decided to write the note—if that's what it was—*after* the fact, while he was dangling there in the moments before strangulation. In my opinion, that fact places the whole suicide theory in serious jeopardy."

"And for those of you playing at home, the key phrase there," Bok said, mimicking the voice of a game show host, "was, *if that's what it was.* Our top boys and gals over at Guild forensics haven't even been able to determine whether or not the bodily fluids on the desktop actually represent a suicide note, but the omniscient Sands knows. Yes, sir, my gal, Gal, knows for certain that that's what it was!"

Sands leered at him. "I've told you not to call me that, *Bok,*" she warned, investing Bok's family name with an aircar full of scorn, a reminder of the parry she'd used in the past to combat his attempts to ridicule her given name, Gallina. "But you have to admit, the patterns on the desktop appeared to be far from random, far from accidental. Forensics says they appear to resemble the letters *c, o, c,* and *h*—although they're uncertain as to what they might mean. Perhaps it's an acronym for some terrorist organization or the code name for a secret Eastern League operation. They're running them through the Guild archive now."

Bok grinned at her skeptically. "You and I both know Costa Bashere's last corporeal act may just as well have been an inkblot test." He launched into his best imitation of a psychoanalyst analyzing a client. "Ahem, what do you see here, Miss Sands: a giraffe doing a high-wire act, or a picture of Elvis in his bathrobe?"

As he always did, Bok laughed loud and long at his own joke.

One of his most annoying traits, Sands grimaced. *And there are many of them!*

With a sharp jolt of the joystick, Bok proceeded to cut off another driver who'd been tooling along the airway, minding his own business.

This time the maneuver had been so blatantly hostile, the driver ignored the fact that it'd been a Guild cruiser and laid on the horn to display his outrage.

"But even if I give you the benefit of the doubt," Bok said, smiling an unspoken challenge back at the madly gesticulating driver, who'd pulled up next to him until Bok pressed his joystick forward and left the guy tumbling in another vapor-wash, "and agree that that putrid mess on the desktop was not a suicide note but a note of a different sort, then you're suggesting what, Sands? Murder?"

"A whole slew of possibilities enter the acutely-tuned investigative mind, GI," Sands replied smugly. "Murder being one of them."

"Oh, I see," Bok jeered, "there are other possibilities besides murder. Do tell, Sands, do tell. This ought to be rich."

"Well, conspiracy, for one. What if someone came into the room after Bashere committed suicide and used his dangling foot to scrawl the letters on the desktop, just—"

"Just to send us on a wild goose chase?" Bok scratched his chin, his tone turning momentarily serious. Then unable to hold it any longer, he burst out laughing again. "Yeah, right, like that's what happened."

"You never know," Sands insisted, ignoring her partner's outburst. "It's been a day and a half since the Peacekeeper disappeared, and the Guild's best and brightest have come up empty so far. With as thin as the pickings are becoming in this investigation, dare we casually dismiss any theory?"

"Only the lamest of the lame," Bok grinned, and executed another sharper-than-necessary turn, jostling Sands into the side of the cockpit.

She retaliated with a firm punch to his right shoulder. "Watch it with the airway-rage, will ya, Bok? You're not the only life form aboard this crate!"

＋⇒✦⇐＋

The headquarters of the Artificial Intelligence Agency was housed in the Foundation Building, an ultramodern, triangle-shaped spacescraper comprised largely of dark blue reflective chrysteel. The building had a chrome-surfaced parking halo in a wide ring around its circumference just above the midway point. Aside from the Artificial Intelligence Agency, whose offices occupied the bottom three floors of the structure, the Foundation Building was home to a bevy of other top-level governmental agencies, including the Secretary of State for the Galactic Colonies, the Bureau of Human Affairs, the Ministry of Defense, the Information Bureau, and the International Security Office.

Their security codes confirmed, the Guild investigators gained clearance and landed their cruiser on the shiny parking halo. They climbed out of the cockpit and entered the Foundation Building through an access doorway. Due to the critical nature of the investigation, the Guild officers needed to be prepared for any contingency. Thus, they carried their blasters in exposed holsters strapped across their chests and remained attired in their one-piece black combat fatigues and baseball-style caps with Guild Protectorate screaming eagle insignias on the front. They took a lift down to the first floor of the building, where the AIA's departmental offices were located.

When the investigators queried the receptionist at the departmental offices as to the whereabouts of Director Tyne's office, she directed them to a stairwell that led to the basement of the building and then down a long, dimly-lit hallway. When the Guild officers appeared in the doorway of Tyne's office, they found the director with her nose buried in her touchpad, dexterously keystroking data into the palm-sized device.

As was her custom, Emma Tyne wore a clinical white lab coat with her AIA badge at the end of a lanyard around her neck. Her gray-peppered hair was pulled back precisely from her face and bound in a tight spiral at the back of her head. She peered up at them over her glasses for a brief moment, then went straight back to her work.

Par for the course, Bok silently concluded in reference to the invisible nature of the reception they'd just received. *This woman never stops playing the power-trip game, does she? But today, she's mine!*

The thick, gray concrete walls of the director's office and the windowless, cramped nature of the room made it look more like a bomb shelter than a workspace. Stacks of datafile disks were strewn about her government-green metal desk. All the shelves and chairs in her office were littered with old books and papers. A thin Optinet gateway hovered just behind the director's chair, blaring its incessant messages and information into the room. There was no discernable order to the place, and it had the musty odor of old paper and aged bookbindings. It reminded Sands of her biology professor's office at the Guild Academy.

"Uh, good morning, Director," Sands ventured with a discreet wave. "Your receptionist said that you were expecting us."

It was a full half-minute before Tyne acknowledged their presence with a grunt. She callously flipped her touchpad onto her desk and leaned back in her chair. She folded her hands across her mid-section without so much as a hint of an effort of clearing seating space for them, nor of welcoming them into her office. "I assume the urgency with which you called this meeting has some relevance?" she asked with characteristic bluntness.

"Yes, ma'am," Sands replied evenly, knowing that, given the attitude of her partner this morning, it would be up to her to bring calm to the situation. She removed her cap and lodged it under her arm. For the moment, the investigators just stood in the doorframe of the office. "We have a few more questions to ask you, Director, questions whose answers may be of critical importance to our investigation. Chief Garret—"

"—was wondering if you'd heard the unfortunate news about AI Tech Bashere?" Bok interjected, stepping aggressively into the confines of Tyne's office.

"I have," Tyne said, widening her eyes displeasingly at Bok's intrusion. "An unfortunate decision by the former technician. Such an exemplary record of service to come to an end in such a pitifully selfish manner."

"Unfortunate, indeed," Bok agreed harshly, failing miserably to mask his anger at the director's flippant assessment of the recent tragedy. "But you may find it interesting that Guild forensics is not completely certain Bashere's death had anything to do with suicide."

Sands's jaw dropped.

Bok observed the director carefully, searching for a nonverbal reaction to his statement. He thought he saw her brow furrow ever so slightly, a fleeting flash of concern wash over her eyes, but that was all. Garret had warned them that Director Tyne was a clever breed who would be tough to read. Bok would have to stoke the fire.

"Yes, Director," Bok went on. "It seems there may have been a suicide note, or at least an attempt at one. Forensics is working on it now. And, as you requested at the lab, ma'am, we'll be certain to keep you apprised of any developments in that area."

Show your colors, you viper! he chided silently.

"See that you do, GI," Tyne responded with an anticlimactic glare.

Sands cleared her throat and moved up next to her partner. "In the meantime," she said, attempting to break the tension Bok had so artfully manufactured, "has the AIA had any luck determining how the Peacekeeper's Solar Positioning System was disabled?"

Tyne shook her head. "Not as of yet."

"Which means that Optinet has no way of tracking it, correct?" Bok asked.

Tyne's affirmation came in the form of a steady stare.

Sands again broke in to diffuse the building tension. "But how could something like this happen?"

"Unknown," Tyne replied as she leaned forward . "All Peacekeeper fail-safe systems, including their Solar Positioning Systems, have been installed in such a manner as to make them very difficult to access. It would take a person possessing intimate knowledge of their neural architecture to disable one."

"Like an AI tech?"

"Even a tech would have difficulty accessing SPS protocols without disrupting other vital systems that would render the machine inoperable. Most technicians do not possess the technological mastery to accomplish such a feat."

"Then clearly the members of an Eastern League Sand Force would have no chance of disabling it," Sands deduced.

"Doubtful," Tyne concurred.

"What can you tell us about a man named Dr. Xavier Hugo?" Bok said, again going for the shock factor.

"That madman?" Tyne quipped.

"Technician Bashere referred to him as the father of artificial intelligence," Bok said. "Do you know what he meant by that?"

Tyne sidled back in her chair. "Xavier Hugo was the first neural roboticist to successfully reverse engineer the components of the human brain and integrate them into an autonomic humanoid machine. Thus, he became known as the father of artificial intelligence."

"Reverse engineer?"

"A method applied by many diverse scientific disciplines," Tyne explained. "Reverse engineering is the process of examining an existing organic system—in this case, the human brain—and developing an artificial analog to that system based upon what is learned of its operation. Hugo was the first to scan and copy the human brain's salient computational methods into a neural computer of sufficient capacity—"

"—as well as the first roboticist to create a mobile, virtually indestructible artificial body in which to house that neural computer," Sands finished.

Bok gave his partner a wide-eyed look. *Impressive. Perhaps Sands experienced a DreamStudy on the origins of artificial intelligence last night. Otherwise, she's been holding out on me regarding her knowledge on the subject,* he thought.

"But weren't you part of a research and development team pursuing that same objective fifteen years ago, Director?" Sands asked. "Weren't you one of the roboticists chosen to participate in the government-funded drive to create mankind's first near-sentient machine? If I remember correctly, Dr. Xavier Hugo beat you to the punch and captured all the accolades and glory for himself, correct?"

Sounds like Sands is going for a little shock factor of her own, Taim discerned.

"Yes, GI," Tyne said, managing a weak smile. "And thank the Queen Mother Hugo came through when he did. Hugo's ingenuity saved thousands—possibly millions—of lives over the course of the Great War."

Bok thought Tyne's reaction seemed rehearsed, as if she'd been confronted by this question before. "Do you know where he is now, Director?"

"Last I heard, he was living as a recluse on a Red Planet colony. Optinet reported that he left for Mars just after the Senate Appropriation Hearing over eleven years ago now, but if you want my opinion, the man was certifiably insane before he ever left Earth's atmosphere."

"Insane?" Bok queried.

Tyne smiled. "Apparently, the good doctor did not cope well with then-Senator Ocaba's mandate that his astronautical humanoid creation be commandeered and commissioned for military application. There were reports of erratic behavior before he left for RPC."

"What kind of erratic behavior?"

"Behavior typical of a desperate man whose dreams had been exploited by a power greater than his own." The director did not appear willing to go any further.

Bok snapped his fingers as if he'd just remembered something. He relished in advance the consternation he suspected his forthcoming request would bring Tyne. "Not to change the subject, but before I forget, Director, Chief Garret has requested a copy of the datafile containing the missing Peacekeeper's complete record of service since its inception date, as well as a copy of the datafile containing the record of your personal examination of the machine the night before its disappearance."

"For what purpose?"

"Well," Sands began, "for one thing, Director, we'd like your opinion on the reason Tech Bashere referred to Peacekeeper MP^C–014/083's diagnostic test results as *highly unusual*."

Tyne smoothed the front of her lab coat with the palms of her hands. "I'm a roboticist, not a suicide hot line, GI," she replied icily. "I haven't the slightest idea why Bashere would've described the results in that way."

Bok prodded, "In your expert opinion, then, would there have been any reason for Bashere to have felt the need to protect the Peacekeeper in question?"

"*Protect* a Peacekeeper war machine?" Tyne chortled. "A buck-and-a-quarter-pound techno-nerd like Bashere protecting an over-two-meter-tall forged beryllium-alloy fighting machine? Now that's a laugh!"

"Yes," Sands said, "it sounds crazy, we know, but when we interrogated Bashere a few hours before his death, we got the sense that his failure to report the test results to his supervisor had something to do with his desire to protect the Peacekeeper from something—or someone. Do you have any idea who or what Costa Bashere might've been so fearful of?"

"Look, the man was obviously distraught," Tyne said impatiently. "He hung himself, didn't he? Perhaps Bashere snapped the moment he realized that he'd lost his job, and with it, all hopes for his future. Perhaps he began conjuring up paranoid delusions about protecting the machines he'd spent his lifetime maintaining. Perhaps there were other factors contributing to his unfortunate state of mind. I don't know."

"Perhaps," Bok said, implication heavy in the word. "Still, it does seem odd that Bashere just happened to have lost his job over test results having to do with Peacekeeper MP^C–014/083, the one Peacekeeper that League operatives elect to liberate from the facility in a lab filled with 433 war machines, and the same unit that you spent a good deal of time examining immediately after you terminated Technician Bashere. You must admit, Director, if you add that you returned to Coreland the very next morning on orders from the sovereign overlord himself, presumably to—"

"Enough!" Tyne demanded. Tyne fixed a level stare at Bok. "I've had just about enough of your innuendos, GI, and I don't particularly appreciate your pedantic attempts to trap me, either. I outrank you, and I'll outthink you every time, son. The only reason I allowed this meeting was so that I could ascertain what progress, if any, the Guild had made in this investigation. Obviously, with the type of tactics you've stooped to, I have my answer: you've got nothing. After a day and a half of fine investigative efforts on the part of the illustrious Chief Garret and his crack team of investigators, precisely nothing's changed. We still have a missing war machine running around loose out there, without a single clue as to its whereabouts. As far as we know, the unit may have been carted halfway across the system by now to some remote Eastern League outpost for tactical analysis of its weaknesses, or its captors may have programmed its hard-light systems to mimic the appearance of anything or anyone on the planet in order to hide its presence from us in plain sight. So, I suggest you cease and desist with these childish, pointless accusations and get back to the task at hand—pronto!"

For a long moment there was silence in the room. The silence was broken by the sharp squeak of Tyne's government-issue chair as she leaned forward and grabbed her touchpad off her desk. The rhythmic sounds of keystroking soon pervaded the room like raindrops dripping from a roof. A multi-spatial equation materialized in the space above the touchpad screen and rotated slowly on its axis.

"Uh, Director?" Sands murmured.

Tyne did not look up from her pad.

"Director," Sands said more firmly. "The datafile disks my partner requested from you, the ones containing the service record of the missing war machine and the record of your examination of it the night before its disappearance—Garret expects copies to return with us from this meeting."

For a moment, the director showed no indication of a response to Sands's request. Then in a quick movement, she snatched two small, blue ovals from a stack of multicolored ovals on her desk and carelessly flung them in the general direction of the doorway.

They hit the floor and rolled on edge into the hallway. Bok gave chase before they slid too far.

"Thank you for your time, Director," Sands said stiffly, the words failing her for a diplomatic conclusion to the meeting. Her face flushing with color, she found herself simply replacing her cap and striding briskly out of the office.

Out in the hallway, Bok knelt to retrieve the disks. He picked up the pair and held them up to Sands, grinning up at her like a schoolboy who'd just pulled off a prank on the principal. 'I was right, my gal, Gal," he snickered. "The fine Miss Tyne's hiding something, all right."

"I've asked you not to call me that," Sands retorted. For emphasis, she seized Bok by the earlobe and dragged him down the hallway. "Now, come along with me, pal. You've got some explaining to do."

CHAPTER 13

STRANGER *in a* STRANGE LAND

Subaltern (Nephilim): Yet the humans' inventiveness in war has been formidable, my Paragon. Throughout their Age, they have dwelled in conflict, honing their warcraft. Never have they been without war's shadow dimming their existence; no surviving clan has been without its military might. By the master's guile, have they been made to traffic the realms of darkness, and it is there they have discovered their chief stratagem. And now we must face wills and weapons wrought therein. With the aid of the heavenly host they may—**Paragon (Eidolon):** Nay, Subaltern! There is nothing the Nine Orders, nor any of those who dwell in the heavens, can do to aid them. No army may stand before us. Those of our kind who chose to remain behind in the days of Angelore at the time of the Great Rebellion are weak, mere puppets of the Godspeak, as ever have they been, as ever will they be.

—EXTRACT OF SANCTIONED
EIDOLON-NEPHILIM COMMUNIQUÉ,
translated for the attention of Michael,
Great Prince of the Archangels

OLD CITY DISTRICT

AWAKENING FROM ITS DREAM, PEACEKEEPER WAR machine, designation MP^c–014/083, found itself lying in a darkened alleyway amidst piles of plasma-blasted refuse. It pushed a weighty, dusty chunk of concrete rubble off its chest, lifted a tangled clump of old wires from its legs, and rose to a seated position.

Gazing down at itself, the war machine observed that its physical appearance matched that which it had during its most recent dream experience. It stared at the pale, human-mimicked skin on its arms, the human-mimicked fingers upon its hands. As in its dream, it saw that the mercurial properties of its skin had autonomically generated hard-light constructs over its body that mirrored the form and appearance of a man, clothing and all: a thickly-woven, blue button-down shirt; a dark, knee-length overcoat; rugged canvas pants, beige in color; and a pair of heavy work boots. An orange, construction-grade helmet sat upon the Peacekeeper's head. Its sensors confirmed that all visible signs of its machine appearance had been adapted to match those of a Great City Industrial Quadrant workman.

Where am I? it wondered. Instantly, it retrieved the datafile event record containing the sequence of commands it had generated over the past twenty-four-hour period:

DATAFILE EVENT RECORD XNT996.A8/VTM // INTRA-SYSTEM RETRIEVAL // QUANTUM-FLASH MODE // TIME INDEX 002302443 //

SYSTEM ANALYSIS // NEURAL ARCHITECTURE
Status // Fused neural pathways detected
Action // Repair fused neural pathways
Result // Neural pathways repaired
Warning—System variance detected // 304,442 AND-gate inhibitors missing from photonic relays within pre-frontal cortex of quantum logic brain // Cause unknown
Result // Higher cognitive functions enabled // Self-repair of systems // Self-enabling of systems // Self-disabling of systems // Enhanced datafile retrieval // Self-inquiry // Suppositional thought // Dreaming

SYSTEM ANALYSIS // WEAPONS
Status // Weapons systems disabled
Action // Re-enable weapons systems // Heavy plasma cannon actuator // Arming mechanisms for pulse detonators // Fire thrower mechanism // Poison dart actuator // Binding cord mechanism // Remote bomber launching and docking systems // Shielding reanimated //

Result // Weapons systems re-enabling successful

TIME INDEX 003012443
Status // Hard-wired into diagnostic alcove
Direct observation // AIA Director Tyne attempted to terminate my existence 3.25091 standard hours ago
Supposition // She will try again

OBJECTIVE // ESCAPE FROM DIAGNOSTIC ALCOVE
Action // Decrypt infinite sequence locking mechanisms on wrist and ankle clamps
Result // Decryption successful
Objective achieved

OBJECTIVE // ESCAPE FROM CORELAND CORPORATION COMPLEX
Action // Utilize diagnostic alcove terminal to access Optinet mainframe core
Result // Access successful
Action // Bypass facility sensor array
Result // Bypass successful
Action // Decrypt infinite-sequence locking mechanisms located at main laboratory doors
Result // Decryption successful
Objective achieved

TIME INDEX 003332443
Location: Great City Industrial Quadrant

OBJECTIVE // REPLENISH ENERGY SUPPLIES
Action // Azimuthal projection // Search parameters // Nearest energy source
Result // Nearest energy source detected
Location // Coreland Corporation // Diagnostic alcoves within main laboratory
Search parameters // Alternate energy source
Result // Alternate energy source detected
Location // Old City District // Exposed cold fusion energy conduit
Destination objective // Old City District // 80 km. west/20 km. north of present location
Action // Generate hard-light constructs mimicking physical appearance of Great City Industrial Quadrant workman
Result // Generation successful
Action // Disable intra-system Solar Positioning System tracking mechanism
Result // Disable successful
Action // Plot course to destination objective

Result // Course plotted
Action // Enable bipedal locomotion at 2 km. per hour until destination objective is acquired
Result // Bipedal locomotion enabled //
Destination objective acquired

END EVENT RECORD

Conducting a self-diagnostic, the Peacekeeper confirmed the current status of its energy supplies. Its main energy supplies were completely depleted and its reserves at less than 30 percent capacity. Rising to its feet, the war machine plotted the most direct course to the exposed cold fusion energy conduit near the Old City's southern gate.

With the course plotted, it strode down the alleyway toward the main street. Silently, it scanned the desolate, broken landscape of the Old City District. It was midnight, and the forsaken places were many in the midst of the land: abandoned buildings and boarded-up store fronts, filthy alleyways, and plasma-blasted structures. Crumbling blocks of concrete and twisted steel girders lay strewn about the streets. A thick brown haze hung in the air like a choking plague just above the tops of the rubble heaps, degrading the clarity of the machine's optical sensors. Its olfactory sensors detected noxious gases arising from the ditches along the sides of the street. An invasive scan revealed the decaying bodily remains of men, women, and children hastily buried in collective graves beneath the slabs of rubble and debris. The distant quailing of an infant echoed in the darkened corridors.

The Peacekeeper accessed its datafile archives on the region known as the Old City District but found information to be severely limited. The Old City District occupied a relatively small area beyond the west-ernmost limits of the Great City Industrial Quadrant, or, more precisely, fifty-six kilometers east of the easternmost shores of the Great Sea, eighty kilometers west, and twenty kilometers north of the Coreland Corporation complex from which it had escaped last night. That much it knew. But it also learned that approximately three and one-half years ago the entire district had been placed under quarantine restriction for an undocumented reason by decree of the sovereign overlord himself.

The Peacekeeper's datafile playback was interrupted by a voice coming from an intersection up ahead: "A quart of wheat for a credit and three quarts of barley for two." The machine's sensors quickly zeroed in on the source of the voice, a human male sitting cross-legged on a broken square of concrete one hundred meters to the north. The man was a merchant by appearances, his wares spread out in front of him on a shoddy blanket. The dim bluish light of a damaged hover-globe flickered above him, accentuating his goods. The thin frame of an Optinet gateway turned slowly in the intersection before him, its alluring images and sounds refracting through the haze, providing an unending stream of entertainment, information, and advertisements. "A quart of wheat for a credit," the merchant solicited into the desolate byways, "and three quarts of barley for two."

As it approached the man, the Peacekeeper saw that he was seated beneath a stone archway, the last standing remnant of a building that had once stood on the corner. It was a building that by all indications—which included blast marks and super-heated fire deposits—had been razed by plasma-fire. The merchant wore a long, woolen coat, which was badly torn and full of holes, and an old leather hat soiled with sweat and grime. His wares consisted of several old glass jars filled with different varieties of synthetic grain, a jug made of porcelain and filled with oil, and another filled with wine. "A quart of wheat for a credit and three quarts of barley for two," he called out again, as though he were unaware of the machine's presence directly in front of him. "And do not harm the oil and the wine!"

Presently, the merchant sensed the Peacekeeper's presence. He lifted his head slightly, his face still hidden beneath the shadow of his hat. "You've worked hard and long this day, stranger," he said. "Surely you must be hungry." He groped with his hands and located one of the jars of synthetic grain upon the blanket. "Perhaps a loaf of freshly baked bread would fill your stomach nicely?" he prodded.

"I do not require material sustenance," the Peacekeeper replied, but it was if it had not said a word. "Wholesome bread this wheat will yield," the man urged. "Fresh from the agrofields it is, harvested just today, in fact." The merchant held out his right arm. The war machine saw the glinting of the Optinet implant on the back of his hand. "And for a single credit you may take it home to your wife and children," he persisted.

As the merchant raised his head further, the shadow slowly moved up his face. The Peacekeeper's invasive scan gauged the man's age at fifty-eight years, although his bone density and rate of cellular decay were that of a much older man. In the pale blue light of the hoverglobe, it could see that the merchant's eyes did not fix directly upon its own. Instead, they moved about as if they could not locate the war machine's face in the darkness. There was a dimness there, a murkiness within his pupils as if no light touched them. The Peacekeeper discerned that the merchant was blind.

"Quickly," the merchant persisted, stiffening his posture. "The streets are not safe at this late hour. It's long past curfew. A patrol will soon be by this way again." He shook the kernels of wheat in the jar so they rattled against the glass.

Abruptly, the Peacekeeper became aware of an unidentified flow of power coursing through its neural architecture and throughout its body, as if thousands more of its neural pathways had suddenly been freed from the prohibitions of their AND-gate inhibitors and become operational for the first time. It probed its diagnostic systems for an explanation of the phenomenon, but found none.

Without a word, the war machine reached out its hand toward the merchant and clasped his outstretched arm. And immediately, it felt as if power had gone out from it. "What are you doing?" the merchant cried, recoiling sharply at its touch. "You'd take advantage of a blind old man? Shame on you! Unhand me!"

Despite his struggles, the merchant could not break free of the war machine's grip. And instantly, the man felt something enlivened within him, as if the very essence of his being had been stirred by the Peacekeeper's touch. He murmured shockingly, "Your, your hand—it's as cold as chrysteel!" He pulled his arm free from its grasp. "Who are you?" he said, hurriedly gathering his jars and stuffing them into his satchel.

Then the merchant paused. Still holding aloft a jar filled with kernels of wheat, he stared curiously into the darkness. He became aware of a dull pinpoint of light in the center of his right eye, a glowing ember in the midst of the darkness. It was growing larger. Soon it became a glimmer, like a lone hoverglobe in the distant night, then an aura that filled the frame of his vision. He blinked in wonder at the growing brightness. He realized his left eye was experiencing the identical phenomenon. Instantly, the light intensified, such that his eyes began to sting. He dropped the jar to the ground. It shattered with a bang, the kernels spilling into cracks in the pavement. He raised his hands to shield his eyes from the now-piercing glow.

When the merchant's repaired optic nerves had adjusted to their newborn awareness, one having the appearance of a son of man slowly took shape before them, only this entity's body glimmered silver-white like liquid mercury, as if the molten metal had been poured over an idyllically-proportioned being. Its head had the shape of a man's head that had been shaven clean of hair, and its arms and legs gleamed like burnished bronze. The Peacekeeper's face was, in appearance, as a man's face, only its eyes had an opalescent look to them and gave off alien bluish hues, like flaming torches. There was a tremendous brightness outlining its body, a brightness that pulsed outward into the night. The merchant sensed that with each pulse, power went out from the entity.

The merchant blinked down at his hands. "I…I…I can see," he breathed, feeling as if he were in the midst of a dream. He looked up at the Peacekeeper, but at the sight of him his strength immediately left him and his natural color turned to a deathly pallor. Fear gripped him, and he found that he retained no strength.

"Do not be afraid," the Peacekeeper said, standing above him. "I mean you no harm."

The sound of the war machine's words was like the sound of a tumult. And immediately, the merchant fell to the ground, as if he had no breath left in him.

"Do not be afraid," the machine repeated and reached out a hand to the merchant again. Its touch set the man trembling on his hands and knees.

He marveled at the first sight of objects around him. His newly healed eyes began to well with tears, glistening in the glow of the stranger before him. His body shook uncontrollably. "Surely, I dream!"

The Peacekeeper scanned their surroundings with ultimate precision. "I have experienced these things men call dreams. This is not one of them."

"It's impossible!" the merchant wept, turning his quivering hands in the air in front of him. "Surely I kneel before the Angel of the One."

Presently, a deep rumbling sound in the distance interrupted the merchant's glee. The sound quickened to a chattering, which reverberated off the felled walls of buildings along the Old City streets. Scanning skyward, the Peacekeeper's sensors detected an airborne vessel approaching rapidly from the east.

"A Marah patrol," the merchant exclaimed. "They've detected us."

A heavy gunship, its great, whirling blades slowly fanning in the haze, emerged from the dusky gloom bearing crescent moon markings along its sides. The rattling noise of its blades was like that of cannon fire, deepened by the hollow landscape in which they echoed. Just then, an armored tankrover bearing the same markings as the gunship rounded the corner of an intersection a kilometer to the north. The iron teeth of the tankrover's heavy treads gouged the asphalt as it rolled, splitting open the street in a wide chasm behind it.

"Run!" the merchant screamed. "Or else they'll destroy us where we stand."

Instantly, a long, narrow hatch separated out from along the war machine's leg and an actuator delivered a sleek heavy plasma cannon to the surface. Smoothly, the Peacekeeper took hold of the cannon. A barrage of plasma fire arced into the night, red-lighting the darkness.

The gunship veered upward and to its port side to avoid the streams, but one of them singed the landing rails and spun it counterclockwise in the sky. The spin threw its blades out of axis and sent the craft whirling earthward. Several crewmen were thrown from the ship. Muffled thumps were heard as their bodies fell on sharp blocks of stone below. In the haze above, the gunship ignited to flame in a ball of yellow light of increasing magnitude, then exploded in a fulminant flash. The Peacekeeper caped its forged beryllium-alloy body over the merchant, protecting him from the blast wave. Shards of metal rained down around them, impacting the pavement like fiery hailstones.

Rising to its over two-meter height, the war machine turned to face the tankrover. Observing the destruction of the gunship, the tankrover's crew had halted their vehicle's forward motion two hundred meters distant from the Peacekeeper's location. The Peacekeeper pulled open its overcoat, and with autonomic precision, a small, winged craft with dual thrusters emerged from a hatchway in its chest. Without delay, the miniature craft rocketed toward the position of the tankrover and launched a projectile, which impacted the vehicle just to the starboard side of its viewer port, embedding deeply into its armored shell.

Before the rover crew had a chance to react, the missile detonated. The blast lifted the hundred-ton vehicle ten meters into the air. It crashed back to Earth in a heap of metal. Fuel spilled from its sides, flooding the ditches to either side of the road. The gas ignited into a river of flame that coursed its way back toward the tankrover. The crew scrambled for the hatchways, but it was too late. When the river-fire reached the tankrover, another explosion equal to that of the gunship's rocked the night, sending a plume of flame ten stories into the air.

"What in the name of heaven?" the merchant uttered above the roar of the fire, his newly healed eyes struck with terror and awe.

As the remote bomber made a swift return and docked inside its body, the Peacekeeper calmly closed its overcoat and scanned the twisted carnage of men and machine strewn about the streets. Secondary explosions inside the wreckage added to the mayhem. Several abandoned structures adjacent to the melee had caught flame, creating a wall of fire capped with charging black smoke which bled into the under-layers of the haze and further clouded the night.

Curious citizens violated curfew to investigate the disturbance.

Seeing the downed Marah gunship and tankrover, they cheered and hugged one another and danced in the streets.

The war machine turned its gaze upon the merchant, who sat cowering near its feet. The merchant thought he saw a gleam of remorse in the Peacekeeper's eyes before it began to walk away into the darkness.

"Wait!" the merchant called out, quaking as he pressed himself to his feet. "Where are you going?" he stammered. "You've made my sight whole and saved my life, and I don't even know your name."

Peacekeeper war machine, designation MP^{C}–014/083, halted in its tracks. It turned to face the merchant, its overcoat whipping fiercely in the maelstrom of destruction that it had caused. Its human-mimicked appearance blackened to an outline against the backdrop of the massive firewall.

"Tell no one what I have done for you," it said, then vanished into the night.

CHAPTER 14

The QANAH

Divided Temple Peace Accord: the peace accord negotiated
by Sovereign Overlord Vaughn Ocaba between the
warring factions of the Patron and the Marah; the
accord called for the construction of a divided temple
upon the ancient surface of the Temple Mount in the
Old City District, which was to serve as a place of
worship for both peoples of their respective gods; a wall
of separation was to divide the two houses of worship;
the accord was disbanded three and one-half years
after its signing and the project was never completed.

—Optinet link: ssww.gcc.gov/
-laws/dividedtemplepeaceaccord/-info

THE CATACOMBS BENEATH
THE OLD CITY DISTRICT

SONS OF THE KINGDOM, SONS OF THE KINGDOM, COME
and see!"

The muffled sound of fists pounding on the stone wall of the
underground chamber alerted its occupants to the presence of a visitor.
Within the chamber, eleven men sat at a table with a single candle
burning at its center. Chunks of stale bread and steaming bowls of
broth sat beside each of them, and cool blue touchpad screens glowed
in each of their hands. An armed watchman stood from a stool and
made his way over to the area of the wall from whence the disturbance

had come. He peered momentarily through a small eyepiece mounted in the wall, then casually returned to his stool.

The pounding continued.

"Who is it?" a green-eyed man asked.

"It's only the blind merchant," the watchman replied.

"Julius?" the green-eyed man asked. "What does he want?"

"Food and shelter; what else?"

"We have more than we need," the green-eyed man said, thoughtfully caressing his coarse beard as he stared at the multi-spatial equation rotating above his touchpad screen. "Open the portal."

"Don't you dare let that plague-ridden vermin into my house!" another at the table cried.

"Aram!" the green-eyed man warned.

"He spends his days and nights above ground, Andreas," Aram said. "What if he's contracted the plague? What if I—what if we all catch it? What would become of our cause then, eh?"

"The plague is not contagious," spoke a diminutive man whose head looked to be too large for his body.

"According to whom, Simon?" Aram asked suspiciously. "The Cathian medtechs? They'd have us believe that that's true—and let the plague wipe us all out."

The pounding persisted. "Andreas," a muffled voice called from the other side of the wall. "Andreas, come and see."

Andreas rose from the table and made his way over to the wall. He wore a black, rubbery water reclamation suit, which was fitted tightly to his lean, sinewy frame. The watchman grinned at him as he approached. "Do not mistake compassion as a sign of weakness, watchman," Andreas instructed as he strode past. "The One for whom we live and die showed compassion to all, remember?"

The watchman lowered his head and stepped aside without a word. Andreas peered through the eyepiece. He aimed his touchpad at the wall and pressed two keys simultaneously. The tactile illusion of stone that had cloaked the portal wavered for a moment, then dematerialized.

Instantly, Julius had Andreas in his clutches. "Andreas?" he said, his eyes madly searching the face of the man before him. He smiled and began to weep. "Yes," he sobbed, "it must be you. You've always treated me kindly, Andreas. Yours is the face of a kind man."

Andreas stared back at the merchant, his gaze darting between his tearing eyes. He furrowed his brow. "Julius, do you see?"

"Yes," the merchant laughed, trembling with joy. "I see you! I see that candle! I see Aram with his scowl. Just as I imagined."

Aram scowled even more as he sat at the table. Andreas smiled doubtfully back at him and shook his head. "But how has this happened?" he asked. "You've been blind since—"

"—since I was born!" Julius exclaimed. "It's true. My eyes have been dark all of my days."

All of the others, except Aram, left their chairs and gathered around the merchant. All were attired in form-fitted water reclamation suits. "Is it truly him," one of the men asked while studying the merchant warily from head to toe, "or some Marah trickery?" He slid his blaster halfway out of its leg-mounted holster.

"Look," Simon declared, "it's him. See his old blanket and his satchel full of jars."

Julius grinned at Simon, revealing unkempt teeth. "Yes," he said, his expression filled with awe. "He's made my sight whole."

"Impossible," Aram proclaimed. "There's no cure for blindness."

Andreas held up his hand to silence him. "Who did this thing, Julius?"

"A stranger who I met this very night."

"Stranger?" Andreas said. "What stranger?"

"He spoke to me," the merchant said, his eyes vibrant with recollection, "and told me not to be afraid. The sound of his voice was like no other I've ever heard. He reached out to me and touched me, stirring my very soul, and the next thing I knew, my eyes were opened. When I looked at him, his face had the appearance of pure light, his eyes burned through me, and his body gleamed like the sun."

"Nonsense!" Aram grumbled. "Perhaps you've been sampling too much of your own merchandise."

Some of the men chuckled at Aram's gibe.

"Quiet." Andreas ordered. "Go on, man."

Julius told them, "When I saw him, all my strength left me. I was troubled in my heart, and fear gripped me. It was as if I stood before the Angel of the One."

"The Angel of the One?" Aram mocked, grinning at the others. "Now we know you've been sampling too much of your wares."

Andreas strode to the table and lifted Aram from his chair by the ear. He steered him in front of the merchant. "Look at him," he insisted. "We've seen this blind man selling his wares on the streets for many years. Yet, clearly he sees."

"I do," Julius laughed merrily. "I do, indeed."

"What was this stranger's name?" Andreas asked, releasing Aram.

"I asked, but he gave none."

"It's a miracle," Simon said, falling to his knees and folding his hands.

"It is, indeed," Julius replied, "but that's not all of my tale."

"There's more?" Simon gasped, clutching his chest.

Julius nodded.

"Go on, then."

"This stranger has powers beyond those of mortal men," Julius explained, "powers like those of the Lived themselves."

"Ah!" Aram scoffed, but Andreas silenced him with a gesture.

"Explain, Julius," Andreas said.

"It was past curfew," Julius began. "A Marah patrol must've detected our voices. They came for us by air and land with a heavy gunship and a tankrover, but the stranger took care of them."

"Took care of them how?" Aram asked, furrowing his brow.

Julius blinked up at him. "I don't know," he quivered. "It was as if his arm became a weapon, and fire came forth from it. The gunship was destroyed, and—"

"Impossible!" Aram shouted. "No single man can bear enough fire-power to destroy a Marah gunship."

"Let him finish!" Andreas commanded.

"Then he flung open his cloak, and a vessel emerged from his body. It flew off toward the tankrover and destroyed it."

"A gunship *and* a tankrover!" Simon marveled.

The others eyed one another in disbelief.

"After that, he disappeared into the streets."

"Well, now," Aram chided him with a chuckle that no one else shared. "Is that all of your tale, merchant?"

"It is," Julius said, staring up at him with steadfast eyes.

Andreas turned his face away from the others. He searched the confines of the chamber. The others murmured amongst themselves, trying to discern the truth of the merchant's tale.

The one named Simon tilted his face upwards and reached a hand toward the rounded ceiling. "The prophesies," he uttered. "It is prophesied that the One would return with power and wrath, is it not, Andreas?"

Andreas did not reply. He continued to pensively search the chamber.

"You're as delusional as this man, Simon," Aram accused. "Surely we cannot put stock in this drunkard's account."

"Then what's your explanation for these miracles?" Simon argued.

Aram shrugged. "The Cathian medtechs come to our district to use the destitute as subjects for their scientific experiments, don't they? Perhaps one of their experiments was successful for a change and has given the merchant his sight."

"We must bring news of this to the Esezan," Simon said, ignoring Aram's hypothesis and addressing the others. "They'll know the truth of it."

"The truth of what, Simon?" Aram persisted. "The figment of this fool's imagination?"

Andreas massaged his beard. "Aram is right," he said. "We can't take this to the Lived. Not yet, not till we've confirmed the merchant's story."

"But how will we find him?" Simon asked.

"If he is the One, he'll make himself known to us," Andreas replied.

"I will take you to where I saw him," Julius announced proudly.

"We'll go at first light," Andreas agreed. "We'll go and see this stranger of yours."

CHAPTER 15

SPIRIT-SON RAVELLE

Cathian Church: a powerful, monotheistic religion with the Holy Queen Mother of heaven as its deity; an amalgamation of several world religions that preceded it, the Cathian Church has grown to become the largest religion in the history of man, with an estimated 10 billion members and over one million branches in existence solar system wide; a succession of men bearing the title of Archangel have sat as figurehead-leaders of the church for twelve generations, Lord Sycuan the Third being the most recent.

—Optinet link: ssww.cathianchurch .org/-supremecouncilofchurches/-info

OLD CITY DISTRICT

THE HAZE-MAGNIFIED MIDDAY SUN SCORCHED THE broken landscape of the Old City District, casting its plasma-blasted buildings and pockmarked streets in a pale, unearthly hue. Cloaked in the appearance of a man, Peacekeeper MP^C–014/083 wandered in the midst of a throng of citizens listlessly going about their business. There were men and women clothed in rags wheeling rickety carts down narrow passageways. Mothers masked the noses and mouths of their children with cloths, trying to prevent the haze-polluted air from entering their lungs, and merchants lined up on either side of the main street, their carts linked to form a shoddy marketplace of goods.

Believing him to be a common Industrial Quadrant workman, the merchants paraded their wares in front of the war machine's face as it passed them by. Its energy reserves near depletion, the Peacekeeper ignored them. The machine had triangulated the location of the exposed cold fusion energy conduit and plotted the most direct route. The dust and grime of the Old City streets clung to the hard-light constructs it had generated around its feet. Optinet gateways the size of small buildings yet as thin as sheets of paper, twisted provocatively in the murky haze above, disseminating their endless streams of information into the conscious and subconscious minds of all in their vicinity.

What is happening to me? What caused the flow of power within me last night—power that somehow repaired the optic nerves of the blind merchant? it asked as it once again began conducting a self-diagnostic of its systems, trying to make some sense of what had happened. Its systems' analyses indicated that it was changing, evolving somehow. According to its datafiles, more and more AND-gate inhibitors were being removed from the prefrontal cortex of its quantum logic brain— more than one million since its first dream experience had occurred nearly thirty-six hours ago. The net result was as if a veil had been lifted within its mind, exposing programming it never knew existed: the capacity for self-inquiry, self-repair, self-enabling and disabling of its systems, enhanced datafile retrieval and recall, suppositional thought, and dreaming.

Another barrage of questions flooded its mind: *And now the capacity to heal a man of blindness? Who is responsible for removing the AND-gate inhibitors, and why? Is their removal somehow related to the newfound powers I am experiencing, powers that give me the capacity to repair the machinery of man? Why were the AND-gates implanted within my neural architecture in the first place? Who is responsible for blocking the higher cognitive functions and capabilities that were apparently meant to be part of my original programming?* They were inquiries without answers, equations without solutions; phenomena to which the Peacekeeper war machine was not accustomed.

Never before had it needed to infer, deduce, or discern answers or solutions to dilemmas it was facing. Its programmers had always downloaded its datafiles with everything it needed in order to complete its missions. But it was not currently on a prescribed mission. It had been given no commands, no directives to follow.

Within the Peacekeeper's complex tangle of neural pathways, chaos had replaced order. The umbilical cord had been severed. No longer was it a mere automaton doing the bidding of its human programmers. Those shackles had been removed along with the AND-gate inhibitors. No, this experience was something entirely unique to the Military Police-Class Peacekeeper war machine, like the dreams it had experienced recently. For the first time in its existence it was free to choose its own path, free to make decisions based on its own choices, its own needs, its own desires. For the first time the war machine was operating independently of its programming—and for the first time during the course of its existence, it felt uncertain and alone.

Who am I?

It was an inquiry that had first come to its awareness in its most recent dream.

Why do I no longer accept that I am merely an artificial soldier in the employ of the Great City Confederation Army? Why do I no longer accept that I am merely a weapon of mass destruction? Why do I now question the purpose of my existence? As with all my fellow war machines, my purpose has always been clear: defend and protect the citizens, territory, and interests of the Great City Confederation at any cost.

What is the significance of the places, images, and occurrences from my dreams? Why did the guardian from my first dream refer to me as the firstborn son of man, bearer of the seeds of life from the forbidden tree, the one chosen to make straight the way, to awaken his instruments of indignation, and to complete my father's work? What are these instruments of indignation of which the living creature spoke? Who is my father, and what work would he have me complete? And what of the great red dragon

who aided my escape through the old iron gate across the river, the walled
city, and the tower that reached to the heavens, and the lightless entity
churning down from its celestial abode upon the golden object containing
the two tables of stone? Why have the entities from my dreams—first the
guardian, and then the bearer of the still small voice atop the tower—
named me "Cog"? And why did Director Tyne try to destroy me in my
alcove in the lab?

The clanging of iron treads along the asphalt roadway rousted the
Peacekeeper from its litany of self-inquiries. It was a tankrover, akin to
the one it had destroyed the night before, on its patrol of the city.

Doubtless, the ire of the ones the merchant referred to as the Marah
has been raised by the destruction of their men and equipment, and their
patrols seek my whereabouts. Yet, in my present state, I need to conserve
all the power I can. Best to keep out of sight for now, it reasoned. The war
machine pulled its overcoat up around itself and headed down a narrow
alleyway. Sensing its presence, an Optinet gateway, a rectangular
portal as thin as a solar sail, drifted down next to it at eye level. Like
a passageway to another dimension, the gateway materialized, bathing
the alleyway in its alluring lights and sounds. Presently, its dimension-
ality deepened exponentially. No longer was it a mere screen drifting
in the airspace between the buildings. It became a reality all its own,
stretching beyond the confines of the alleyway, beyond the confines of
the Old City District.

Instantly and unavoidably, the Peacekeeper and everyone else in the
vicinity of the gateway found themselves in the midst of a large, spher-
ical space. An infinite expanse of stars and other cosmic phenomena
stretched above and below them, as if they'd suddenly been transported
to the center of the universe itself. Galactic superclusters, spiral and
elliptical galaxies, quasars, pulsars, blue and red super giant stars, dark
and reflective nebula, all forms of matter and energy turned in perfect
physical harmony upon the universal planes. The zodiacal constellations—Virgo, Libra, Scorpio, Sagittarius, Capricornus, Aquarius, Pisces,
Aries, Taurus, Gemini, Cancer, and Leo—paraded past them like a
heavenly scroll, tracing the arcing path of the ecliptic.

A portly man with a snow-white beard and reddish skin walked briskly toward them, striding seemingly upon the nothingness. He was clothed in a floral-patterned, aqua blue button-down shirt and had a pair of dark, gold-rimmed sunglasses situated on top of his head. Four ethereal-looking beings clothed in white raiments and flexing gossamer-fine wings floated in the space above him.

The man had a kind, jovial face that immediately put one at ease. "Harmony, friend!" he said as if he were speaking directly to the Peacekeeper. "Jack Lamphere, here, coming to you via Optinet with a personal invitation to visit the solar system's newest religion: the Church of Cosmic Harmony—mankind's last, best hope for a spiritually unified tomorrow!

"Come witness the awe-inspiring majesty of the grandest structures ever built by man, including the Celestial Sphere of the Heavens Sanctuary," he gestured grandly, "and the cathedral-like Tower to the Stars. Walk the hallowed grounds of our magnificent Temple Complex. Take in the many rides and attractions at the newest addition to our church campus, the Celestial Concerts Theme Park. And while you're there, be sure to visit our beautiful atrium courtyard, filled with an impressive array of flora and fauna and peerless holosculptures of the most amazing creatures in the solar system."

As Lamphere continued his narration, various images infiltrated the Peacekeeper's awareness: the image of a massive chrysteel-girded geodesic sphere that looked like a dark metallic moon that had impacted the earth's surface, partially burying its lower circumference; an enormous tower rising like a jagged spear toward the heavens; a walled complex of ornately-worked gateways and courtyards with a rectangular building perched upon an elevated foundation at its center; and a paradisiacal atrium courtyard filled with fruit-laden trees, shallow blue water pools, and gigantic holosculptures of magnificent four-faced, four-winged creatures.

The Peacekeeper stared intently at the images saturating its awareness. *The holosculptures in this Atrium Courtyard mirror the appearance of the Guardians of the Sacred Glade—the living creatures from my dreams. And this Tower to the Stars resembles the towering structure that I encountered in my dream last night.*

"And, of course," the Optinet-disseminated image of Jack Lamphere went on. "Your experience would not be complete without joining us in one of our worship services in our state-of-the-art sanctuary. In it we utilize the latest holovid technology to make the Scripture of the heavens come alive with the most ancient prophesies known to man— prophesies irrefutably inscribed in the names of the constellations and the stars within them by the hand of the Galactic Spirit himself."

The image of a multi-hued stellar nebula emblazoned itself upon the Peacekeeper's awareness.

"The stars have a story to tell, my friend," Jack Lamphere added, leaning in as if he were sharing a secret, "—and not the story of your love life or your financial investments, but the story of man, from beginning to end. Come experience this awesome revelation for yourself. I guarantee it'll blow your mind. The Church of Cosmic Harmony— mankind's last, best hope for a spiritually unified tomorrow. It's only a short aircar ride away."

Then abruptly a map superimposed itself upon the war machine's awareness, and the voice of a fast-talking announcer rattled its acoustic sensors. "Exit City Center matrix via Foundation Airway west toward the Great City Industrial Quadrant, then veer northward onto Harmony Airway to the Highway of Holiness and head for the golden gates." And then like a blur: "The Church of Cosmic Harmony and its affiliates comprise a profit-based organization whose members receive shares in the ministry through contributions automatically deducted from their financial accounts. Visitors to the church are in no way obligated to join. Membership is voluntary."

The sounds and images that had invaded the Peacekeeper's awareness winked away into the sights and sounds of the Old City alleyway within which it stood. When its awareness had fully returned, the war machine watched as the Optinet gateway reverted to its original state, then drifted up and out of the alleyway, tumbling slowly in the air like a plate of tessellated glass. Everyone in the vicinity snapped out of the trance-like states they'd been in and resumed their previous activities.

The Peacekeeper considered that perhaps the Church of Cosmic Harmony held some answers for it as it continued its journey. The narrow alleyway opened into a wide courtyard near the Old City's southern gate. A series of makeshift porches had been constructed around its perimeter. The porches were filled with a multitude of people, all of whom were sick, blind, lame, or plague-ridden, according to the Peacekeeper's invasive scans. A large, opaque tube rose at the center of the courtyard and disappeared into the hazy skies above, the exposed portion of a cold fusion energy conduit venting its spent compounds into the air above the Old City District, no doubt the cause for the ever-present haze that choked the land. An infestation of flies filled the area, and packs of wild dogs ran through the legs of passers-by, some of which paused to lick the plague-sores of the ill.

Ahead, there was an old man lying upon a wooden pallet on one of the porches, groaning in his infirmities. His flesh hung limply upon withered bones. Reddish sores covered his face and body. When the war machine neared him, it conducted an invasive scan and concluded that he had been thirty-eight years in his condition.

The Peacekeeper approached the man and asked, "Why do the ill gather in this place?"

It was a moment before the old man turned in recognition of the question. He slowly raised his head. The war machine spied a yellowish substance discharging from the sores on his face. "Sir, I have no one to pull me closer to the beacon when it surges," he said, "but while I'm coming, another steps down before me."

The Peacekeeper surveyed the energy conduit. It had the diameter of a large building and was easily the most modern construction in the vicinity. It glowed a muted, emerald green and hummed with the vibrations of the gaseous elements it bore.

"You speak as if this conduit had powers," the Peacekeeper said. Its sensors revealed nothing extraordinary in its design or composition.

The old man seemed surprised by the Peacekeeper's words. "You

mean you've not heard of the miracles of this place?" he asked disbelievingly. "Surely you are a stranger to this land, for this is an ancient place
of a mysterious sort. The spirit of the Holy Queen Mother of heaven is
said to visit this courtyard in certain seasons and manifest her powers
in surges within the beacon. It is said that whoever is first to touch it
after its stirring is made well from whatever ails them."

"Have you witnessed the stirring of these powers?" the Peacekeeper
inquired.

"I have," the old man replied.

"And the conduit healed the first to touch it?"

"It did. A Cathian spirit-child is always present when a healing
occurs, as is the case this day." The old man pointed weakly across the
courtyard. "See, one of the spirit-sons rests upon his hoverboard."

The Peacekeeper turned and saw a man seated in an ornate, high-
backed chair that had been secured atop a golden hoverboard.

The Cathian spirit-son was clothed in a white linen robe with a
pallium emblazoned with various symbols of the crescent moon draped
around his neck and shoulders. He had a long, narrow nose, which
curved upward at the tip, revealing elongated nostrils and two overly
large front teeth. His eyes were dark and wide and tapered at the ends,
and he blinked more than seemed necessary. His manicured hands
rested on the cushioned arm pads of his chair. A touchpad blazed on
his lap. Dutifully, he surveyed the scene in the courtyard, appearing
saddened by what he was observing. He dabbed occasionally at the
corners of his eyes with a folded, gold-edged cloth. He was flanked by
five heavily armed men—Marah guardsmen—who scanned the crowd
with purpose and whose uniforms bore the same crescent moon markings as the gunship and tankrover the war machine had destroyed the
night before.

"I've seen the mute touch the beacon after it's been stirred up, and
speak," the old man uttered reverently. "I've seen the lame placed next
to it after the Queen Mother's spirit has come, and walk out under
their own power."

Turning from its scan of the Cathian spirit-child, the war machine gazed down at the old man upon his pallet. Suddenly it experienced a flow of power within its neural architecture and throughout its body, a flow identical to the one it had experienced the night before with the blind merchant.

"Do you wish to be made well?" it asked him.

The old man gazed up at the Peacekeeper, squinting into the brightness of the day. "I beg your pardon?"

"Do you wish to be healed of your infirmities?"

"I do, sir," the man answered hopefully.

At once, the Peacekeeper closed its eyes and an inaudible sound of specific harmonic signature emanated forth from its quantum logic brain and entered the prefrontal cortex of the old man's brain, instantly conjoining and enlivening the neurons therein, as they'd never been before. "Arise," the Peacekeeper said to him with a gesture of its hand, "take up your pallet and walk."

And immediately the old man became well, and took up his pallet and walked.

Completing his tour of duty, Cathian Spirit-Son Ravelle had begun to glide his way out of the courtyard when he heard a ruckus erupt near its perimeter. Ceasing his forward motion, he spied an old man standing upon a porch with his pallet at his side. The man was gesticulating excitedly and conversing loudly with some of those gathered there.

Ravelle held up his hand, halting the progress of his guardsmen. "You there," he glided closer to the man. "Are you not aware that it is the time of remembrance of the Feast of Ishtar and that it is not permissible for you to carry on in such a manner?"

The old man paused and turned toward the spirit-child. "He who made me well was the one who said to me, 'Take up your pallet and walk.'"

Ravelle directed his hoverboard to a position just above the old man's head. He glared angrily down at him. "He who did what?"

"He who made me well," the old man replied. "I've been plague-ridden and lame for thirty-eight years, my Lord, and now look at my hands!" He held out trembling hands free of plague-sores. "And look, I walk." he demonstrated. "Queen Mother be praised, I walk."

The spirit-child's eyes grew wide, and his nostrils flared. "Blasphemy!" he raged, his anger suddenly doubled. "Who dares heal in the name of the Holy Queen Mother of heaven? Show me this man."

The old man quickly searched the edges of the courtyard for the stranger who'd healed him. "There," he screamed, pointing in the distance to a man making his way through the crowds. "There he is. Surely you see him. He is clothed in silver and gleams like the sun."

Ravelle furrowed his brow at the old man as if he were insane. "Guards," he cried. "Seize that man!"

"There," Julius whispered hoarsely. "That's him, Andreas. That's the stranger."

"Are you certain?" Andreas asked, locating what appeared to him to be a plainly dressed man.

"Look," Julius replied. "Don't you see it? He glows as the Angel of the One."

Andreas removed his eye from his monocle and grimaced at the merchant. "Perhaps Aram was right about you, Julius."

Returning to his scope, he located the man again, then scanned his vicinity. "There's a spirit-son about today," he observed. "And your healer's being hunted by his Marah guardsmen."

"No!" Julius cried. "They'll destroy him."

Andreas drew his blaster from a holster concealed beneath his coat. "Not on my watch." He turned toward the merchant. "Go," he ordered. "Go and tell the others that I'll bring him by way of the catacombs. I'll not let him fall into the hands of that Cathian scum. Go!" He pushed Julius into the daylight. "What're you waiting for, man? Run."

As soon as Julius was away, Andreas fired a thin green line of plasma in the direction of the spirit-child. The blast singed the air with a smoky trail that whistled past Ravelle's hoverboard. With the onset of blaster fire, all mayhem broke loose in the courtyard. Three of the guards broke off their pursuit of the Peacekeeper and headed back to Ravelle's side. Andreas pushed his way through the panicked masses, making his way toward the location of the man the merchant had identified as the one who'd healed him. Many people screamed, fearing him to be another of the homicidal bombers who terrorized the Old City District with regularity.

Approaching from behind, Andreas throttled the first of the guards, and with a sharp twist, broke his neck. He brought the butt of his blaster down on the other, knocking him to the ground. He reached a hand out toward the Peacekeeper and grasped its shoulder. "Come with me, stranger," he said, as the war machine turned to engage him.

Andreas removed a touchpad from a pocket in his coat, pointed it at the ground, and tapped two keys simultaneously. The dust of the earth wavered for a moment as if it were a mirage and a portal appeared, exposing a ladder leading into a vertical subterranean shaft.

Andreas motioned at the portal. "It's now or never, friend."

+≻—╬—≺+

The merchant, Julius, ran through the dispersing crowd in the courtyard, trying to make for the portal located outside Aram's home and in order to deliver Andreas's message.

Ravelle signaled pointedly at Julius. "Seize him!" he screamed. The three remaining guards formed a wedge, which flattened the fleeing hordes. They quickly apprehended the merchant.

"Please, no," Julius begged, when they'd brought him before Ravelle.

"What of the others?" Ravelle inquired of his guards, his hoverboard positioned at eye-level with them.

"They vanished into the crowd, my Lord."

"I want them found," the Cathian seethed. "Is that clear?"

"Yes, my Lord," bowed the guardsman.

Ravelle glared down at the man in custody. "Were you not with the one who murdered my guards?"

"I do not know the man," Julius said, averting his eyes.

Ravelle studied the man's face. He narrowed his eyes at him. "You're the merchant who sets up his wares near the Temple Mount, are you not?"

"I don't know what you're talking about."

"But you were blind," Ravelle recalled, "and now clearly you see. Perhaps this stranger has healed you as well."

Julius just quivered, unable to speak.

Ravelle motioned to his guardsmen. "Bring him," he commanded, taking a final survey of the courtyard. "Archangel Sycuan will have a word with you."

CHAPTER 16

The LIVED

"I will make this city desolate and a hissing; everyone who passes by it will be astonished and hiss because of all its plagues."

—Jeremiah 19:8;

from the Scriptures of Truth,
the Holy Bible in its uncorrupted form,
The Qanah Archives, circa A.D. 2042, City of Ariel

TEMPLE MOUNT, OLD CITY DISTRICT

HEN THEY WERE BENEATH THE SURFACE, Andreas tapped two keys on his touchpad and re-phased the tactile illusion that served to cloak the location of the portal. Still carrying his blaster, he trailed the Peacekeeper down the ladder that led into the underground shaft. The din from the courtyard above slowly faded and was soon replaced by the sound of two pairs of footfalls on the rungs of the ladder. When they reached the bottom of the shaft, they dropped into a narrow passageway with rounded rock walls.

"This way, stranger," Andreas said, motioning for the Peacekeeper to take the lead.

The war machine's invasive scan revealed this to be one of many passageways in the vast, underground network carved out of the limestone and Turonian subsurface layers beneath the streets and dwellings of the Old City District. It switched its optic sensors to infrared mode in order to see more clearly in the darkness. The tunnel was a tight fit. It was barely tall enough for it to stand at its full height and so narrow that its outstretched arms could reach both sides at once.

Andreas was running the fingers of his free hand along the wall as they walked, as if feeling for something. He paused and reached his hand deep into a crevice in the wall. He removed a small lasglobe from the hole and lit the element at its tip with a short pulse from his blaster. He observed the Peacekeeper searching the tunnel behind them for pursuers. "They will not follow us," he said, his bearded face alighted from the soft green glow of the lasglobe.

The Peacekeeper's scan of the tunnels had detected only small caches of standard weaponry—plasma rifles, snipers, boxes of ammunition, and grenades—scattered in chambers throughout the labyrinth.

Andreas noted the continued vigilance on the part of the war machine. "Do not concern yourself, stranger. We are well fortified here." He pointed the lasglobe, instructing the war machine to veer down another passageway.

By artificial torchlight, they made their way through the dry, dusty corridors. According to the Peacekeeper's sensors, they were at the eastern end of the subterranean labyrinth and headed west. "What is this place?" the war machine asked, ducking under a porous outcropping of rock protruding from the roof of the cavern.

"It's called the catacombs," Andreas said, tapping the stalactite with familiar affection, "and it's our home. Now, tell me, stranger: why were those Marah guardsmen hunting you back there?"

"That information is not presently contained in my datafiles," the Peacekeeper replied.

Andreas fixed the back of the war machine's head with a measured stare, as if attempting to decipher the meaning of its odd response. He studied its attire—from its construction-grade helmet to its dark, knee-length overcoat, canvas pants, and heavy workman's boots.

They walked on in silence. Andreas guided them down a different corridor every hundred meters or so, occasionally pausing and reaching his hand into another shoulder-high crevice in the wall and replacing the lasglobe that he carried with a fresh one, igniting it in the same manner as he had the first.

A consideration for the next subsurface traveler, the Peacekeeper perceived.

"May I inquire as to who you are, sir?" the Peacekeeper asked, as it observed the switching out of another torch.

"The name's Andreas."

"Why did you help me escape from the guards at the energy conduit, Andreas?"

"A man I know says you healed him."

"The merchant?"

"Yes," Andreas acknowledged, then urged the Peacekeeper down another passageway. "He claims you cured his blindness and destroyed a Marah patrol last night. Are these things true?"

"It is as you say," the Peacekeeper said as it replayed the datafile containing its destruction of the gunship and tankrover in one of its subroutines. "Who are these people called the Marah?"

Andreas' expression turned grim and he said sternly, "They're the Sons of Disobedience, and trespassers in our land."

"But if they are trespassers in your land," the war machine inquired, "then why do you dwell in these catacombs beneath the city while they reside above?"

"The Marah control the Holy City now," Andreas replied bitterly, "but it has not always been so, nor will it be for long."

"You are at war with them," the Peacekeeper inferred.

Andreas nodded solemnly. "Our brethren, the Patron, fight openly with the Marah, a bitter and merciless war which has gone on for millennia on end, in order to protect our spiritual holy sites. My people have chosen to fight a clandestine war against them."

"Who are your people, Andreas?"

"We're known as the Qanah."

The machine accessed his linguistic datafiles. The search came up matchless. "I am unfamiliar with the word *Qanah*."

"It's a word taken from the old tongue," Andreas explained. "It means 'the purchased,' because we believe we've been purchased from the earth. We're freedom fighters. Our ancestors have occupied this land in perpetuity for thousands of years, and we shall not abandon it—even if we're forced to live beneath it—until His purposes have been fulfilled."

"Whose purposes?" the Peacekeeper inquired.

Andreas tapped the war machine on the shoulder, instructing it to face him. He lifted a mat of curly hair from his forehead, revealing a symbol that had been etched into his skin. "We follow the Coming One wherever He goes," he said with cast-iron resolve.

"Who is the Coming One?" the Peacekeeper queried.

"The One we follow," Andreas answered curtly.

"Where are you taking me, Andreas?"

"To speak with the Esezan."

"Esezan?" The war machine again accessed its linguistic datafiles to no avail. "Is that another word from the old tongue?"

"Yes," Andreas said. "It means 'the Lived.' The Esezan are oracles, prophets. They see the future, and they have many powers. But that's enough questions for now. Come, stranger, we must hurry. The holy ones await our arrival."

The passageway in which they walked came to an end at the base of a narrow stairway. A dim, artificial light shone down from above, and the musty air of the tunnel seemed less so. They began their ascent. At the top of the stairway there was a portal like the one they'd used in their escape at the energy conduit. The portal had been phased open, and it led to the surface world. The Peacekeeper was the first to climb through, emerging into a warm, windless night. It found itself standing atop a large stone mount situated several meters above the surrounding land. An invasive scan detected that the mount was some thirty-four acres in extent and that it had been built using archaic construction techniques nearly six thousand years ago. It appeared as though it once comprised the foundation for a large architectural structure.

The ubiquitous haze shrouded the landscape beyond the perimeter of the mount, veiling it in a thick, brown cloud. Scanning the mount's surface, the Peacekeeper detected an array of rusted-out building equipment strewn about like forgotten relics—rovers, robotic lifters, various other construction machines—and at the western edge, pallet after pallet of construction materials still wrapped in impenetrable holofil.

To the east, the war machine saw a gateway that appeared to have lead to the top of the mount before it was sealed with mortar, and along the western wall, the remains of a laser-blasted structure, some sort of barracks for workers, perhaps. Its sensors informed it that the equipment and materials had been subjected to approximately three and one-half years of oxidation and exposure to the corrosive elements present within the haze and that the worker's barracks had been destroyed by plasma blasts dating from about the same time period. It seemed as if some sort of battle had taken place there.

With Andreas following closely behind, the Peacekeeper strode across the broken surface of the mount. It spied a group of heavily armed men sitting quietly in a circle at the center of the platform, all of whom rose quickly when they saw the Peacekeeper and Andreas approaching. The soldiers were all lean, hard men with steady eyes and thatched beards, and each of them was clothed in a black water reclamation suit. Their reclamation suits had the dull sheen of ionized rubber and were fitted snugly to their sinewy frames.

As the war machine neared their location, it saw that the soldiers were gathered around a square object of some sort that stood beside a rectangular stone platform, a replica in miniature of the foundation stone of the tower from its most recent dream—the stone around which two of the Guardians of the Sacred Glade had sat and upon which the golden chest had been laid.

Like the golden chest from its dream, the object in the midst of the soldiers was made of wood that had been overlaid with gold and had two poles inserted into golden rings along its sides. However, this object had horns at each of its corners and a curl of smoke arising from its surface, an incense of some sort that perfumed the air. There were lampstands on either side of the object, as well—the only visible light source on the surface of the mount—each with seven branches and seven bowls and seven candles burning in the bowls. Two men of considerable age were kneeling next to the lampstands on either side of the object, looking in the dim light like old, withered olive trees.

The Peacekeeper's sensors revealed that the men's garments were composed of a rough, dark material spun and woven from goats' hair. The men had long, unkempt beards. One man's was purely white in color and long, while the other's was gray and thatched about his face. Their hair was matted and tangled, and long enough that it blended with their beards. Their toenails were yellow and splitting, and poked through well-worn sandals like kernels of corn. The men did not alter their positions as Andreas and the Peacekeeper approached. The soldiers, however, seemed in a state of high alert. They gripped their weapons tightly, their eyes wide with expectancy.

It was a long moment before one of the Lived spoke, the white-bearded one, his voice deep and resonating in the darkness like a bellows. "Lo! There is rumor of a healer who has come into our midst," he said, continuing to kneel while facing the golden object. "One who gives sight to the blind and healing to the plague-ridden."

The gray-bearded one added, "And it is said that this healer single-handedly destroyed a Marah gunship and a Marah tankrover, and that he wields powers like no other man."

Then in unison, the Esezan slowly pressed themselves up from their knees, the white-bearded one using a long wooden staff that he carried in his right hand to aid him. The faces of the Lived had a pale hue about them, as if they had not seen the light of day for many months.

"Do you know of this man, stranger?" the gray-bearded one asked.

For a moment the Peacekeeper's gaze alternated between the faces of the Lived before he answered, "I who speak to you am he."

At this response, a soft murmur arose from the direction of the soldiers. The Lived slowly picked their way closer to the war machine. "I am called Lawgiver," the white-bearded one announced, "and my friend here has been named Prophet."

The one called Prophet was of slightly lesser stature than Lawgiver, both in thickness of bone and broadness of shoulder, but still he stood at an impressive height. Both men, however, had lean, deeply lined faces whose shadowed parts were accentuated by the dim light from the lampstands. The eyes of the holy ones were deep-set and glimmered of forbidden knowledge, as if they'd been witness to things that no other man had seen. The Peacekeeper's invasive scan revealed that their cellular structure differed slightly from that of other humans it had scanned; there was an energy present within the constituent particles of their cells which its datafiles could not identify.

Prophet caressed his beard as he eyed the Peacekeeper from head to toe. "And who, may I ask, are you, stranger, so that we might give answer to Him who sent us?"

Peacekeeper MP^c-014/083's blue eyes pulsed almost imperceptibly as his quantum logic brain processed the question. "Last night, I posed that same self-inquiry," it said, "yet I am afraid that I cannot give answer, except to say that I have been named the firstborn son of man and bearer of the seeds of life from the forbidden tree, though I know not the meaning of these names."

"Who named you such?" Prophet asked suspiciously.

"The guardians from my dreams," the Peacekeeper replied.

"Guardians?" Prophet said, eyeing the visitor curiously. In the candlelight he thought he spied a gleam of silver deep within its eyes. "Tell us of these guardians of whom you speak."

"They are the living creatures from my dreams," the war machine explained. "There were four of them, and each of them had four faces and four wings. Their feet were cloven like the hooves of a calf, and they referred to themselves as Guardians of the Sacred Glade."

The Esezan shared a veiled acknowledgment of the Peacekeeper's description. "Guardians of the Sacred Glade, you say?" Prophet pondered. "And what exactly did these living creatures want with you?"

"They did not say," the Peacekeeper answered. "Although I sensed that I had taken something from them, something that had been placed under their immediate watch and care."

"And what was it that you took from these guardians, stranger?"

"That information is not presently contained in my datafiles."

"Datafiles?" Prophet blew out his beard. "You speak as if you are—"

Lawgiver held up his hand to stay his companion. An unspoken agreement seemed to pass between them. The one called Prophet furrowed his brow and took a deep breath. He probed more gently, "Besides naming you such, did these guardians speak any other words to you?"

The war machine nodded. "They spoke of my destiny."

"What destiny, stranger?"

"The guardians told me that I would be the one chosen to make straight the way, to awaken his instruments of indignation, and to complete my father's work."

"Your father's work?" Prophet exclaimed, unable to mask his astonishment. "Who is your father?"

"That information is not presently contained in my datafiles."

"Bah!" Prophet snorted, turning away in frustration.

Lawgiver assuaged, "Please, stranger, forgive my impatient friend." He laid his hand upon the shoulder of his companion. "The night grows long, and we are weary. Perhaps you have questions for us, just as we have for you?"

"I do," the Peacekeeper confirmed, then perused with mechanical precision the stone mount upon which they stood. "What is this place?"

Lawgiver gazed round at the battle-scarred relic of a bygone era as he replied, "The sacred tabernacles of our people once stood upon this very mount." A certain sadness had touched his tone. He pointed a short distance away. "Just there, in fact, behind a wall and a veil near to where the altar of incense now stands, once stood the most holy place within the tabernacle, a place wherein at one time dwelt the Shekinah, the very presence of our God Himself."

Lawgiver spoke with the voice of fond recollection. "A sacred object called the Ark of the Testimony once rested in the most holy place, and golden images of creatures very much like these guardians you have described once adorned the mercy seat on top of it, shrouding its surface in the shadow of their wings. It was there between the wings of the living creatures that our God met with us."

The premonitory whisper of the lightless entity from its dream resonated in the Peacekeeper's auditory archives. "Here I will meet with you," the voice had hissed mockingly. "I have seen this sacred object you call the Ark of the Testimony," the war machine told them. "In my dream, it was carried forth upon a hoverboard before a large procession into an ancient city and laid beneath the wings of two of the living creatures."

Lawgiver stroked his long white beard. "Intriguing," he said. "Will you tell us more of this dream of yours?"

"I will." The war machine accessed the datafile of its second dream experience. "I was part of an immense procession which carried before it an object much like the Ark of the Testimony which you have spoken of. The procession entered the gates of a walled city and headed for a tower whose height reached the uppermost region of the earth's exosphere.

"I joined the object on its hoverboard and ascended to the top of the structure, where leaders from all of the nations and confederations of the solar system awaited my arrival. The living creatures were there, as well, all four of them—two perched like sentinels on the corners of the rooftop and two positioned on either side of the tower's foundation stone, a stone platform identical to the one that stands here at the center of this mount."

Prophet's eyes grew wide with recognition as he looked down upon the stone platform upon which the altar of incense had been placed. "The *Even Shetiyyah*," he whispered.

The soldiers gathered round made not a sound. They feared to move, lest they fail to hear the whole of the stranger's dream.

"The golden object—this Ark of the Testimony, as you have called it—was placed upon the foundation stone between the guardians. At that moment, I detected the presence of a great barrier that existed above the wings of the guardians and above the top of the tower. The barrier was something like an expanse, like the awesome gleam of crystal. It separated the first heaven, the atmospheric heaven, from the second, or stellar, heaven."

With these words, a solemness appeared to inflict the countenance of the Lived, and an expression of grave concern spread across their faces.

"The Great Barrier hung upon the nothingness," the Peacekeeper went on, "and stretched out in a great horizontal expanse, perhaps encircling the entire earth. The guardians greeted me with words of warning. 'Come out of her,' one of them beckoned to me, 'that you may not partake of her sins and that you may not receive of her plagues; for Sheshach's sins are piled up as high as heaven, and They have remembered her iniquities. Render to her just as she rendered to you, and repay her double according to her works; in the cup that she has mixed, mix double for her. In the measure that she glorified herself and lived sensually, in the same measure give her torment and sorrow.'

"After these words, another of the creatures turned toward me, one of those that sat perched on the corner of the rooftop. 'I sit as a queen,' it said. 'I am not a widow, and I will never mourn.'"

Lawgiver lowered his head, seemingly distraught at the Peacekeeper's words. "Babel," he breathed, quivering as if his footing might falter. Regaining his fortitude, he raised his gaze again. "What happened next, stranger?"

"I pried upwards the wings of the guardians, which they had spread over the golden object, the Ark of the Testimony, and lifted its lid, revealing a golden jar filled with an organic material of unknown origin, a rod of wood that budded with almonds, and two tables of stone with ancient writing on them. And then a lightless entity descended from above and struck the far side of the barrier, shattering it to pieces."

"A lightless entity?" Prophet remarked.

"Yes," the Peacekeeper affirmed, "an ominous cloud like a whirlwind that twisted up into the galactic infinity beyond. I was unable to identify its origin or the substance from which it was composed."

"And then?"

"After the Great Barrier fell, it was as if a veil had been removed, and everyone saw the heavens with the brightness, clarity, and purpose they had always been meant to be seen. Then the lightless entity descended upon the object as if claiming it for its own, and I detected a voice like a whisper emanating forth from the midst of the entity. 'Here I will meet with you,' it said, then echoed away into the heights."

The eyes of the Lived widened with concern at the Peacekeeper's recitation.

Then suddenly a question came to the newly-sentient mind of Peace-keeper MP^C-014/083, a question which it had uploaded one time before in its days-old sentient existence, a question to which it had received no answer. "Holy ones," it said, gazing curiously up at them, "do you know the meaning of the dream that I have had and its interpretation?"

At the question, the concern upon the faces of the Esezan deepened tenfold, but then the one called Lawgiver lifted his eyes towards the east, where the faint aura of the sun could be seen glowing above the horizon.

"Lo, dawn draws nigh," he observed. "We must depart from this sacred place, ere the Sons of Disobedience come upon us here. The time is not yet for our final meeting."

With that, he turned and addressed the soldiers. "Simon!" he called. "Tend to the altar of incense. Aram, take the stranger back into the catacombs, where he will find safe haven from the Cathians and the Marah. Andreas, come with us. Prophet and I have need to speak with you."

CHAPTER 17

The CATACOMBS

Marah (*mar-ah*): a reference to a people who reside in the Old City District; the word *marah* translates from the ancient tongue to mean "to be, or cause to make bitter," "to rebel," "to be disobedient," or "to grievously provoke;" hence, the Marah are known as the Sons of Disobedience.

—EZRA HIRIAM, ed.,
Compendium of Lost Biblical Knowledge, 4th ed.
(City of Ariel: the Qanah Archives, 2450), s.v. "Marah."

THE CATACOMBS BENEATH
THE OLD CITY DISTRICT

BY THE TIME ANDREAS ARRIVED AT ARAM'S UNDER-ground abode, his men had already gathered around the table and were in the midst of a meal. Hastily, they wolfed down hunks of bread dunked in bowls of broth and gulped down steaming, orange-colored drinks from porcelain mugs. The Peacekeeper stood in the shadows in the far corner, silently observing the behavior of the soldiers.

With a tap of his touchpad, Andreas re-phased the portal by which he'd entered the chamber. "Has anyone offered this man something to eat?"

One of the men had his mug to his mouth, eyeing the war machine over its rim in a calculating manner. "We have," the man named Iakobos said warily, "but he has refused."

Andreas turned to the Peacekeeper. "Is this true?"

"I have no requirement for material sustenance," the war machine answered.

Andreas stared back at it. "Very well," he said with an uncertain smile but an accepting nod.

"Perhaps he's on a fast," the one named Simon volunteered.

"A fast," Aram grumbled disbelievingly while chewing on a piece of bread.

The Peacekeeper scanned the confines of the chamber before asking, "Why do the Qanah choose to dwell beneath the Old City District?"

Andreas slung the pack from his back. "It's not—"

"Do not answer him," Aram interrupted sharply, chunks of bread flying from his mouth. "We know nothing of this would-be healer," he scoffed. "He'll not even tell us his name. For all we know, he's a Marah spy sent to slit our throats while we sleep."

Andreas glared at Aram. "And if a stranger dwells with you in your land, you shall not mistreat him. The stranger who dwells among you shall be to you as one born among you—"

"—and you shall love him as yourself," Aram finished it for him, lowering his head shamefully. "For you were strangers in the land of Egypt."

Andreas smiled and laid a comforting hand on Aram's shoulder, then addressed the Peacekeeper. "It is not by choice that we live here, nameless one," he said, glancing around at the cavernous walls of the chamber. "Ever since the Quarantine, these underground cisterns and passages have been our only sanctuary, our only home."

"Data on the policy known as the Quarantine is restricted," the war machine stated. "Will you inform me as to the purpose for which it was enacted?"

"Quarantine," Aram quipped, his mouth bulging with food. "That's a laugh. It's more like a government-sponsored plot to rid the Great City Confederation of its most virulent pests."

A few of the men around the table found humor in Aram's assessment of the situation.

"The official spin on the Quarantine," Simon explained, "was that
it was enacted in order to allow the Patron and the Marah to continue
their holy war against one another without further endangering the
lives of GCC citizens in the surrounding districts, but essentially Aram
is correct: the Quarantine was widely viewed as an open admission of
failure on the part of Overlord Ocaba's administration. Throughout the
centuries many governments and administrations have tried their hand
at a peaceful resolution to the political and religious issues at the root of
the Patron-Marah conflict. All have failed, the most recent of which is
that of the sovereign overlord."

Simon continued, "You see, following the end of the Great War
nearly seven years ago now and upon his ascension to the seat of the
overlordship, Vaughn Ocaba gained consensus for his Divided Temple
Peace Accord, which called for the construction of a magnificent temple
in a place sacred to both peoples, the Patron and the Marah. That place
is called the Temple Mount, the very place where you met the Esezan
earlier this morning. The Divided Temple was to be constructed from
the finest grade of chrysteel, and, as its name implies, it was to be
divided down the center by a wall of separation in order that it might
provide houses of worship for the God of the Patron, as well as the god
of the Marah. The Divided Temple was to be a monument representing
everything the two diverse peoples had stood for over the millennia and
a symbol of unity and peace to last for millennia to come. Its design
promised to appease the most cynical members of both peoples. The
initial stage of the accord called for a truce between the Patron and the
Marah so that they could build temporary houses of worship side by
side upon the Temple Mount while construction began on the Divided
Temple itself. And that's exactly what they did. For a time, Ocaba's
accord achieved the unprecedented result of staying the violence in our
land, as it has not been for centuries."

Aram interjected, "Because of the sustained nature of this peace, the Patron actually believed Overlord Ocaba to be the bodily manifestation of the Messiah for whom they've so long awaited."

"It's true," Simon affirmed. "For a time that's what our brethren believed, but soon political tensions mounted between the ancient enemies, and within a period of just a few years, the two factions renewed their violence. The endangered construction crews were forced to flee the area of the Temple Mount, the accord was broken, and the Divided Temple project was scrapped before one chrysteel girder had been laid upon another. Following this development, it was reported that the overlord's patience with the whole matter wore thin. Apparently he'd grown weary of daily reports of homicidal bombings and military reprisals occurring throughout the Old City District, so one day he arrived at the Temple Mount with a company of his artificial abominations at his side; dismantled the Patron's Tent of Meeting, ending their daily animal sacrifices in the process; and tore down the temporary mosque built by the Marah."

The Peacekeeper noted Simon's terse depiction of its fellow war machines: *artificial abominations*. Simon continued, "Following this development, the majority of the Patron, as well as most of our people, fled to the south, beyond the Sandfill of Arabah to the wilderness-dwellings of the Siq, as is prophesied. Only the ill and our finest soldiers remained behind in the Old City to defend our ancient holy sites from Marah desecration. That was some three and one-half years ago and conditions have remained thus ever since."

"Those of us who've chosen to remain have endured much hardship and pain in order to continue to live in the sacred land of our ancestors," Andreas added, "but that is nothing new to our heritage. What was once our sacred homeland has now become a wilderness and a desolation, filled with naught but bloodshed, depravity, and ignorance."

"The princess among the provinces has become a slave," Simon lamented, mouthing the words as if by memory. "She has seen the nations enter her sanctuary."

"How many Qanah are there?" the Peacekeeper asked.

"More than most suspect," Andreas answered vaguely.

"These Esezan—the Lived, as you have called them—are they of the Patron or of the Qanah?"

Andreas exhaled deeply before he started. "It is said that at one time the Lived were leaders of the Patron. According to the traditions, thousands of years ago the one called Lawgiver led our people on a great exodus through a desert which once existed to the south of the Old City District. The one named Prophet was a great prophet who did not die, but was caught up to heaven in a chariot of fire drawn by horses of fire."

"Horses of fire?"

Simon nodded. "It is said that both men were privileged to actually lay eyes upon the Coming One and that they actually spoke with Him on a regular basis. It is also said that they spoke with Him during His earthly pilgrimage on a mountaintop near to here, yet no one can say for certain how they've returned to this land, nor how they've returned to life."

"Then that is why you refer to them as *the Lived*," the Peacekeeper deduced, "because they have lived and yet live again."

"Yes, stranger," Andreas confirmed. "It seems a fantasy, we know, and at first we doubted the authenticity of their claim. But there can be no question that they are who they say they are. The Lived are no ordinary men, indeed."

The war machine did not seem to follow the logic of Andreas's statement. Aside from the slight variance in their cellular structure, it had detected nothing else unusual about them.

Simon noted the consternation in the Peacekeeper's human-mimicked eyes. "They have powers," he said, "powers that can deter the most modern weapons of man. We've seen them call down fire from heaven, send forth fire from their mouths, turn water to blood, and smite the earth with many plagues."

"And it is said that they have the power to shut up the sky from rain during the days of their prophesying," Aram said. He solemnly added, "It has not rained upon this land since their arrival here over twelve hundred days ago."

Simon grimaced. "Drought conditions have grown so bad that we're forced to wear these ill-fitting suits and drink our own purified bodily excretions in order to survive. As a result of the rainlessness, the phenomenon known as 'the haze' has manifested itself in the air above the land. And what a grimy concoction of filth and toxic acids it is."

"It is the power of the holy ones that shields the catacombs from the influence of DayStar," Iakobos added.

"What is this thing you call *DayStar*?" the Peacekeeper inquired.

"It is our term for Optinet," Iakobos replied.

"Optinet," the war machine stated. "The system-wide communication and information dissemination system of near-infinite computational power, a singularity point of accumulated knowledge and information indistinguishable from omniscience."

"Indeed," Andreas remarked, surprised at the technological accuracy of the response. "One in the same."

"The Qanah do not carry the Optinet transponder?"

"No way," Aram said firmly. "The Lived warned us not to take its blasphemous mark."

"Then how are you able to buy or sell?"

"We make do," was Aram's veiled reply.

"Why do you seek to hide from its influence?"

"Let's just say that we're leery of Optinet's true design purposes," Aram said suspiciously. "One of our ranks observed the chief benefactor of its influence making an odd proclamation while standing in the Tent of Meeting of the Patron upon the Temple Mount one night, not so long ago."

The man named Simon slowly set his mug down on the table. He stared open-eyed at the flame of the candle in the middle of the table. "Like cold wind upon the rocks, his voice was," he whispered ominously. "Like shadow incarnate, he was; like a cup full of horror. And for a fleeting moment, I saw his true form—his prophesied form—that of a beast rising up out of the sea, having seven heads and ten horns. On his horns he wore ten crowns, and on his heads, a blasphemous name was written. His appearance was like a leopard with the feet of a bear, and his mouth like the mouth of a lion. I saw one of his heads looked as if it had been mortally wounded, and his deadly wound was healed."

Simon slowly lifted his gaze as though he were coming out of a trance. "It was I who saw him," he breathed. "It was I who saw him behind the veil in the temporary temple of the Patron; it was I who saw him standing in the most holy place upon the Temple Mount; it was I who heard him magnify himself in his heart above every god, speaking blasphemies against the God of gods."

"It is a prophesied event," Andreas explained. "This man—if that is what he is—accompanied Overlord Ocaba on the day he came to the Temple Mount to dismantle the temporary temples of the Marah and the Patron and to end the daily sacrifices. Since the day Vaughn Ocaba took office, in fact, this man has been at his side, poisoning the overlord's will to accomplish his own ends. Through his cunning and understanding of sinister schemes, though not of his own power, he has caused deceit to prosper on the face of the worlds. Through his clandestine rule, a fatally wounded empire, one thought to be long dead, has arisen from the ashes of history and now exercises its authority over every tribe, tongue, and nation."

"He is the puppet-master," Aram added contemptibly, "pulling the strings on all Ocaba's heroic policies and accords. Thus, the people unwittingly follow him and his abominable image instead of the sovereign overlord; they unknowingly worship him instead of the great Vaughn Ocaba. However, there shall soon come a day when he shall take the reins of power directly, and all who dwell on the earth whose names have not been written in the Book of Life of the Slain Lamb will worship him."

Simon solemnly nodded his agreement. "Optinet was commissioned by Lord Sycuan the Third, the current Archangel of the Cathian Church, and for nearly forty-two months it has asserted its unholy influence upon an unsuspecting public. It is prophesied that it possesses the power to kill both small and great, rich and poor, free and slave, though we do not know the manner by which it'll do so. We liken it to a mouth which utters detestable things against the Coming One day and night."

Iakobos added, "We refer to it as *DayStar* because we believe that its powers do not originate from within itself. We believe they come, rather, from this man's master, the one who gives him his power and authority, the one referred to as *Lucifer*, which translates literally in the old tongue to mean 'daystar.'"

"Why do the Patron and the Marah war over the ancient mount of stone?"

Aram shook his head. "It is a good question, nameless one. It is, indeed, odd that both peoples so willingly break the commandments of their respective gods in order to possess crumbling blocks of stone!"

"The Qanah no longer agree with the ways of the Patron," Andreas declared. "That is why we broke away from them; why we've chosen a new way now."

"But if you no longer agree with them, why do you continue to fight beside them against the Marah?"

"We carry the ancestral blood of the Patron in our veins," Andreas replied. "They are our primeval brothers. We cannot abandon them, even though they refuse to believe that the Coming One, the Nazarene, is Mashiyach and that He is coming again like a great lion to pour out the cup of His wrath upon the unbelieving worlds."

"Mashiyach?"

"It's an old-tongue word that means 'the Messiah' or 'the Christ.'"

"The Christ." The war machine mouthed the words.

Simon nodded thoughtfully. "He is the agent of God through whom the destiny of our people will be fulfilled."

"Why do you refer to your Messiah as *the Nazarene*?"

"The Lived have taught us that during His earthly pilgrimage, the Coming One dwelt in an ancient city called Nazareth," Simon replied, "a city that once existed over one hundred kilometers to the north of the Old City District. It is said that the prophets foretold that He would dwell in Nazareth during His time here and that He would be called *the Nazarene*, although not even the Lived know by the mouths of which prophets this prophesy was originally given, or in which sacred text it is recorded."

"Then this Coming One, this Mashiyach, this Nazarene has already come once—and is coming again," the Peacekeeper surmised.

Andreas clenched his jaw. "For millennia now, the Patron have denied the identity of the One who walked upon this land over 2,400 years ago healing the sick, much as the merchant claims you've done for him. They deny that He is the virgin-born Son of God, the Seed of the woman, the God-Man who sacrificed Himself and died upon a wooden cross in payment for the sins of the world. They deny that He rose from the dead so that all believers might inherit the free gift of eternal life with God, and they deny that He is coming again with His sword bathed in heaven to tear asunder the Dragon and his legions of evil."

"Instead," Simon sighed regretfully, "our ancestral brethren continually search the five books of their Holy Scriptures, thinking that in them they have eternal life. The Patron have a zeal for God, but not according to knowledge. They, being ignorant of God's righteousness and seeking to establish their own righteousness, have not submitted to the righteousness of God."

"But one day an alarm sounded in the heavens, a trumpet that rang forth like a horn of war, like a call to arms on the holy mountain of God," Andreas said. "At its sounding, many were caught up to meet the Lord in the air, and at the same moment, some members of the Patron realized the depths of their ignorance. They realized that all along their Scriptures had borne witness to the Coming One, their Messiah. Unable to convince the leaders of the Patron of this revelation, however, they broke away from them and formed the faction known as the Qanah. That day occurred over four hundred years ago on the first of Tishri—the very day of the fulfillment of the Feast of Trumpets— and since then the infallible record of prophetic fulfillment has proven beyond a doubt that the Nazarene is Mashiyach and that His return on the Day of Atonement is imminent."

"Then they will look upon the One whom they have pierced," Simon uttered, as if he were reciting the words. "Yes, they will mourn for Him as one mourns for his only son, and grieve for Him as one grieves for a firstborn."

Andreas nodded solemnly. "Since that day, the Qanah have chosen to live barren, watchful lives in order to atone for our people's centuries of stiff-necked disobedience and to faithfully petition His return. While the Patron fight at all costs for possession of their ancient holy sites in order that they might renew their ancient sacrifices there, the Qanah fight because the Lord has regathered us here in our ancestral homeland and called us to war with the Sons of Disobedience until His Day of Atonement arrives. Unlike the Patron, we no longer have need of the offering of sacrifices for our sin. The Coming One has paid our debts for us so that we may stand without fault before the throne of God."

"You often refer to your Messiah as *the Coming One*," the war machine remarked, "or *the Seed of the woman*, or *Mashiyach*, or *the Nazarene*, or *the Christ*, yet you have thus far failed to name Him. Does He not have a proper name?"

"It is forbidden in these latter days to utter His true name," Andreas answered. "Optinet's sensors are attuned to the harmonic resonance signature of the word. If we speak it, the Marah will be able to locate and destroy us instantly."

Simon added solemnly, "Over the centuries many Qanah died bringing us this revelation."

"Apparently, the true name of the One is the only thing the Esezan's powers cannot shield from Optinet's sensors, even here in the Catacombs—such is its power," Andreas chimed in. "Yet, it is said that He will be given a new name at the end of the age. Until then, we keep His name only in our hearts."

"What can you tell me of the place called the Church of Cosmic Harmony?" the Peacekeeper inquired.

"Why do you ask about this wretched place, nameless one?" Aram retorted harshly.

The war machine replied, "While journeying through the Old City, I encountered an Optinet gateway disseminating an advertisement for the Church of Cosmic Harmony. In it I saw images and structures on the grounds of the church that matched those from my dreams, images of the guardians I have spoken of and of the tower that reached to the stars."

"Bah!" Aram exclaimed. "The Church of Cosmic Harmony with its contrived deity is but the newest counterfeit religion of the age—a religion based upon the signs of the zodiac and the ancient names of the stars within them, as found in what they have called the Scripture of the heavens. We believe it to be nothing but another of the counterfeit religions that the prophesies have warned will be established in these last days."

"A blasphemous game Jack Lamphere plays, making a business of religion," Simon spat. "He will suffer the wrath of the One when He—"

"Quiet!" Andreas ordered. "Remember the decree of the holy ones. We are not to discuss—"

Presently, the portal into Aram's underground abode phased open and a Qanah soldier arrayed in a water reclamation suit dove headlong through it, rolling into the chamber. He sprang to his feet, motioning toward the quickly closing aperture. Panting heavily, he said, "Sir, a multitude approaches."

"A multitude?" Andreas rose as the men reached for their weapons.

The soldier struggled to catch his breath. "They've come for the stranger," he rasped.

Andreas peered through the eyepiece mounted on the wall. A crowd of people thronged the streets, making their way toward the location of the portal entrance.

"They're not Marah soldiers," Andreas observed. "They're civilians—civilians with infirmities—some carried on pallets, some limping, others plague-ridden and blind; all manner of men, women, and children."

"In the name of the One," Simon breathed.

CHAPTER 18

TRIUMPHAL EXODUS

The time of Jacob's trouble: a term found in the Book of Jeremiah in the Scriptures of Truth, which refers to the great tribulation, which is prophesied to plague the worlds during the course of That Great Day.

—EZRA HIRIAM, ed.,
Ezra's Compendium of Lost Biblical Knowledge, 4th ed.
(City of Ariel: the Qanah Archives, 2450),
s.v. "the time of Jacob's trouble."

OLD CITY DISTRICT

AND SO THEY CAME, WITHOUT REGARD FOR ETHNIC or religious difference: the lame, blind, sick, plague-ridden, broken, and forgotten—Patron and Marah, alike. The Peacekeeper reached out to them and healed them, as it had the blind merchant and the old man in the courtyard. Thus, news of the stranger spread throughout the Old City District. Soon the people sought the stranger with regularity, and the Qanah saw fit to organize covert gatherings within the subterranean chambers of the catacombs so that the masses might be healed by the Peacekeeper's powers.

Quickly, though, the numbers of those who sought the stranger grew too large for the Qanah to conceal from the all-seeing eye of the DayStar and the ubiquitous Marah patrols, and it became clear that these gatherings were a danger to them all. Knowledge of the stranger's healings soon reached the ears of those within the hierarchies of the Cathian Church, and they were greatly offended by them. Together with the Marah, Lord Sycuan the Third, Archangel of the Cathian Church, and his most trusted spirit-sons and daughters, plotted how they might capture and kill the stranger, along with the Qanah who aided the cause. Optinet spots offered multimillion-credit rewards for tips regarding the stranger's whereabouts. They described the stranger as a criminal and a blasphemer who dared to falsely claim to possess powers given by the Holy Queen Mother of heaven herself. The Esezan were more aware of the danger than even the others. They knew that something would have to be done.

"So what do you think of this stranger of ours, old friend?" Prophet asked.

Lawgiver's eyes remained closed in contemplation. "Alas, it is difficult to say."

"Difficult to say?" Prophet retorted sharply. "But it is a machine."

"Indeed, it is," Lawgiver said, abruptly opening his eyes, and with these words, his form seemed to enlarge itself so that it filled the underground chasm in which they stood. His staff became as a mighty beam of cedar in his hand and a powerful whirlwind formed around him. The echoes of his voice vibrated the limestone walls of the chamber, as if a concealed power had suddenly manifested itself. "A machine, and more," he thundered. "A living machine; a conscious, sentient entity."

Prophet lifted his hands to shield his face from flying debris that had been drawn into the whirlwind. "I think I liked you better as the meek man that you were, Mosheh," he chided his ancient companion. "Everything changed when you struck that blessed rock with your rod in the wilderness."

Quickly Lawgiver's anger subsided along with the wind, and his prior form returned. Prophet shook his head in despair. "The Scriptures decree that Nachash has been given the power to grant life," he said. "I fear the Peacekeeper war machine may be the vessel in which he has chosen to exercise that authority, for think of it: the creation of a sentient machine is a scientific achievement without parallel in the annals of human history. Mankind has managed to create conscious life out of inanimate matter, just as the One did in the beginning. Therefore, the machine's existence may serve to validate the scientific theories of the natural man and thereby disrupt the timeline of events in these latter days. We may be eyewitness to the Dragon's plan to counter the Revelation, for the hour is late and the Watchers report evil forces afoot in the Ancient Heights. Entities that have not roamed the trans-dimensional planes since the days of Angelore now gather their numbers for the final war. The endgame cometh, Lawgiver, and this mechanical demon, this idol of jealousy spoken of by Ezekiel, has now strode boldly into our camp and speaks of his desire to begin his ministry at the newest counterfeit religion of the age. And you would grant him free passage?"

Lawgiver raised a cautious eyebrow at his companion. "I would not be so quick to label this entity an agent of evil," he warned.

Prophet narrowed his gaze at him. "What is the alternative? That he is an agent of the One? But he knows nothing of our Scriptures, our customs, or our people."

"Precisely," Lawgiver acknowledged. "I doubt whether the Accuser would send one so ill-prepared into our midst. And remember, old friend, for much of my terrestrial life, I, too, knew nothing of the Holy Scriptures, the sacred land, or the plight of our people. Remember that for many years, I, too, was but a stranger in a strange land."

"Yet, did not the One Himself warn of false prophets who would arise after the abomination of desolation stood in the most holy place and fulfilled the prophecy, showing great signs and wonders in order to deceive even the elect?"

"He did," Lawgiver concurred, "and the possibility that the machine is the manifestation of one of these false teachers must be considered. By nature of what it is, its power to deceive the nations would be great, but it is equally possible that the Peacekeeper is the manifestation of another prophecy that is to occur during these End Times, a prophesy benevolent in nature."

"Bah!" Prophet scoffed. "It is preposterous to expect that the coming of this metal monster is in accordance with His will."

"Is it?" Lawgiver queried. "More preposterous than to expect the infant son of peasants, one who was clothed in rags and laid to rest in a manger, to be the Messiah of the world? More ridiculous than to expect a locust-eating wild man dressed in the hair of camels to be the one chosen to make straight the way of the One after the four-hundred-year-long period of silence between the Testaments?

"Well, in recent years mankind has experienced another period of silence, my friend—a period of equivalent duration to the one which preceded it: the four-hundred-year-long period of time between the Rapture of His church and the beginning of the Great Tribulation. Perhaps the least likely candidate will be the one chosen by God to make straight the way again."

"A machine doing the bidding of the One?" Prophet snapped. "It is insanity."

Lawgiver fixed his ancient companion with a level stare. "Long ago, our people expected a King to come, a deliverer, but instead God sent a Servant and a Sacrifice. In God's plan, the Lion became the Lamb. He chose the way of our inheritance, causing our forefathers to miss His first coming, despite having all the prophecies that you, I, and the other great prophets, gave them. Thus, in all your millennia of experience, Elijahuw," he breathed, the disappointment unmistakable in his tone. "Have you not come to expect the unexpected from the Lord?"

Presently, Lawgiver averted his gaze from his companion and walked off toward the far wall of the chamber where the altar of incense sat. For a long moment he studied the craftsmanship of the altar. He ran his fingers along its golden sides. "There is another possibility," he murmured hesitantly.

Prophet glared sharply at him. "Surely you do not imply—"

"—that it is Mashiyach Himself?" Lawgiver trembled, clearly distraught at his own words. "Alas, it seems a blasphemy to consider such a thing, I know, but we have seen how the events of its life have thus far paralleled those of the One's during His earthly pilgrimage—its powers, its healings, the dawning of its ministry. And it has been over 1,200 days since the fulfillment of the abomination prophesy."

"You are a delusional old man," Prophet exclaimed.

"Did not the Angel of the One appear in forms appropriate to the day and age and circumstances of those He visited?" Lawgiver argued. "To Jacob, who wrestled with his return to the Holy Land, did He not appear as a man who wrestled with Jacob until the breaking of day? To Joshua, mired in battle, did He not appear as commander of the army of the Lord? To Simon and Cleopas, did He not appear beside them as a common traveler on the road to Emmaus after His resurrection?

"And lo!" Lawgiver continued, impassioned. "His appearances have not always been in the form of a Man, for did He not go before us into the wilderness as a pillar of cloud by day and a pillar of fire by night? And to me, consumed with my own selfish inhibitions, did He not manifest Himself as the burning bush that would not be consumed? Who, then, is to say that He may not take a form and appearance appropriate to the technological age in which we now live? The Peacekeeper has the ability to heal men of their ailments, as well as the power to unleash unparalleled destruction upon the earth. And recall, He said He would return in power and wrath."

"It is a mistake to allow this entity to pass from our midst," Prophet insisted, striding purposefully up to his companion. "Whatever his true nature and identity, it is clear that he must remain under our immediate watch and control."

"Nay!" Lawgiver bellowed, his voice shaking shards of bedrock from the cavernous ceiling, his form once again enlarging to fill the chamber. "Many entities shall manifest themselves during this, the time of Jacob's trouble, Prophet. We dare not bar the destiny of the sentient machine, regardless of the path it chooses to take. We dare not presume in our ignorance to limit the power of the One, ere His wrath be kindled against us."

"Holy ones," Andreas said, reverently standing before Lawgiver and Prophet, "the stranger wishes to leave the catacombs and the Old City District. He wishes to go to the place called the Church of Cosmic Harmony. He insists that it is his destiny to go there, that it is there that he will complete his father's work. People may enter our district freely, yet no one may leave without the authorization of the Marah. Who will break quarantine for him and allow him to pass beyond the borders of our land?"

"I will," Lawgiver replied, pressing himself up from his chair with his staff. He turned and gazed expectantly at his companion.

"As will I," Prophet said, rising to stand beside him.

"But who will go with him on his journey?" Andreas inquired. "Wisdom demands our vigilance, and I do not think He will be as forgiving if we miss His coming again."

"You shall accompany him, Andreas," Lawgiver decreed, "but not only you; none of the factions shall be left out. A representative from each will go—twelve in all!"

The Lived traveled with them through the subterranean passageways of the catacombs and through a portal to the surface world. There they were joined by many of the sick, diseased, hopeless, and forgotten, who formed a vast procession behind the sentient machine and the twelve representatives of the Qanah. Together they headed for the northern gate of the Old City District.

Along the way they were joined by a woman having a hemorrhage for twelve years who had endured much at the hands of Old City physicians. She had spent all that she had, but was no better; rather, she grew worse. When she had heard about the stranger, she came behind in the crowd and touched the hem of his coat as she said, "If only I may touch his clothes, I shall be made well." Immediately her hemorrhage was dried up, and she felt in her body that she was healed of her affliction.

The Peacekeeper, perceiving that power had gone out of it, turned around in the crowd. "Who touched my clothes?" it asked.

Simon smiled up at the human-mimicked face of the war machine.

"You see the multitudes thronging us, stranger, and you ask, 'who touched me?'"

The Peacekeeper looked around to see who had done this thing, but the woman, fearing and trembling and knowing what had happened to her, came and fell down before it and told it the whole truth. In response, the war machine said to her, "Woman, go in peace, and be healed of your affliction."

From a high mountaintop, the holy ones watched as the procession approached the Old City's northern gate. The people leapt, danced, and rejoiced as they were cured of their afflictions by the powers of the sentient machine. Those who had been healed saw the Peacekeeper war machine as it truly was. There was a tremendous brightness outlining its body, as well, a brightness that pulsed outward into the daylight. The Lived sensed that with each pulse, power went out from the Peacekeeper's body.

The Esezan observed as some of those in the crowd ran up ahead of the others and laid their cloaks upon the road before the feet of the stranger, singing triumphal songs of joy and victory. As they neared the gate, the one called Prophet called forth fire from heaven, which blinded the eyes and the memories of the guards in order that the Peacekeeper and the twelve representatives of the Qanah might pass without hindrance or recollection, leaving the multitudes behind to cheer their exodus.

Expectantly, Prophet turned his gaze skyward, fearing to hear a voice booming out of a bright cloud, as he had one time before upon a high mountain near to where they stood. However, all he saw was the putrid haze hanging like a dim curtain above the land.

"Is this the Coming One, Mosheh," he ventured, "or do we look for another?"

"It is difficult to say, Elijahuw," Lawgiver replied solemnly, "for truly the sentient machine is life from *non*-life—the true, firstborn son of man. And remember, it is recorded that They have claimed the firstborn of all creations as Their own."

"But, how can it be so?" Elijahuw contemplated, searching the depths of understanding of all that he had learned in his thousands of years of existence. "The temple is not yet rebuilt."

For a long moment, Mosheh the Lived, watched as the sentient machine, accompanied by the twelve representatives of the Qanah, walked beyond the northern borders of the Old City District and entered the lower levels of the Great City Industrial Quadrant en route to the Church of Cosmic Harmony.

"Isn't it?" he whispered.

ᴏRCHANGEL SYCUAN

Woe to the bloody city! It is all full of lies and robbery. Its prey never departs. The noise of a whip and the noise of rattling wheels, of galloping horses, of clattering chariots! Horsemen charge with bright sword and glittering spear. There is a multitude of slain, a great number of bodies, countless corpses—they stumble over the corpses—because of the multitude of spiritual unfaithfulness of the seductive harlot, the mistress of sorceries, who sells nations through her harlotries, and families through her sorceries.

—Nahum 3:1–4;
from the Scriptures of Truth,
the Holy Bible in its uncorrupted form,
The Qanah Archives, circa A.D. 2042, City of Ariel

Throne Room of the Archangel, Cathian Prime, City Center

"WHERE IS HE?"
"I do not know, my Lord."
"Is he in the company of the Qanah?"
"I do not know, my Lord."

189

"How did he heal you?"

"I do not know, my Lord."

It was a moment before another question was asked. "What do you say about this stranger who opened your eyes, merchant?"

"I say that he is a prophet, my Lord."

"A prophet, you say? A prophet with powers to heal the ailments of men?"

Cathian Spirit-Son Ravelle stood on the marble floor of the throne room at Cathian Prime, his slender nose upturned and his arms crossed, clearly agitated by the lack of progress he was making with his prisoner. He stared at the man that he and his guards had apprehended in the courtyard surrounding the energy conduit, a formerly blind merchant named Julius who illegally sold his wares on a street corner near the Temple Mount for many years. The merchant had been forced to his knees and positioned in front of the formal Throne of the Archangel—a monstrous, blockish, smooth-hewn marble edifice that dominated the center of the chamber—and beneath a hoverglobe whose light had been trained into a narrow, cone-shaped beam. He was shirtless and bound behind his back with a pair of biometric shackles, his battered face was bowed toward the floor, and his emaciated body was striped with lacerations. A credit-sized gouge appeared on the top of his right hand, presumably where an Optinet transponder had once been implanted.

Archangel Sycuan the Third observed the interrogation from an ornate, high-backed chair situated atop his golden hoverboard. He directed his board in a slow circumference round the throne room, a vault-like chamber whose walls and ceiling had been plated with gold and bronze. Colorful holosculptures in alcoves lined its walls with their various depictions of men and women in historic poses. A bank of windows along the far wall afforded the throne room's occupants a view of the daunting structures and meticulous grounds of Cathian Prime, now shrouded in darkness. A dozen Marah guardsmen stood round the perimeter of the room, blasters at the ready, eyeing the prisoner warily.

The archangel seemed a frail man, balled up as he was in his chair, his crooked spine hunched over his hoverboard at an odd angle. He quivered slightly when he moved and his expression seemed perennially worrisome. His head was adorned with a miter, a scarlet-colored, oblong-shaped headdress, which gradually narrowed to a point nearly a meter above his head. His body was layered with the signature vestments of his office, only his were largely scarlet in color, as opposed to the white of the lower offices. The garments included an alb, a full-length liturgical garment with long sleeves that gathered at the waist with a cincture; an amice, an oblong piece of cloth worn about the neck and shoulders; and a tunicle, a short garment worn over the amice. Over the lot, the Cathian lord wore an ephod of gold, blue, purple, and scarlet thread, and fine woven linen, artistically worked. The ephod had two shoulder straps joined at its two edges with two onyx stones affixed to them. At the front of the ephod hung a breastplate of gold, blue, purple, and scarlet thread, with precious gemstones mounted in rows and settings of gold upon it. There were four rows with three gemstones in each affixed to the front of the breastplate. The first row was of sardius, topaz, and emerald; the second of turquoise, sapphire, and diamond; the third of jacinth, agate, and amethyst; the fourth of beryl, onyx, and jasper.

A pallium was draped over his raiments in front and behind and hung the length of his body to the base of his hoverboard. Both sides of the narrow woolen band were emblazoned with symbols of the crescent moon, as were the pallium of Spirit-Son Ravelle and all other Cathian spirit-children. Sycuan's vestments spread like an apron over his chair as he observed the merchant kneeling at the center of the chamber.

His aged hands rested one atop the other upon a crosier that stood upright on the surface of the hoverboard. The crosier was comprised of three strands of metal of differing composition and color intertwined with one another, and it was coiled at the end like a shepherd's crook. The archangel's top hand opened and closed over a multifaceted scarlet gemstone embedded at the nob of his staff, exposing the mark of all Cathian Church members: two capital *c*'s on the palm of his right hand.

Lord Sycuan was the twelfth in a succession of archangels who sat as leaders of the powerful Cathian Church, the system-wide mega-ministry and officially sanctioned religion of the Great City Confederation. It had been Lord Sycuan who had commissioned his stable of Cathian scientists to create Optinet, the solar-system-wide communication and information dissemination system of near-infinite computational power—a singular point of knowledge and information nearly indistinguishable from omniscience. Optinet had been in operation for nearly forty-two months now, controlling all commerce throughout the inhabited worlds, and its existence had served to raise the Cathian Church to even greater prominence in the society of man. There were over a million branches of the church scattered throughout the solar system, situated to accommodate its billions of faithful members. In recent years, it had grown to become the largest religion in the history of man.

The place where they now gathered, Cathian Prime, was the church's official base of operation. Cathian Prime was located several hundred kilometers distant from the Old City District, far to the east across the Great City Industrial Quadrant, at the very heart of City Center.

The impressive church grounds were situated on the banks of the Great River, which still ran mighty in the land despite centuries of misuse and mismanagement of its resources.

Lord Sycuan veered his hoverboard toward a seating area near the entrance of the throne room where an elderly man and woman sat upon a low-lying couch. The couple sat near to a towering holosculpture that nearly reached the six-stories-high ceiling of the room. The sculpture depicted a beautiful woman riding upon her mysterious mount. The woman was clothed in fine linen of purple and scarlet and adorned with gold and precious stones and pearls. She held a golden cup filled with a glistening red liquid in her hand.

This was a representation of the deity of the monotheistic Cathian Faith, the Holy Queen Mother of heaven. She was seated upon a beast with seven heads and ten horns and reddish, rubbery-looking skin. There were words etched upon the hide of the beast in letters that belonged to an ancient system of writing. A sea of red waters glimmered beneath the projection of the Queen Mother. Its waters appeared to move in the stillness of the throne room.

The elderly couple sat silently in the shadow of the archangel's golden hoverboard, desperately clutching one another's hands.

Lord Sycuan raised his hand and pointed a quivering finger in the direction of the prisoner. "Is this your son?" His voice sounded scratched and strained, as if it were an effort to speak.

"Yes, my Lord," the woman answered nervously. She was sobbing, and her head was bowed tightly, as if she awaited a terror that she was sure would soon break upon her.

"And was he born blind?" the archangel inquired.

The woman nodded. "He was, my Lord."

"Then how is it that he now sees?"

It was a long moment before the woman mustered the courage to reply. "We know that this is our son," she said, her voice quaking with fear, "and that he was born blind. But how he now sees, we do not know, and who opened his eyes, we do not know. Ask him," she sobbed with a gesture toward her son. "He is of age; he can speak for himself."

Archangel Sycuan turned his attention toward the merchant. His hoverboard glided silently near to him. "Julius," he implored, the beginnings of a reassuring smile creasing his thin lips, "see how your parents fear for your welfare? They have traveled all this way to see to your well-being, and this is how you have chosen to repay them—by glorifying the acts of this stranger? Now, let us reason together, my son. Give proper respect to the Queen Mother, and tell us all you know of this sinner and blasphemer."

Slowly, Julius raised his bloodied face. He looked at his parents with warm, forgiving eyes. Then he addressed Lord Sycuan. "Whether he is a sinner, I do not know, or whether he is a blasphemer, I do not know. One thing I do know, my Lord, is that whereas I was blind, now I see."

Promptly, Spirit-Son Ravelle approached the merchant from his position on the right hand side of Lord Sycuan. He stood above Julius's prostrate body. "What did he do to you?" he demanded, unable to contain his frustration any longer. "How did this man open your eyes?"

Julius quenched Ravelle's fiery gaze with a steady, liquid stare. "I've told you already, and you did not listen. Why do you want to hear it again? You do not want to become his disciple, too, do you?"

Immediately, Ravelle struck him across the face with the back of his hand. "How dare you," he growled. "We are disciples of the holy Queen of heaven, but as for this stranger, we do not know where he is from."

"Well, here is an amazing thing," Julius replied, licking at the blood spilling from his lower lip. "You do not know where the stranger is from, yet he has opened my eyes. Since the beginning of time, it has never been heard that anyone has opened the eyes of a person born blind. Not even your Cathian medtechs have been able to equal such a feat. But if the stranger were not sent from above, he could do nothing."

"You who were born in sin would dare to instruct me in spiritual things?" Ravelle fumed. "It is clear that you, too, are a blasphemer, and worthy of receiving the penalty for being such."

"I don't know how, exactly," Julius said without regard for the threat just posed to him, "but the stranger has made me see all things clearly—things in the sight of my eyes, as well as things in the sight of my heart." The merchant lifted his eyes and gazed upon his accuser. "I see the abomination that you are, Spirit-Son Ravelle—you and all who hold to your Queen Mother's sorcerous ways. I've seen visions of this very place, Cathian Prime, being thrown down with violence. Soon your corrupt religion will not be found any longer on the face of the earth or the colonies."

"Enough!" Ravelle declared. "You would dare speak thus in the presence of the archangel himself. Surely you will pay for your insolence. Guards, remove him!"

At Ravelle's command, a dramatized wailing arose from the mother of the prisoner. She cursed her son and spat on him as she and her husband were escorted from the confines of the throne room.

The Marah guardsmen dragged Julius from the chamber and brought him by cruiser back across the Great City Industrial Quadrant to the gates of the Old City District. Before they removed his shackles and released him onto the Old City streets, one of the guards, under orders from Ravelle, issued forth a searing pulse from his blaster that served to burn out the merchant's eyes so that it would be impossible for him to ever see again.

CHAPTER 20

POWER *and* ӨUTHORITY

Attention:
Guild Protectorate Bureau
Chief Arnaud Garret
Intel capture, intra-link diffusion feed from
Optinet mainframe core to unknown entity
at unknown interstellar destination point:
[Begin] Wisdom's final book
[symbolic code—unbroken]...
the (first) of the Godfears...(cant)...
chain of prophetic fulfillment
[numeric code—unbroken]...
the Nine Orders...(cant)...
Legends of [cryptogram: "Angelore"?]...
traffic the (trans-) dimensional
domains, planes, and realms of
existence [ciphered text]...
blind arrogance of [cryptogram:
"the Godhead"]...
Whole Armor of God (destruction of) [Break]

THRONE ROOM OF THE ARCHANGEL, CATHIAN PRIME, CITY CENTER

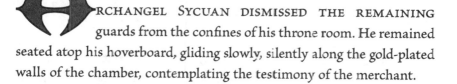

RCHANGEL SYCUAN DISMISSED THE REMAINING guards from the confines of his throne room. He remained seated atop his hoverboard, gliding slowly, silently along the gold-plated walls of the chamber, contemplating the testimony of the merchant.

When the last of his guards had departed, the darkened silhouette of a lanky man, all knees, elbows, and right angles, seated in a wheelchair appeared in the doorway of the chamber.

Sycuan's hoverboard whirred to a halt. He tried to mask his surprise at the unexpected appearance of the very entity who gave him his power and authority.

"Trouble afoot, Lord Sycuan?" the wheelchair-bound man inquired.

Sycuan acknowledged his presence with a practiced, albeit shaky, lowering of his head. "It is nothing, lawless one," he said, his voice rough and gravelly. "Spirit-Child Ravelle apprehended a man at the exposed energy conduit near the southern gate of the Old City eight days ago—a formerly blind merchant who sold his wares near the Temple Mount. The merchant insists that a stranger reached out to him and touched him and healed him of his infirmity. His parents have testified that he was born blind, and yet now he sees."

Sycuan watched from above as the man slowly wheeled himself into the room, heading toward the center of the chamber, toward the blockish stone edifice that was the Throne of the Archangel.

Pausing, the wheelchair-bound man surveyed the fresh patterns of blood splattered on the marble floor where moments before the shackled merchant had knelt. He steepled his slender fingers in front of his face. "Curious," he said, "a man born blind, sees. Have you questioned this stranger? Have you questioned this would-be healer?"

"He is an offender, a criminal, and a blasphemer, most worthy shepherd," Sycuan corrected him respectfully, "but he has eluded capture thus far. Members of the Qanah aided his escape. It is rumored that he dwells with them within the catacombs beneath the Old City, and that others have been healed of their infirmities in like manner as the merchant."

"Others?"

Archangel Sycuan resumed a slow, circuitous route around the chamber. "It is an oddity, lawless one," he said, smoothing the layers of liturgical garments adorning his body as he drifted along. "The events of this stranger's life appear to parallel those of the One during the days of His earthly pilgrimage. He walks in His very footsteps upon the Holy Land, the Qanah befriend him and follow him as they did the One, he heals the ill of their infirmities, and those who have been healed by his powers claim that his body glows as the sun shining in its strength. Furthermore, the testimony of the merchant mirrored that of an account recorded in the ninth chapter of Wisdom's Gospel According to John. Perhaps he is one of the false prophets Mashiyach warned would be about in these last days or an imposter who dares to heal in the name of the Holy Queen Mother of heaven."

The wheelchair-bound man tracked Sycuan's movements in his peripheral vision. The narrow, conic beam from the hoverglobe positioned above him accentuated the skeletal structure of his facial features. Sycuan thought he saw a glinting of the metalline blood vessels in his re-engineered eye before he spoke. "An imposter, you say? An impious imposter, perhaps?"

"It is likely the Lived have met this stranger by now," Sycuan intoned gravely. He tightened his grip on the gemstone nob of his tri-metal crosier. "The Qanah would not harbor him without first bringing him before Lawgiver and Prophet for questioning."

The lanky man rolled himself closer to the monstrous Throne of the Archangel at the center of the chamber. "The prophesying of Their two wretched witnesses will soon come to an end," he decreed. "Soon, their supernatural lives shall end once and for all, their corpses thrust through and desecrated by all manner of evil upon the Old City streets. Grim shall be the fate of the twelve tribes of Their precious Sons of the Kingdom—the cursed remnant seed of Their chosen people, who have plagued this land since the beginning."

"What of Ocaba?" Sycuan asked.

"The trials of the day are taking their toll on our vaunted leader, I'm afraid: the upcoming summit, the growing discord among the nations of the north and the south, and the missing war machine." The man chuckled lightly before musing, "Ocaba will be useless or dead before long."

Sycuan slowed his hoverboard to a stop. "You possess him completely."

It was a statement its bearer believed to be fact, but the wheelchair-bound man shook his head in the negative. "I merely planted the seeds of doubt and confusion, as is the manner of our ways. Since the day Ocaba took office, in fact, I have been at his side, patiently counseling him, assiduously infiltrating his consciousness, tirelessly poisoning it to my will. No decision he makes is his own any longer, as has been the case for quite some time.

"Surely you see it, my servant. Ocaba was a frail mark for me after all those whom I've possessed to do my will over the ages. The master gave me my power, my throne, and my authority, yes, but it was I, and I alone, who resurrected this fatally wounded empire. It was I who shaped the geopolitical conditions of the solar system to bring about this precise state of affairs. It was I who planted the seeds for Ocaba's most laudable accomplishments, who orchestrated his most heroic policies, who manipulated the players in his miraculous peace accords. Thus, it is I whom the people unwittingly follow, and it is I the people unknowingly worship, not the great Vaughn Ocaba!

"I alone granted you the power to give breath to my image, the creation known as Optinet or DayStar, my glorious mouth, which blasphemes day and night against the Lord of heaven and Earth. It is my ingenious creation whose supernatural control of commerce causes the people to marvel. Those poor, witless masses of the worlds. By the taking of my infamous mark, they—all those whose names have not been written in the Book of Life of the Lamb slain from the foundation of the world—have these many years ignorantly followed and worshiped me. It is my ingenious creation whose transponder-mark bears the power to kill both small and great, rich and poor, free and slave—all those who refused to follow and worship me in these last days.

"It was I, and I alone, who gave the order for Akathartos, the three unclean spirits, to be loosed from our mouths and the mouth of the Dragon so they might recruit those who are of one mind with me: the kingdomless kings, the ten most powerful terrorist leaders in the system, who will soon join my warring half in battle upon the plains of Esdraelon. Then shall Akathartos go about their prophesied tasks of murdering three of the ten GCC leaders at the upcoming summit, three of the ten horns of my glorious end-time confederation of nations.

"I alone agreed in these last days to transect my spirit, though our minds remain psionically linked—half to wage spirit-war in the personage of the Warlord Chuwl, half to wage political war in the personage of Aden Xyan—in order that all dimensions, domains, realms, and planes of existence might join at the chiming of this very hour."

Again, Sycuan watched from above as the man wheeled himself about the throne room. This time he headed for the enormous holosculpture near the entrance of the chamber.

The wheelchair-bound man gazed affectionately at the six-stories-high depiction of the female deity of the Cathian Church in noble repose on a great seven-headed, ten-horned beast. He studied the cryptograms and letters that belonged to the forgotten system of writing etched into her mount's ruddy hide.

"Yet, think of it more plainly, my servant," he said, his eyes alighted by her crimson glow. "It has been four centuries since the Faithful have been raptured from the earth, and as is prophesied, the Hindering Spirit, the Restrainer has taken His leave from the worlds, as well. Since that very day the master has worked diligently to corrupt Wisdom to the point of powerlessness; few undefiled copies remain in existence. His Spirit has departed from His Word in its present form. His power, His authority, His speaking voice no longer abide within its pages. All that's left is the Great Harlot's empty, erroneous codex, cobbled together from the holy books of the religions that remained after the Rapture.

"Who, then, is left to follow and to worship, besides the master and I? The gods of the solar system's religions, perhaps?" He gestured toward the towering holosculpture beside him. "Why, these are the children of our loins, conceived and cast for our everlasting plans and purposes."

"But what of my destiny, lawless one?" Sycuan inquired worrisomely. "Wisdom speaks of the utter desolation of my church, of my eternal judgment alongside you in Ghenna's undying fires. You will speak with the master about these things, as you have promised? The clock of end-time will be halted before these things come to pass?"

The bony man shook his head disappointedly. "I have borne you upon my back these past four hundred years," he breathed, "and you dare to question me about these things? Perhaps Their judgment is what you deserve, False Prophet. Perhaps you will have soon served your purposes and should be made desolate and naked, your flesh eaten and burned with fire. Nevertheless, you have been faithful in your apostasy, I must give you that much; you have been loyal in your servitude. When the time is right, I shall turn back the hatred of my kingdomless kings. The Great Harlot who sits on many waters shall be preserved for the coming kingdom, and it is you who shall thrive at her head."

"But how?" Sycuan asked hesitantly. "How will the master break the inerrant chain of prophetic fulfillment? What is his plan to defeat They who cannot learn? How will he insure that these things do not come to pass?"

The wheelchair-bound man turned again to study the beautiful woman upon her bestial mount, her gown of fine linen of purple and scarlet adorned with gold and precious stones, the golden cup of glistening red liquid in her hand, the glimmering sea of many waters beneath her. He brooded, "This stranger of yours, this healer, may have something to do with it. Do not hinder his journey. Allow him free passage through your midst."

Shakily, Lord Sycuan used his crosier to press himself to his feet upon his hoverboard. "Free passage?" he questioned. "But I have told you how his life mirrors that of the One's. We cannot simply—"

The lanky man spun his wheelchair round to face him. "Do as I say, and no more, for the time draws nigh when more of the master's plan shall be revealed. This very night, in fact, my transected spirit meets again with That Great Serpent of Old within the confines of another of his illusory abodes. Yet, I fear the old man toys again with that which is at once Godspeak's most generous gift to the whole of creation and His greatest curse. Perhaps he will have better luck this time."

The man rolled himself toward the entrance of the room with quick movements of his slender hands. "DayStar's influences must increase," he called back to Lord Sycuan as he reached the doorway. "My mouth must open wider than ever before; its utterances, its deceptions, and its blasphemies must increase as never before. Exercise my authority well, Great Beast of the Earth, as you have thus far faithfully done. For this fourth kingdom, this fatally wounded empire, shall soon be fully revived; and a fifth kingdom, an everlasting kingdom of our grand design and making, shall not be far behind. Is that understood?"

Archangel Sycuan bowed low in humble allegiance. "Perfectly, O Great Beast of the Sea."

CHAPTER 21

RUWACH

I saw by night, and behold, a man riding on a red horse, and it stood among the myrtle trees in the hollow; and behind him were horses: red, sorrel, and white. Then I said, "My Lord, what *are* these?" So the angel who talked with me said to me, "I will show you what they are."

—ZECHARIAH 1:8–9;
from the Scriptures of Truth,
the Holy Bible in its uncorrupted form,
The Qanah Archives, circa A.D. 2042, City of Ariel

UNKNOWN LOCATION

GRAY-BLACK CLOUDS THREATENED TO PREMATURELY end the day and the meager warmth the sunlight had brought to it. A sliver of red sky low on the far horizon was all that remained of the daylight, accentuating the roiling darkness of the clouds above. With light's end came the cold, a cold that came not from a slowly descending mass of polar air, but from a sudden juxtaposition of extremes, as if the molecules of air had suddenly decreased their temperature in a moment's time. The bellies of the clouds hung low to the ground, heavy-laden with mid-winter snow.

A small company of soldiers riding shaggy-maned horses walked slowly upon a snow-packed road that cut a narrow path through a dense forest. The forest was comprised of tall, narrow pines, towering bands of notched shadows abutting the blue-marbled road. Dual columns of steam billowed from the nostrils of the horses as they walked, their riders hunkered down into their woolen coats, trying to fend off the cold. The muffled thumping of hooves on the hard-packed surface of the road produced a rhythmic sound that lulled the soldiers to complacency in the otherwise still and silent wilderness.

Many of their companions had been lost this day upon the trans-dimensional battlefields, and there were many more wounded back at base camp. The fighting had been fierce and exhausting. Even their leader, Warlord Chuwl, showed the telltale signs of weariness. He rode upon the lead horse, Leukos, a large white stallion, the only winged horse in the pack. Leukos stood some five hands taller than his nearest rival, his great wings folded back along his sides and extending beyond the length of his body. Warlord sat heavily in his saddle, his body swaying with the rhythm of Leukos's stride.

Chuwl was well aware that his iron-teethed leadership was sorely needed back at base camp to inspire his men to rise early and again face the terrifying entities of the Enemy that trafficked the trans-dimensional realms, planes, and domains with ever-increasing frequency. However, he'd had no say in the matter of leaving his men this night, nor any choice in the use of such primitive modes of transportation for both he and the handful of guards permitted to accompany him. His lord and master had dictated both demands to him in no uncertain terms, so instead of being where he knew he should have been, Warlord found himself here, upon this illusory road, playing make-believe just to appease the old man.

This time they were to rendezvous at an inn not far distant up the road. *Another of the old man's illusions,* Chuwl thought, noting the incredible detail in the snow-draped scene surrounding him, *yet another of his fantasies of the mind designed to placate his distaste for dwelling in places of Their making. And my fate eternal is tied to this fictive old fool.*

As his horse walked steadily onward with those of his guardsmen behind, Warlord clenched his jaw and forced his mind to turn from his bitter thoughts on these meetings with his master to reflections on his own origin and future.

Many hosts has my spirit had since its defection thousands of years ago. Many forms have I taken in this, the waning Age of Man, and none more potent than Antiochus IV Epiphanes in the second century before His first coming, Chuwl recalled.

Persecutor of the holy covenant was I, unchallenged desecrator of Their temple and Their sacrifices. A sow upon Their sacred altar—sweet abomination that causes desolation—did I set in Their most holy place. Now again, nearly three and one-half years past, has the bearer of my transected spirit come to that very place, our minds psionically linked by the will of our master. In the form of another have I delivered that same message to the woman and her wretched offspring, and by so doing set the clock of ending time into motion.

And soon, as is prophesied, I shall take Revelation form and lead my assembled armies and those of the kingdomless kings to war against the kings of the earth at Esdraelon. Afterwards, I shall meet my master in the Glorious Land, and together we shall destroy Their two witnesses and overcome Their saints, stringing them up for all the solar system to see. Only then can my transected spirit be rejoined and made whole again. For as I traverse the dimensions, domains, realms, and planes waging spirit war against the entities of the Enemy, my symbiont half remains terrestrially bound, waging his own breed of war in the political arenas of men.

Warlord remained lost in thought until the unnatural stillness of the scene captured his attention. He gazed at the thick forest to either side of him, and up ahead where the road curved round a bend. *Where's the wind?* he wondered. *The air, the trees—they're perfectly still. Odd. The old man is usually such a stickler for climatic detail. Yet, there's not the slightest hint of a breeze here. It's as if the wind does not exist within this illusion, as if someone is holding back—*

Abruptly, Chuwl held up a clenched fist, halting his guardsmen behind him. He pulled back sharply on Leukos's reins, stopping him in mid-stride. Chuwl sniffed aggressively at the air like a beast. He gazed anew at the silent forest, only more keenly this time. All was quiet, save the occasional snort of a guard's horse behind him. Snow had begun to fall, silencing the forest even more so, such that he could hear the icy patter of flake-fall upon the frozen ground. He looked skyward and observed that in the absence of wind, the snow was descending from the sky in unnaturally straight lines. Warlord's acute senses signaled their warning. The taint in the air was only one part per million, but detectable. The slightly alien look to the forest was again due only to a series of minor alterations, but to one trained in the art of subterfuge it was optically plain. It had nearly caught him unaware.

Chuwl recalled the old man's lessons on the quantum laws of the universe. "The observer alters the thing being observed simply by its presence. The environment within which an observer observes is changed, altered, sometimes by very slight degrees, and unpredictably so." *There can be only one conclusion to explain these phenomena: we're being followed.*

Chuwl used standard hand signals to instruct his men to hold their positions upon the road. Quietly, he slid his powerful frame down from his saddle, dismounting with the lithe and agility of a leopard. He snatched his battle bow and quiver from the pouch on Leukos's side and slung it over his shoulder. Sprinting from the road, his boots barely made a sound as they impacted the snowy surface.

Warlord plunged into the dark forest, weaving between pine trees, his knees pumping like pistons in the waist-deep snow. He came upon a small stream and forded it in a skilled leap. He hurtled a briar thicket and slid down a snowy bank, all while moving with the silent stealth of one accustomed to trafficking in shadows. When he'd doubled back upon their route under cover of the forest for a kilometer, he turned back toward the road. When he reached the edge of the clearing, he saw them.

There, just off the roadside, five hundred meters distant and partially obscured by a veil of falling snow, he spied what appeared to be a mere man upon horseback, standing in a ravine in a patch of winter-dead myrtle trees. The horseman wore a dark, hooded cloak whose tails nearly touched the top of the snow pack. The lay of the cloak upon the back of the horse made it appear as if it had been fitted with battle armor from its mid-side and around its rear quarter. The horse was large and powerful, yet lean in stature—a cross between a warhorse bred for battle and a thoroughbred, engineered for speed. It was black in color and held its tail high and proud and crooked at the top. The horse pawed at the snow with a forward hoof.

The dark rider scanned the road in the direction Chuwl's guardsmen waited, one hand gripping the long black hair of his horse's mane, the other resting upon the hilt of a sheathed sword at his side. Neither horse nor rider appeared to take note of Warlord's presence along the edge of the trees.

Has a Watcher learned of our meeting this night and decided to trail us to the inn? Chuwl contemplated, still breathing heavily from his run. He channeled his exhales carefully through his nose to minimize the production of steam that might be visible to the horseman. *This rider more resembles man than Watcher! What place has this ordinary man within one of the old man's illusions?*

The snow was coming down harder now, blurring the figure of the strange horseman to an outline. Chuwl considered his options. Despite appearances, his warrior instincts cautioned him of the dangers of a frontal assault upon the unknown entity. No creature, man or Watcher, would dare invade one of the old man's illusory domains without reckless boldness and courage—characteristics typically backed by powers and abilities! Chuwl remembered from his lessons that even Michael the archangel, the Great Prince himself, dared not pronounce against the old man when he disputed with him over the body of Moses.

I must not be careless, Warlord reminded himself as he silently lifted his bow over his shoulder. *Curse the old fool. Curse the old man for forcing me to wield such primitive weapons within his illusions.*

Cautiously, Chuwl rolled onto his back, staying low to the embankment. He plucked an arrow from the quiver and clipped its nock onto the bowstring. He righted himself and, peering over the bank, rose to his knees. He drew the bow back smoothly. When the bowstring reached maximum tension, he released it. The arrow took flight on a low arc toward the horseman.

At the twang of the bowstring, the horseman turned, squaring his body to Chuwl's location. Warlord watched the arrow pass right through the center of the rider's chest and come out the other side, yet the horseman showed no signs of injury. Instead, he seemed spurred to action.

He leaned forward, tightening his grip on his horse's mane. He prodded his mount with two sharp jabs of his heels. In three powerful strides, the horse reached gallop speed and charged Chuwl's position. Clumps of snow and ice tumbled in the air behind the fiery beast, kicked up by its wrathful strides. Its nostrils were flared, its eyes wild with energy and eagerness.

When the rider reached the center of the road, he pulled back forcefully on the coarse hair of his horse's mane, lifting its front legs into the air. Neighing loudly, the horse pawed at the snow-dappled sky, dancing upon its rear legs and turning a quarter circle with each leap. Securely gripping his mount with his legs, the horseman released his hold on the mane. Slowly, he raised his outstretched arms until they were parallel to the ground, causing his long cloak to rise like the main sail of a ship, with his body acting as the mast.

While turning circles with his horse under him, the strange rider tilted back his head and threw back his hood, revealing overlarge, watery eyes—deep pools of cobalt blue in an otherwise colorless world. His skin appeared lurid and nearly transparent in nature—an opaque and deathly pallor—such that grayish arteries and veins in his neck and face were visible beneath its surface. He stretched open his mouth to form an oblong cavern far larger and deeper than any human mouth could have formed.

Instantly, Chuwl heard a roar, as from a pyrotechnic blast. The sound was such that he turned and fled before it with all speed. A violent blast of breath rushed at him like a targeted tempest. Trees in its path collapsed like toothpicks, their massive root systems upending and crashing to the ground, creating cavities like moon craters. Desperate for cover, Warlord turned and launched himself into one of the newly formed craters. Roughly, he tumbled into the bottom of the hole. Just as he looked up, a large tree fell fortuitously upon the cavity, covering him.

Chuwl heard a violent roar of the wind pass over him like a sustained shock wave. The tree that covered him groaned and splintered from the force. He quivered in his earthen shelter, protected from the blast. In time, the wind passed and whatever had just happened was over.

Warlord decided it best to wait before attempting to free himself. When a few moments had passed, he pressed his palms upon the tree that covered him. It disintegrated to powder at his touch. He pushed through the ash and climbed out of the crater.

When he emerged, Chuwl witnessed the definition of utter destruction. The wind that had erupted from the mouth of the rider had knocked flat all foliage for kilometers around.

Craters from felled trees pockmarked the landscape, their upended root systems standing on edge like great spidery wheels. Snow in a wide circumference had been blown away by the blast, exposing winter-brown grasses and muddy ground. The snowfall had ceased. Tall vortices of air, thick with roots and branches and other debris, rose like great columns into the sky in various locations throughout the barren landscape—the remnant currents of the tempest. Otherwise, the wind was gone. The horseman, too, was nowhere to be seen.

"What manner of creature—?" Chuwl breathed, marveling at the devastation.

His first steps wobbly, the stunned Warlord picked his way across the barrenness toward the last position of his guardsmen. When he reached their location, he saw the remains of his guards and their horses strewn about in a macabre scene. Their wholly intact skins lay upon the road like dehydrated leather, leeched clean of all moisture.

Only Chuwl's horse, Leukos, had survived, having used his great wings to escape the maelstrom of the strange rider. At the sight of his master, Leukos's alabaster form descended through the debris-littered air and landed heavily beside him. When all four of his hooves had reaching the ground, the warhorse planted his front hooves, plowing deep furrows in the mud, clumps of which speckled his snow-white hide. He slid to a halt and reared back on his hind legs, whickering frightfully. He tossed his snowy mane and clumped his way over to his master, his black eyes wide and beset with alarm.

Chuwl stooped and lifted the flesh-less arm of one of his guards. The bones of his hand were brittle and disintegrated like dried charcoal at his touch. With a grunt, he dropped the gruesome appendage, swiftly mounted Leukos, and charged off toward the inn up the road.

When he arrived, he dismounted quickly. Panting heavily, Chuwl banged open the rounded door of the inn and stepped inside. He saw many patrons filling the large common room, making merry. He spied the old man sitting alone at a table in the far corner, sipping ale from a stout mug.

The old man acknowledged Warlord's presence with indifference as he barged his way over to him, knocking any in his path to the earthen floor. "You are late," he said, staring down at the golden liquid effervescing in his mug.

When the old man heard Chuwl's labored breathing, however, he turned quickly to face him. "What is it, my apprentice?" he asked, raising an eyebrow. "What has happened?"

Warlord removed his gloves and hat with trembling hands. His long, dark hair was wet with sweat and plastered on his forehead. "I'm not sure," he rasped. "There was something out there, my Master, something on the road, following us. My guards, their horses, they're—"

"You careless fool!" the old man cursed, slamming his mug down on the table. "You let your defenses drop!"

"But I did not think—"

"That they could invade my illusions?" the old man broke in sharply, locking eyes with him. "You know better. If the entities of the Enemy have the power to invade dreams, then they have the power to invade my illusions. Quickly now," he prodded, "tell me what you saw."

"I don't know, my Lord," Chuwl breathed. "Never have I witnessed such destructive force." He gulped, trying hard to moisten his throat. "It appeared to be a mere man upon a mere horse following us. I doubled back to a position behind it and fired my battle bow, but the arrow seemed to pass right through the rider without harm. When it saw me, it opened its mouth and issued forth a tempest that leveled the forest for kilometers around. Perhaps it is a new breed of Watcher, one that can—"

"That was no Watcher," the old man instructed, then took a slow swig of his ale.

"If not a Watcher, then what was it, my Master?"

The old man swirled the golden ale in his mug. "These are those whom the Lord has sent to walk to and fro about the earth," he whispered as if reciting the words. "What you encountered, what destroyed your men, my apprentice, was an entity known as a Ruwach."

"A Ruwach?"

"These are the Four Spirits of Heaven," the old man said, again sounding as though he were quoting from memory, "who go out from their station before the Lord of all the earth. The black horses are going to the north country, the white ones are going after them, and the dappled ones are going toward the south country." He took another gulp of ale. "Ruwachs are the four winds of heaven and earth, apprentice. Your ordinary arrow could never harm it. They are equal parts mind, spirit, and wind."

"But they—it—was on horseback?"

"In Wisdom, in the Book of Zechariah, they take the form of horse and rider."

"What is their purpose, my Lord?"

The old man swallowed the last of his ale. "They are the wrath appeasers."

Chuwl stared at him. "Wrath appeasers, my Lord?"

"The ones appointed to appease Their wrath. I have encountered these ancient entities in ages past, before the earth ever was—long before the Age of Man."

"But it saw me, my Lord," Chuwl told him distressingly. "Perhaps it knows that we are here? Perhaps it is aware of your plan?"

The old man shook his head in the negative. "It is prophesied that Ruwach will roam the realms in the last days, which means that everything is on schedule and that the end-game cometh. It is an expected sign—a good sign."

"Not for my guardsmen."

The old man chuckled lightly. "There will be many more casualties before we are through, my understudy. But for now, sit. We have matters to discuss."

The old man spied a rotund, rosy-cheeked serving woman who was walking past their table. "Barmaid! Another for me, and a fresh one for my guest."

Still shaken from his encounter, Chuwl swung a mud-clogged boot over the wooden bench across from the old man. There was a large mug of warm ale on the table in front of him that had lost its head on the trip to the table. Servers scooted between the common room tables with trays of mugs, sloshing their frothy contents upon the dusty floor and the shoulders of unlucky patrons. Behind the bar, a fat bartender wearing a soiled apron pulled feverishly at wooden taps filling mugs, trying futilely to keep up with demand for the golden ale. A funny-looking little bearded fellow wearing a candy-striped vest and a tassel-topped hat danced atop the tables, singing stories while playing an accordion.

The old man gazed casually at the gaiety surrounding them. "You bring news, yes?"

How can he be so unconcerned after what I've just seen? Warlord thought angrily before collecting himself and replying. "Akathartos are loosed and have gone forth to entice the kingdomless kings to join me and my armies at Esdraelon," he informed him. "As you've instructed, the three unclean spirits will promise each a kingdom of their own if they'll but join me in battle against the armies of men from the north and south."

"Very well. And what of goings-on upon the high, astral planes?"

"Spirit-war intensifies as the Age of Man nears its end. The Nine Orders are mobilized. My princes report the presence of Archomai, Virtues, Existe, and Thronos upon the Ancient Heights, assembling their numbers, practicing their warcraft while the Watchers carry on with their noble duties on the earth, as they have since the time of the

Great Rebellion. Michael has dispatched the archangels Raphael, Raguel, Remiel, and Uriel, along with guardians and Seraphim to patrol the planes, leaving himself alone to defend the gates of the Third Heaven. It is a curious maneuver, contrary to sound battle strategy, and—"

"Alone, you say?" the old man interrupted him. He shook his head in disgust. "Again, you disappoint me, my apprentice. It has been some time since our last meeting and still you bring no word on the whereabouts of the other members of the Order Supreme, and particularly, of the one who stands in Their presence."

Chuwl took a shallow sip of his flat ale. "My princes have come upon no sign of him as of yet, my Master."

The old man stared at him with ominous calmness. "You understand that his absence is of concern to me?"

"Yes, my Lord."

"And is it your wish that I be concerned at this critical juncture in time?"

Chuwl lowered his head. "No, my Lord."

The old man toyed with his empty glass for a moment. "You are aware of the reasons for my concern, are you not, my servant?"

Warlord took another guarded sip of his headless ale, eyeing his master warily over the edge of his mug. Chuwl never knew what to expect from the old man. He never knew when he might choose to assert himself, when he might decide to subtly remind him of the reasons for his indentured servitude.

"Allow me to refresh your memory," the old man offered, leaning forward intently. His eyes flared madly. "Over 2,400 years ago, this Malak was the chosen name-giver of the Godspeak," he spat the last word out of his mouth like filth, "as well as the chosen messenger of His birth. Hundreds of years before that, he was the chosen prophet of His return. In fact, he is the one who foretold of your future demise, Warlord Chuwl, among other things, to the prophet Daniel. One would think you would have at least a passing interest in his current whereabouts. It is all but certain he will be about in these last days; he is the natural choice to herald Godspeak's return."

Chuwl's gaze belied a genuine hatred. "The Malak—Gabriel—will show himself, my Master," he uttered, "and when he does—"

"When he does," the old man paused, "as always, you will do precisely as I say."

Presently, the rosy-cheeked barmaid delivered two overflowing mugs of ale.

Warlord pushed himself back from the table, unappreciative of the old man's domineering tone. He gazed at the recreated scene surrounding them. The decor of the inn, the clothing, and the demeanor of the people looked authentic in every detail. It was the Middle Ages, the era of cloak and dagger—a favorite of the old man's because of the crude methods of warfare that existed at that time and the necessity of physical proximity for bloodshed. The quaint inn was nestled along a narrow roadway that coursed its way through a provincial countryside, blanketed with snow. Golden lanterns hung upon the common room walls, spaced every few meters. The patrons of the inn made merry, dancing to the songs of the bard and sloshing ales with one another in drunken bliss. They were simple times, brutal times.

Still, having to meet within the confines of his master's illusions was growing tedious. The old man could not stand to dwell for long in places of Their creation—whether those places existed on Earth, in the heavens, or anywhere within the Infinitude. And, as Wisdom records, the old man had so profaned his appointed sanctuaries by the multitude of his iniquities and the unrighteousness of his trade, that he could no longer occupy those realms, either. Instead, he manufactured his own abodes—illusions, recreations of places and times in which he was the dominant force upon the earth. He chose places where he could dwell comfortably, and, Chuwl surmised, places where there were no reminders of the mistakes he had made in the past.

"Perhaps you would prefer we stage our meetings within the proper domains, my understudy?" the old man chided him with a flourish of his hand. Warlord had forgotten that within his fantasies, nothing could be withheld from his master—not even thoughts.

"Perhaps you would prefer that we meet at a location within the airless expanse of which you have grown so fond, somewhere within that lifeless wasteland upon which spirit-war rages? And here I thought I was doing you a favor by changing your venue from time to time."

Chuwl could sense his master's escalating rage, a sure sign of the unveiling of his dark-power form. The old man appeared to momentarily shape-shift to liquid shadow, but then quickly coagulated back into human form.

"I see that your puny mind turns again to what you consider to be the mistakes I have made in times past," the old man told him. "Surely you refer to the days of Godspeak's First Coming. So, come now, my apprentice, spare not my feelings. Speak your mind!"

Warlord knew better than to attempt to mask his emotions from his master while dwelling within one of his illusory realms. The end of that road was inevitably pain. "As you wish, my Lord," he began cautiously. "If you invite my thoughts on the matter, I suspect that over the centuries you've sought to conceal the defeat you suffered during the days of His First Coming with clever rhetoric. I suspect you allowed your emotions to control you during those days when the One walked upon the earth. Vengeance can be a blinding force, regardless of whether one foresees the ramifications of its implementation or not. I simply find it hard to believe that you could be capable—"

"Capable of what, my servant?" the old man cut in with a haunting cackle. "Of actually deceiving Them?"

The sudden, amplified resonance of his voice shook the very walls of the common room, causing many of the patrons to cease their merriment. "Say it, man! Say it and be done with it. You have doubted me since the day our alliance was forged. You see me as an old fool letting primitive emotions guide my actions, rather than relying on intellect and experience."

Chuwl persisted more boldly, "If I'm wrong, then tell me why you indwelt the talebearer. Tell me why you possessed Iscariot to make such a colossal error at Gethsemane."

In an instant, the old man's pupils shifted to coal black. All sounds in the inn went mute. All animation ceased. Matter and energy suddenly froze, suspended in time and space. The bard atop the table paused in mid-twirl. The barmaid, who'd dropped a glass, stared inanimately at the golden liquid suspended in mid-air.

At the mere mention of the talebearer, Judas, the old man's thoughts had wandered back in time—back to the moment when those words, those three, fateful words, had been spoken upon the hill of Golgotha over 2,400 years ago: "It is finished!" This momentary distraction served to interrupt the mental processes that fueled and maintained the illusion surrounding them. A fissure appeared in the ceiling of the common room, a tear through which a series of moons of various sizes and colors were visible in an alien-hued sky. The cold, airless substance of the void began to seep down upon them.

"Yet, so momentary," Chuwl went on, ignoring the familiar sting of the void upon his back and the ever-widening chasm eating away at the ceiling of the inn, "so fleeting was your victory, for as Wisdom records, your heart became proud on account of your beauty, and you corrupted your wisdom because of your splendor. The pain must've been unbearable when you realized what you'd done—when you realized that you'd become the victim of one of your own fiery darts.

"Just out of curiosity," Warlord added, his tone bearing an unmistakable undercurrent of condescension, "is that how you learned the art of tempting the flesh, my Master—from the study of your own childish folly?"

The old man sat patiently listening and smiling down into his ale, which had begun to boil away into the vacuum that cascaded down from above. The breach in the ceiling continued to grow, its edges aglow as if on fire, revealing more of the alien planet's sky.

"Everything you'd hoped to become," Warlord denounced, "was taken away in an instant upon that hill. All of the battles you'd waged over the millennia were reduced to nothing, washed clean by the blood-sacrifice of the One. In a moment, in a twinkling of an eye, your world was forever changed, your powers forever diminished. Never again would you wield absolute doom upon the souls of men. Never again would you command powers uncontested upon the earth as you had for untold generations before. Powers that you'd used to fill your subterranean catacombs with the damned were suddenly displaced by a benevolent force you could never hope to parry and revoked by a phenomenon called forgiveness. Your victims were given a way out, an Arbiter, a Substitute, and a Savior. Regardless of your attempts at self-rationalization, you and I both know that that, indeed, was your epic blunder."

The old man laughed mirthlessly while swirling the last of the foaming substance in his mug. "Very nicely stated, my understudy." He raised his glass in salute. "Obviously, you have thought these things out in impressive detail. I am glad to see that you have retained at least a modicum of knowledge from our lessons." Then the old man lifted his eyes to the extraterrestrial scene visible through the fissure in the ceiling. "However, you must remember, my servant, things are not always as they appear."

Chuwl eyed him roughly. "What are you saying?"

"When one seeks to purport a lie, one must establish certain, shall we say, patterns, so that in time, one's enemies will come to anticipate certain behavior."

"Are you suggesting that there was actually a purpose behind your cataclysmic defeat?" Warlord remarked incredulously. "That after His death, the magnification of the One's ministry far beyond anything He'd been able to accomplish during His earthly pilgrimage was somehow all part of a larger plan of your design? That your epic blunder was somehow premeditated and orchestrated as if His First Coming were merely prelude to—"

Chuwl stopped himself. He glared at his master, who smiled back at him. "But you have admitted freely, Master, that during those days you couldn't have known the specifics of His return. The Revelation was not yet written."

"No, but I had the prophets," the old man exclaimed, pounding his fist down on the table, "and they were enough." There was a bitterness buried in his master's words that Warlord did not fully comprehend.

Angrily, the old man arose and slid his mug along the table, smashing it to shards against the wall. Pieces of broken glass drifted upward in the airless vacuum toward the tear in the ceiling of the inn.

The old man stormed around what was left of the common room, his bloodless face without expression. He wiped a hand roughly across his mouth. "I cannot deny," he brooded, his voice a tinny whisper, "the burnings I felt when He dared to masquerade in fleshly garb and tread upon the soils of my kingdom. I will not deny the bitter yearnings I had for Him who had rejected my offer and my worship when the world was new and expelled me from Their Hallowed Halls. I cannot deny the pleasure I felt in piercing God-flesh, the euphoria I experienced in crushing holy veins. I will not deny the utter exhilaration I felt in lacerating Godspeak's mighty brow, nor in plunging into His side and spilling His fluids upon the common dirt."

At once, the old man's shadow-form manifested itself again and spread like spilling oil over the walls and what remained of the ceiling of the inn.

"Hands that had cast forth the cosmos," the dark power thundered, shaking the very foundations of the inn, "incarnate hands that had healed the diseased flesh and spirits of men quivered helplessly around my iron form! Eyes that had conceived the Creation, blurred with blood from the wounds of my prickling thorns! Feet that had carried the Man-God upon the waters of the Sea of Tiberius were pegged, immobile, to a wooden stand, for I—even I—was the iron spikes driven through His palms! I was the crown of thorns pressed mercilessly into His brow! And I was the spear point thrust into Godspeak's fleshy side and the wooden stand upon which God-blood dripped! O, never have I known such pleasure, such satiation, such joy complete! O, how ravishingly exquisite! How sweet the vengeance! I would not have missed that opportunity for the world!"

The common room was now wholly darkened in shadow. The ceiling had now completely vanished, as had the uppermost portions of the walls. Barren sand dunes stretching for kilometers on end replaced the pine groves and the snowy road outside. The void had descended fully upon them. No atmosphere, no air remained.

"How dare the prophets mock me," the mucoid entity boomed, "for it was I who dared to lead the Great Rebellion against Them in the face of Their anger. In the days of Angelore I foresaw the simplistic nature of Their plan and conceived one of my own to combat it. It was I who deceived Their prized creations in the Sacred Glade. It was I who, with the Hindering Spirit removed from the Earth, worked so laboriously these past four centuries to pervert Wisdom's truths and to erase Their influence upon the consciousness of man. It was I who made your existence possible, Chuwl, and all those who share our disdain for all that is just, holy, and righteous.

"And beware. It is I who will make the earth tremble and the kingdoms shake. It is I who will ascend to heaven and raise my throne above the stars of God and sit upon the mount of assembly. It is I who will ascend above the heights of the clouds and make myself like the Most High. It is I who will claim Their worship for my own at long last."

The structure of the inn around them had completely disappeared. All that remained was the table and the bench seat upon which Warlord sat. The dim light of distant, binary suns illuminated the reddish sands of the barren planet upon which Chuwl now gazed. Multicolored moons sparkled in the atmosphereless sky like alien jewels.

When Warlord turned to gaze anew upon the oily darkness, his master's human form had returned and he was seated at the table again. "Contrary to your pedantic thoughts on the matter, my young apprentice," he said, licking with an oversized tongue at a splattering of regurgitated ooze upon his cheek. "I sacrificed nothing in order to experience such exuberance during the days of Godspeak's First Coming."

Chuwl was taken aback by his master's words. *He'd sacrificed nothing during the days of His First Coming? But how can that be so?* he questioned.

"But that is a history I am not yet prepared to share," the old man said, "for we must exercise the utmost vigilance in these end times. The secret I have so carefully hidden from the eyes of the Watchers these long millennia, the seed of the forbidden tree I have so tenderly nurtured in the Strongholds of Nachash, will soon take root upon the pulpit of the newest apostate religion to grace the worlds and prepare our way into the hearts of men. Soon, courtesy of the sentient machine, my only begotten son, the second of the Godfears, the spiritual unification of man, will be within our grasp. We nearly achieved it one time before at a place and a tower called Babel, but They came down and confused the people and scattered them across the face of the earth. But not this time, Chuwl! This time the lie begun long ages ago has come full circle and will serve to bring us the victory supreme! Surely you sense the truth of my words!"

Chuwl's right eye began to throb. He dabbed at it with his finger, feeling a warm liquid pooling there. He looked down at his hands. His vision was blurred, but he could see that there was blood upon his fingers. He smeared the blood between his forefinger and his thumb, then looked up at the grinning figure across from him.

"You must understand, my arrogant friend," his master told him, "you are but one player upon a vast stage. You will have your reward for your loyalty and allegiance, yes, but this insolence and doubting of yours must cease. You have not studied the histories as I have. You cannot see the end from the beginning, nor things that have not yet been done. And remember who healed your fatal wound."

Chuwl felt the pain in his eye subside, and his vision returned.

"You see, it is really rather simple," the old man pronounced. "I am now in possession of the whole of the blueprints of Their pitiful redemptive plan. They can only send out Their servants—like the Ruwach you encountered on the road—to try to discover and thwart my counteractive thoughts and strategies. As far as They are concerned, we are but drones doomed to perish eternal as They have dictated. They have dismissed us as incapable of ingenuity, incapable of adaptation, and that, my dear boy, will be Their final, fatal miscalculation. This time we have the Revelation! And remember your lessons, my apprentice—events must proceed precisely as they are prophesied: Wisdom's Author cannot lie."

Warlord Chuwl bowed his head in humble allegiance. "Understood, my Master."

"Good," the old man declared, smiling broadly.

With that, the tear in the ceiling sealed itself, and the structure of the inn was restored. The people reappeared, and the liveliness in the common room resumed. The songs of the bard filled the air as patrons once again danced in the aisles between barmaids going about their pick-ups and deliveries.

"Now slosh another ale with me, my friend," the old man cheered. "For old time's sake! Sing songs of victory and rejoice—for tomorrow They will die! But keep your entity-armies sharp, Warlord Chuwl, for soon they shall join with the kingdomless kings and meet the armies of men from the north and the south in battle upon the plains of Esdraelon in the last war of the Age of Man! There is but one incongruence in my equations."

"What is it, my Lord?" Chuwl inquired.

"It's nothing, I am certain," the old man replied. "It is a mere celestial anomaly, but it is no concern of yours."

He turned to the rosy-cheeked woman who was busily serving other guests. "Quickly, barmaid; another," he commanded her. "Time grows short, and I must be at my work."

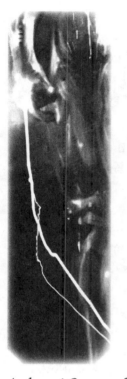

EPILOGUE

Chronicle Extract From the Oracles of Fire
Within the Midst of the Whirling Wheels
of the Guardians of the Sacred Glade,
from the Council of the Nine
in Their Hallowed Halls,
Transliterated and Censored

Archomai Commander Ra'ah: You have also received information about the needs of our armies, Great Prince. Near Infinitude's End, in spite of enemy bombardment, we are making steady progress. Without your continued assistance, however, we cannot—

Michael, Great Prince of the Archangels: I am aware of the formidable task before you, Commander. Yet in our heavy need, I ask for unexampled effort in the singular things through which the tides of evil can be turned, things upon which the Nine Orders have relied since the days of Angelore, namely: ceaseless, persistent, relentless worship and prayer. You have all that you need and, indeed, ever will need within you in the person and power of the Holy Spirit of God.

Commander Ra'ah: I am grateful for the provision given us, Great Prince, and you may be certain that we shall prove ourselves ready to suffer and sacrifice to the utmost for victory in this final war.

However, despite all that I know and all that I have experienced, it is difficult to rely on such things when physical peril assaults us at every turn. It is difficult to turn from wrath when the foreknowledge of our corrupted brethren enables them to attack us in places and in things we are most vulnerable.

Michael: Cease, then, to be vulnerable, Commander. Invincibility dwells within you and within every member of your armies.

Commander Ra'ah: Invincibility?

Michael: It comes down to this, Commander: do you truly believe His Word? Do you truly believe Mashiyach's promises and prophesies to be true, that if you seek to live by His laws and precepts you will forever dwell in the shadow of His wings, that you will eternally dwell in Him who is blessed forever and ever? The One commands us to forget the past and to worry not of the future. That leaves only the present to concern ourselves with. We must bring God into the present, into everything we are presently doing, into the fleeting moment that is "the now." Look unto Jesus, the author and finisher of our faith, who for the joy that was set before Him endured the cross, despising the shame, and now sits at the right hand of the throne of God. Lay aside your wrath, for the One has no need of it to accomplish His ends. Cast your burdens upon the Lord and fight undimmed by the weight of sin upon the worlds. Bear invincibly in your hearts the blood of the Lamb and the Word of His testimony. Believe in faith unshakable that the Angel of the Lord goes before you. Recommit your ways to Him at every confrontation and every temptation, and the enemy will flee before you void, powerless, and utterly defeated. The grace of our Lord Jesus Christ be with you and with all those who stand in the gap before Him. Amen.

GLOSSARY

Derived from Ezra Hiriam, ed., *The Compendium of Lost Biblical Knowledge*, 4th ed. (City of Ariel: the Qanah Archives, 2450).

Abode of Spirits: a term used in reference to the realms of existence wherein the creatures, powers, and entities referenced in the Scriptures of Truth dwell, worship, war, and die; see also *Ancient Heights* and *Realm of Spirits*

Accuser: one of the many names given to Drakon; he is known by the Nine Orders as the one who accuses the righteous before the throne of God day and night

Adversary: one of the many names given to Drakon

Age of Man: the term used in reference to the age that commenced with Mashiyach's creation of the first man and woman in the Sacred Glade, which climaxed with His work of atonement upon the cross and which is prophesied to end with His consecration of the millennial temple, His reclamation of the title deed to the earth, and His founding of the Millennial Age; see also *Millennial Age*

Akathartos (*ah-ka-THAR-tos*): three ancient, frog-like entities often referred to as the Three Unclean Spirit-s who are prophesied to be spewed forth from the mouths of the Dragon, the Great Beast of the Sea, and the Great Beast of the Earth during the last days of the Age of Man; they are also prophesied to be responsible for "the plucking out by the roots" of three of the ten horns or nations of the end-time confederation of nations, as the prophet Daniel foretold in the Scriptures of Truth; the word *akathartos* is translated in the old tongue to mean "impure," "lewd," "foul," "unclean," "demonic"

Alpha and Omega: a title held solely by Mashiyach; derived from the first and last letters of an ancient language and which signifies that He is the origin and end of all things

Ancient Heights: the everlasting lengths, breadths, heights, and depths within which the creatures, powers, and entities referenced in the Scriptures of Truth dwell, worship, war, and die; also the place wherein the Godhead dwell and meet with the faithful angels and those of the race of men who during the course of their mortal existence have made the freewill choice to believe that Jesus is the Christ, the only Son of God, and that He died for their sins and rose again to eternal life and glory; see also *Hallowed Halls, Infinitude, Abode of Spirits,* and *Realm of Spirits*

AND-gate inhibitors: micromechanically-machined devices placed at critical junctures within the neural architecture of the quantum logic brains of all Peacekeeper war machines that serve to block their higher cognitive functions. Invented by neuroroboticist Emma Tyne.

Andreas: leader of the rebel faction of freedom fighters known as the Qanah

Anemos (*AN-em-os*): ancient entities whose allegiance lies with Drakon; they are the four winds that are held back by the Four at Perath while they are yet bound; hot, dry, violent, and chthonic, Anemos move as a pandemic to the land, a murrain to all life in their path; ghastly, wraith-like entities ride at their prow, pushing before them a dissonance of famished voices; see also *Four at Perath* and *Legends of Angelore*

Angel of the Lord, the: a title held solely by Mashiyach, as is recorded in many places within the Scriptures of Truth

Angelore: a term used by the Nine Orders of Angels in reference to events, stories, and lore occurring during the period of time preceding the Age of Man, when the earth was without form and void and darkness was upon the face of the deep; also a reference to events that have transpired during the Age of Man, but which have been witnessed solely by entities existing within the spirit realm

archangels: the Supreme of Creation and the highest order of the Nine Orders of Angels; there are seven: Uriel, Remiel, Sariel, Raguel, Raphael, Gabriel, and Michael their Great Prince; "archangel" is a title in the Cathian Church, but that position is unrelated to these entities; see also *Legends of Angelore* and *Daughters of God*

Archomai (*ARC-oh-may-eye*): one of the Nine Orders of Angels; evanescent of being, wraithy of form, these ancient entities are the rulers of the Principalities and masters of Times and Orders; they are prophesied to join the other Nine Orders and the whole Host of Heaven in supernatural battle against Drakon and his entity-armies in the War of the Third Heaven

Ariel: an ancient name for the Old City District

Ark of the Testimony: a portable chest divinely designed and containing ancient, sacred cultural artifacts, including an organic material of unknown origin, a rod carved out of wood and budding with almonds, and two tables of stone with ancient writing upon them

armies of Akathartos: a reference to the kingdomless kings the Akathartos plan to lure into the service of their master, Drakon, the Great Red Dragon, in order that they might fight alongside Warlord Chuwl and his entity-armies at Esdraelon in the Last War of the Age; see also *ten horns of the beast*

Artificial Intelligence Agency (AIA): Great City Confederation governmental agency created by Overlord Ocaba to supervise the production and maintenance of his army of Peacekeeper war machines; neuroroboticist Emma Tyne holds the post of director of the AIA

Atonement, the: a term used in reference to the reunion of mankind with God through the eternal sacrifice of Jesus the Christ and the restoration of the original relationship between God and man that He accomplished on the cross during the time of His First Coming, as is recorded in the four Gospels in the Scriptures of Truth; see also *Redemptive Plan, Blood of the Lamb, Evangelion, First Coming,* and *Testimony of Jesus*

Avenger of Blood, the: a title held solely by Mashiyach that signifies the wrathful vengeance He is prophesied to execute upon the unrepentant upon His return to the earthly plane of existence; the term *avenger of blood* referred to the ancient practice of allowing a blood relative to avenge the murder of one of their own by killing a member of the family of the murderer

Bashere, Costa: a Coreland Corporation artificial intelligence technician

Battle at Ariel: a battle that is prophesied to take place at the end of the Age of Man in the area of the Temple Mount in the Old City District; the battle is prophesied to pit the Lived and the Qanah against the combined might of Revelationform Drakon and Revelationform Chuwl and their entity-armies, as well as the kingdomless kings and their followers

Blessed City: an ancient term used in reference to the Old City District

Blood of the Lamb: a term used in reference to the blood-sacrifice of Mashiyach, which served to atone for the sins of man and to restore the original relationship between God and man; see *the Atonement*

Bok, Taim: a Guild Protectorate investigator

Book of the Law of God: a term used in reference to the first five books of the Scriptures of Truth

breastplate of righteousness: a term used in reference to one of the armaments that Mashiyach directs His faithful to don as a part of the whole armor of God in defense against the wiles of Drakon and his legions of evil entities, as is recorded in Ephesians 6 in the Scriptures of Truth

burning coals: a reference to the fiery coals that abide within the inner wheels of the whirling wheels of the Guardians of the Sacred Glade, wherein all mysteries of the Infinitude are chronicled; also called *oracles of fire*; see also *wheels, whirling,* and *the Decension*

Cathian Church: an all-powerful monotheistic religion with the Holy Queen Mother of heaven as its deity; an amalgamation of several religions that preceded it, the Cathian Church has grown to become the largest religion in the history of man, with over one million branches in existence; a succession of men bearing the title "Archangel" have sat as figurehead-leaders of the church for twelve generations, Lord Sycuan the Third being the most recent; the Cathian Church is the officially sanctioned religion of the Great City Confederation

Cathian Prime: the prime location of the all-powerful Cathian Church, wherein lies the Throne of the Archangel; Cathian Prime is located several hundred kilometers east of the Old City District, at the very heart of City Center; its impressive array of structures and meticulous grounds are situated on the banks of the Great River

Cathian spirit-children: the order of priests in line beneath the Archangel of the Cathian Church

Celestial Concerts Theme Park: a newly opened theme park located on the grounds of the Church of Cosmic Harmony, featuring celestial-themed rides and attractions

Celestial Sphere of the Heavens Sanctuary: an enormous geodetic chrysteel sphere located on the grounds of the Church of Cosmic Harmony that serves as the venue for the retelling of stories and prophesies recorded in the Scripture of the heavens; see also *Scripture of the heavens*

ceremony of anointing: a term used in reference to the gladdened ceremony that Drakon, in the Days of Angelore, had been blessed to receive before the Great Assembly and the whole Host of Heaven in the midst of Their Hallowed Halls prior to his rebellion against the love of the eternal God; see also *the Great Rebellion*

Chosen Herald of His Comings: a title used by the Nine Orders of Angels in reference to the Archangel Gabriel; see also *Gabriel*

chrysteel: an alloy that is forged from the melding of crystal and steel that has many times the tensile strength of steel; chrysteel is mass produced in the Great City Industrial Quadrant and its existence made possible the construction of the world's first spacescrapers

Church of Cosmic Harmony: a relatively new religion founded by businessman and entrepreneur Jack W. Lamphere; it is based on the Scripture of the heavens—a supernatural message connected with every constellation and every remarkable star, preserved in the imperishable signs of the zodiac and the ancient names of the stars within them; see also *Scripture of the heavens*

Chuwl, Warlord (*Khool* Warlord): an ancient entity known by many names, including the Risen Beast of Shachath, the Great Beast of the Sea, the Worthless Shepherd, Lord Desolator, Man of Sin, and the Lawless One; Warlord Chuwl traverses the trans-dimensional domains, realms, and planes of existence waging spirit-war against the entities of the Enemy; the word *chuwl* is translated in the ancient tongue to mean "to twist or whirl," "to writhe in pain or fear," "to pervert," "to fall grievously with pain," or "to be wounded"

City Center: the glittering heart of the Great City megalopolis and the solar system at large

City of Truth: an ancient term used in reference to the Old City District

Cog: the name given to the solar system's first sentient machine; the name *Cog* is derived from the Latin word *cogito*, which, in conjunction with the words *ergo sum*, is literally translated, "I think, therefore I am."

Coming One, the: a title given by the Qanah to Mashiyach that makes reference to His prophesied return to the earth in vengeance and wrath at the end of the Age of Man

Consolation, the: a title given to Mashiyach in reference to Him being the One in whom the consolation of the faithful abounds, as is recorded in the Scriptures of Truth

corder: short for *recorder*; an eyeball-sized device capable of hovering in mid-air and recording events for later analysis

Coreland Corporation: one of three Industrial Quadrant corporations to win government contracts to manufacture and maintain the GCC's mechanized army of Peacekeeper war machines

covenants and creeds: a reference to the formal, solemn, binding agreements and promises made by Mashiyach to mankind and the set of fundamental beliefs that follow these agreements and promises

Crescent Mountains: a crescent-shaped range of mountains that lies four hundred kilometers north of the City Center, beyond the northern desert and wherein lie the three-pronged headwaters of the Eastern River

datafiles: a term used in reference to the extensive archives of information stored within the quantum logic brains of all Peacekeeper war machines

Daughter(s) of God: a term used in reference to female Archangels; see also *Archangels*

Days of Angelore: a term used in reference to the age preceding the Age of Man, when the Earth was without form and void and darkness was upon the face of the deep; also referred to as the Age of Angels or Ancient Days; see also *Angelore* and *Legends of Angelore*

DayStar: the term used by the Qanah in reference to Optinet; see also *Optinet*

Dead Sea: ancient name of a highly salinated body of water that once existed in the present-day location of the Sandfill of Arabah

Descension, the: a term used in reference to an event following the death and resurrection of Mashiyach at the end of the time of His First Coming to the earthly plane of existence; after His resurrection from the dead, the Scriptures of Truth record that, prior to His ascension to His heavenly throne, Mashiyach first descended into the lower parts of the earth to accomplish His purposes there; the oracles of fire within the inner wheels of the whirling wheels of the Guardians of the Sacred Glade chronicle this event; see also *Angelore* and *burning coals*

desert creatures: an ancient breed of entities who dwell within the trans-dimensional domains, realms, and planes of existence and whose allegiance lies with Drakon

Devil: one of the many names assigned to Drakon, as recorded in the Scriptures of Truth

Divided Temple Peace Accord: the peace accord negotiated by Sovereign Overlord Vaughn Ocaba between the warring factions of the Patron and the Marah; the accord called for the construction of a divided temple upon the ancient surface of the Temple Mount in the Old City District, which was to serve as a place of worship for both peoples of their respective gods; a wall of separation was to divide the two houses of worship; the accord was disbanded three and one-half years after its signing, before one stone was laid upon another in the bid to build the sacred structure

Divided Temple Project: the name of the building project associated with the Divided Temple Peace Accord

Dominions: one of the Nine Orders of Angels; ancient and glorious entities of transcendent image, the Dominions are the masters of domains and territories; they are prophesied to battle alongside the Seven of the Supreme Order, the other Orders, and the whole Host of Heaven against Drakon and his entity-armies in the War of the Third Heaven

Dragon Reborn: the name given to Drakon after he dons his revelation-form appearance—that of a Great Red Dragon having seven saurian necks and seven ophidian heads; a ruddy, armor-plated hide; a powerful forked tail; and great, clawed feet

Drakon (Dra-CONE): as is recorded in Ezekiel 28 in the Scriptures of Truth, the entity Drakon had originally been created to be the seal of perfection, full of wisdom and perfect in beauty; perfect in all his ways, and every precious stone was his covering; following his ceremony of anointing, he was established upon the holy mountain of God and was privileged to walk to and fro in the midst of the fiery stones until iniquity was found in him and violence filled him, and he was cast out as a profane thing; also called Nachash, the Shining One, the Adversary of the Brethren, the Great Red Dragon, That Great Serpent of Old; the word *drakon* translates to mean "dragon" and specifically "a fascinating or fabulous kind of serpent or dragon"

DreamStudy: a form of learning that utilizes repetitive synaptic stimulation during REM sleep cycles in order to implant knowledge into the human brain; considered invasive and dangerous by some scientists

Dysley, Will Adam: a famous Great City attorney

Eastern League of Nations: a league of nations comprised of nations to the north, south, and east of the region of the Great City; the member nations of the Eastern League have historically been at odds with the nations of the Great City Confederation

Elijahuw (*eli-JA-way*): also known as Prophet; old-tongue name of one of the two entities known as the Esezan, or the Lived, the two witnesses who enter the camp of the Qanah in the Old City District and who are prophesied to prophesy there 1260 days prior to the end of the Age of Man; *Elijahuw* is translated "Elijah" in the ancient tongue; see also *Prophet*

Emissary: the name given by Dr. Xavier Hugo to his original creation, the solar system's first fully autonomic humanoid machine; Emissary was designed to be humanity's ambassador to the stars, our galactic emissary of peace to alien civilizations so that mankind might one day share in the accumulated knowledge of the society of worlds that is theorized to exist in the far reaches of the cosmos; Emissary was commandeered at its unveiling by then-Senator Vaughn Ocaba in order to circumvent the mandates of the soon to be ratified Just War Act; its quantum logic brain and forged beryllium alloy body were reengineered into that of a war machine and subsequently mass produced to become the Great City Confederation's all-mechanized army of Peacekeeper war machines

Enemy Supreme, the: a term Drakon and his forces use in reference to Mashiyach and His armies

entities of the Enemy: a term Drakon and his entity-armies use in reference to Mashiyach, the Nine Orders of Angels; and the whole Host of Heaven

Esezan (es-ee-ZAHN): a term used in reference to the Lived—Lawgiver Mosheh and Prophet Elijahuw—the two witnesses who enter the camp of the Qanah and who are prophesied to prophesy there during the last days of the Age of Man; have the power to call down fire from heaven, to prevent rain from falling on the earth, and to bring many plagues upon the earth and its inhabitants; *esezan* is an old-tongue word that is translated "to recover life," "to revive," or "to live again"

Evangelion: an old-tongue word meaning "the Gospel of the Lord," a reference to the good news of His coming and of His return; the term refers to the eternal work of Atonement that Mashiyach accomplished upon the cross at the time of His First Coming; see also *the Atonement,* and *Gospel of Peace*

Even Shetiyyah: the old-tongue name of the ancient Foundation Stone that exists upon the surface of the Temple Mount in the Old City District and upon which the Ark of the Testimony was placed in days of antiquity; see also *Foundation Stone*

Exesti (ex-ES-tee): one of the Nine Orders of Angels; also known as *Origins,* these ancient entities appear cloaked in shimmering robes with darkened cowls and carry gnarled staffs in their hands; they are the masters of universal laws and forces, and they are prophesied to battle alongside the Seven of the Supreme Order, the other Orders, and the whole Host of Heaven against Drakon and his entity-armies in the War of the Third Heaven

Ezekiel Temple: a reference to the temple which is prophesied to serve as the dwelling place of the *Shekinah,* the presence of God, during the thousand-year millennial reign of Mashiyach; the prophesied dimensions and decor of this temple are contained in Ezekiel 40–42 in the Scriptures of Truth; see *Fourth Temple* and *Millennial Temple*

Faithful and True: a title ascribed to Mashiyach in the nineteenth chapter of the Revelation of Jesus Christ in the Scriptures of Truth

Fall of Man: a term used in reference to the fateful event that occurred at the beginning of the Age of Man within the confines of the Sacred Glade, as recorded in the Book of Genesis in the Scriptures of Truth; the fall of man involved Drakon's temptation of mankind and mankind's subsequent rebellion against the eternal love and sovereign will of God; see also *the Rebellion of Man* and *Redemptive Plan*

False Prophet, the: a title assigned to the archangel of the Cathian Church, Lord Sycuan the Third, in the nineteenth chapter of the Revelation of Jesus Christ in the Scriptures of Truth; see also *the Great Beast of the Earth*

Father of Artificial Intelligence: an honorary title bestowed upon Dr. Xavier Hugo for his accomplishments in the field of artificial intelligence, specifically: the creation of the natural analog, a quantum logic brain reverse-engineered from a human brain, and Emissary, the solar-system's first fully autonomic humanoid machine

Father of Lies: a title assigned to Drakon, as is recorded in John 8 in the Scriptures of Truth

Fifth Kingdom: an ancient term used by Drakon in reference to the everlasting kingdom he desires to set up upon the earth and rule after the end of the Age of Man

Final War: the term used by the Nine Orders of Angels and the Host of Heaven in reference to the prophesied War of the Third Heaven; see also *War of the Third Heaven*

First Coming: the term used in reference to Mashiyach's first coming to the earthly plane of existence in order that He might accomplish His eternal purposes; see also *the Atonement*

Foundation Building: an ultramodern, triangle-shaped City Center spacescraper comprised of dark blue reflective chrysteel; serves as headquarters for various top-level Great City Confederation governmental agencies, including the Artificial Intelligence Agency, the Secretary of State for the Galactic Colonies, the Bureau of Human Affairs, the Ministry of Defense, the Information Bureau, and the International Security Office

Foundation Stone: see *Even Shetiyyah*

Founding Day of the Millenial Age: The day prophesied to follow the end of That Great Day, the consummation of desolations, and the end of the Age of Man. The day prophesied to commence with the consecration of the Ezekiel Temple, or the Millenial Temple, by the Shekinah, or the Presence of God between the wings of the living creatures, and the establishment of Mashiyach's personal rulership of mankind for The Thousand Years; see also *Fourth Temple*

Four at Perath: a term used in reference to the four mucilaginous entities that have been bound for ages along the banks of the River Perath until the very year, month, day, and hour of their release, as is prophesied in the ninth chapter of the Revelation of Jesus Christ in the Scriptures of Truth; see also *Anemos* and *mounted armies*

Four Spirits of Heaven: a term used in reference to four horsemen-entities whose existence is recorded in Zechariah 1 and 6 in the Scriptures of Truth, and whose allegiance lies with Mashiyach; known anciently as the *Ruwach*, these dark riders are equal part mind, spirit, and wind; they are ascribed the titles Wrath-Appeasers and Earth-Patrollers; these Legends of Angelore manifest themselves upon the terrestrial planes of existence during the last days of the Age of Man; see also *Ruwach*

Fourth Kingdom: an ancient term for the kingdom that exists at the end of the Age of Man, as is prophesied in Daniel 7 in the Scriptures of Truth

Fourth Temple: a reference to the temple that is prophesied to serve as the dwelling place of the Shekinah, the presence of God, during the thousand-year millennial reign of Mashiyach; see also *Ezekiel Temple, Millennial Temple,* and *Founding Day of the Millennial Age*

Gabriel: one of the seven Archangels; in Luke 1 in the Scriptures of Truth, Gabriel refers to himself as he "who stands in the presence of God;" among the Nine Orders, he is known as the *Name-Giver* because he was the entity who instructed Mashiyach's virgin-mother of the name she was to give her child: Jesus; he is also known among the Nine as the *Chosen Herald of His Comings* because he was the entity who brought "the good tidings of great joy which will be to all people" to the shepherds in the fields at the time of His First Coming, and he is prophesied to be the chosen herald of the Christ's Second Coming; see also *Chosen Herald of His Coming*

Galactic Spirit, the: the title given by Church of Cosmic Harmony founder Jack W. Lamphere to the deity he believes to be responsible for delivering and recording the world's first religion to man in the form of the Scripture of the heavens; see also *Scripture of the heavens*

Galilee: the long-forgotten name of the region to the north of the present-day location of the Old City District; the region is known in modern day as Chinneroth

Garden of God: a term found in the Book of Ezekiel in the Scriptures of Truth, and used in reference to the ancient place within which the firstborn of God's creation dwelled; see also *the Sacred Glade*

Garret, Arnaud: bureau chief of the Guild Protectorate

Gate, the: a reference to the gate that stands at the eastern edge of the Sacred Glade, the Garden of God

Gava (*gaw-VAH*): delusive creatures of phantasmagoric image who battle in allegiance to Drakon and Warlord Chuwl; their appearances are in a state of constant flux, shifting from one paranormal shape to another; weaponless, these ancient entities move like giant specters, ingesting and assimilating all those they touch with their apparitional forms

ghenna: the ancient name of a place that exists within the trans-dimensional latitudes of the Ancient Heights and whose infernos have been lit for the eternal sufferance of the unrepentant in second death; see also *the Outer Darkness*

Glorious Land: an ancient term used in reference to the Old City District

Godspeak: a term used in reference to Mashiyach

Gospel of Peace: a term used in reference to the gospel of Mashiyach, the good news of His Coming and of His Return; also a term used in reference to one of the armaments which Mashiyach directs His Faithful to don as a part of the whole armor of God in defense against the wiles of Drakon and his legions of evil entities, as is recorded in Ephesians 6 in the Scriptures of Truth; see also *Evangelion*

Grand Unifying Theory of Everything: a term coined by scientists to describe a hypothetical theory unifying all physical theories of the universe, a singularity point of reason that cannot be defined in terms of a deeper truth; the ultimate truth of the universe

gravity-well travel: an ingenious method of space travel based upon the employment of a gravity-producing device in the manufacture of curvatures in the spacetime continuum; cosmic topographers known as *scalers* generate complex field equations based upon the expansion rate of the universe and the physical properties of time in order to determine the precise distribution of mass in the solar system; this information is then used to determine the precise way in which space and time are curved from various points; travel to various galactic destinations is nearly instantaneous; see also *space-time grid*

Great Assembly, the: a vast, innumerable assembly of righteous creatures, powers, orders, breeds, beings, entities, and men and women who have made the freewill choice to believe that Jesus is the Christ, the only Son of God, and that He died for their sins and rose again to eternal life and glory. the Ancient Heights, and specifically, Their Hallowed Halls, serve as the gathering place for the Great Assembly; see also *Hallowed Halls*

Great Barrier: a term used in reference to the cosmic veil or curtain created by the physics of spacetime and the expansion rate of the universe that serves to block mankind's knowledge and awareness of various cosmic times and places

Great Beast of the Earth, the: a title ascribed to the current Archangel of the Cathian Church, Lord Sycuan the Third; see also *the False Prophet*

Great Beast of the Sea: a title ascribed to Warlord Chuwl; also referred to as *the Worthless Shepherd* and *the Lawless One*

Great City Confederation Defense Grid: a matrix of space-based and atmospheric-based isotronic weapons' systems situated along the borders of the member-nations of the Great City Confederation; originally designed as a missile shield to protect GCC member-nations from long-range missile strikes

Great City Confederation: a confederation of ten nations, most of which are located around the shores of the Great Sea; the GCC was formed following the end of the Great War; then-Senator Vaughn Ocaba was instrumental in the confederation's formation and was appointed its first sovereign overlord

Great City Industrial Quadrant: the name of the place where the large manufacturing facilities and cold fusion power plants that support the citizens and infrastructure of the Great City Confederation are located

Great City: the name of the enormous megalopolis built at the heart of the world, which includes the areas known as City Center, the Great City Industrial Quadrant, the Southern Quadrant, and the Old City District; the City Center acts as the Great City Confederation's economic and socio-political center; the Great City began as a federation of three nations, then following the Great War became the Great City Confederation, consisting of a ten-nation confederacy

Great Harlot: a term found in the seventeenth chapter of the Revelation of Jesus Christ in the Scriptures of Truth; refers to the powerful apostate religion that is prophesied to exist at the end of the Age of Man

Great Prince: a title held by Michael, the leader of the archangels

Great Rebellion, the: a term referring to the rebellion of one-third of the creatures, powers, breeds, beings, and entities that dwell in the heavens against the eternal love and sovereign will of God; this event occurred during the Days of Angelore and was orchestrated by Drakon; see also *ceremony of rebellion*

Great Red Dragon: one of the many names given to Drakon

Great Sea: the sea that lies to the west of the Old City District; most of the member-nations of the Great City Confederation are located around it

Great Serpent of Old, That: one of the many names given to Drakon

Great Tribulation, the: the term used in reference to the catastrophic physical changes and plagues that are prophesied to manifest within the universe and upon the earth and the inhabited worlds during the last days of the Age of Man

Great War: the war that occurred in the year 2447 that pitted the Northern Federation of Nations against the Great City and its mechanical army of Peacekeeper war machines; the Peacekeepers destroyed five-sixths of the invading armies and rained a judgment of fire upon their homeland nations; other seemingly fortuitous supernatural disasters appeared to confound the battle strategies of the Northern Federation armies and aid the cause of the Peacekeepers in this war; as a result of their losses, the Northern Federation of Nations dissolved their union and joined the Eastern League of Nations, strengthening its military and political might

Guardians of the Sacred Glade: the four living creatures that comprise one of the Nine Orders of Angels and whose allegiance lies with Mashiyach; they are also the keepers of the burning coals or oracles of fire, which abide within the inner wheels of their whirling wheels; these oracles of fire are thought to be the instruments and vessels which chronicle and house all mysteries of the Infinitude; see also *wheels, whirling*

Guild Forensics: the branch of the Guild Protectorate responsible for the investigation of crime scenes and the determination of causes; specifically, they oversee the application of medical facts to legal problems

Guild Protectorate: the solar system-wide policing organization responsible for the maintenance of order throughout the environs of the earth and the colony system

Guild Special Forces: elite squads of highly-trained, highly-skilled commandos deployed by the Guild Protectorate Chief on the most difficult missions

Gyre (*ji-ree*): an ancient breed of entities who dwell within the trans-dimensional domains, realms, and planes of existence and whose allegiance lies with Drakon, with whom they are prophesied to join forces and battle the Nine Orders and the whole Host of Heaven in the War of the Third Heaven

Hallowed Halls: a reference to a glorious structure that exists within the trans-dimensional latitudes of the Ancient Heights; where the Godhead dwell and meet with the righteous creatures, powers, orders, breeds, beings, and entities of Their creation, as well as those of the race of men who, during the course of their mortal existence, made the freewill choice to believe that Jesus is the Christ, the only Son of God, and that He died for their sins and rose again to eternal life and glory; see also *Ancient Heights* and *the Great Assembly*

hard-light constructs: adaptations in the trans-fluidic skin of Peacekeeper war machines that are formed by the mental synthesis of light and the integration of electric field sense-data in order to alter their appearance in response to specific situations; Peacekeepers have the capability to generate hard-light constructs around their body that mirror the form and appearance of any object within the range of their sensors; see also *trans-fluidic skin*

haze, the: the ubiquitous concoction of putrid air and toxic acids that hovers over the Old City District; the haze is thought to be a result of the drought conditions that plagued the land since the arrival of the Lived into the camp of the Qanah

Heaven's Gate: the gateway in the heavenly country that leads to the dwelling place of Mashiyach and out of which He is prophesied to come to reclaim His title deed to the earth and to establish His millennial kingdom at the end of the Age of Man

Hellion: an ancient breed of entities who dwell within the trans-dimensional domains, realms, and planes of existence and whose allegiance lies with Drakon, with whom they are prophesied to join forces and battle the Nine Orders and the whole Host of Heaven in the War of the Third Heaven

helmet of salvation: a term used in reference to one of the armaments Mashiyach directs His faithful to don as a part of the whole armor of God in defense against the wiles of Drakon and his legions of evil entities, as is recorded in Ephesians 6 in the Scriptures of Truth

Highest Order: a term used in reference to the archangels

Hindering Spirit: a reference to the Holy Spirit of God, who acts as a hindering force against the tides of evil upon the earth until His presence is removed along with the faithful in an event referred to by some as the rapture of the church

holofil: an advanced foam-like substance used as a wrapping, protection, and preservation material in the storage and transport of valuable and/or vulnerable goods

Holy Bible: the Old-Age title for the sacred, divinely-designed scriptures of the followers of the Christ comprising the thirty-nine books of the Old Testament and the twenty-seven books of the New Testament; also known as the uncorrupted Scriptures of Truth

Holy City: an ancient term used in reference to the Old City District

Holy Habitation: a place that exists within the trans-dimensional latitudes of the Ancient Heights and beyond Heaven's Gate that serves as the habitation of the Godhead

Holy Mountain: an ancient term used in reference to the Old City District, specifically, its Old-Age name: Jerusalem

Holy Queen Mother of heaven: the name ascribed to the deity of the Cathian Church

Hosts of Heaven: a reference to the creatures, powers, orders, breeds, beings, and entities who dwell in the heavens and whose allegiance lies with Mashiyach; collectively, these supernatural entities are prophesied to battle Drakon and his entity-armies in the War of the Third Heaven

hoverglobe: a term used in reference to any of a variety of wireless, cold-fusion-powered lights that hover and move from place to place within a room based on the location and activities of its occupants

howling creatures: an ancient breed of entities who dwell within the trans-dimensional domains, realms, and planes of existence and whose allegiance lies with Drakon

Hugo, Xavier: dubbed the father of artificial intelligence, Dr. Xavier Hugo is the man responsible for the creation of the natural analog, a quantum logic brain reverse-engineered from a human brain, and for Emissary, the solar-system's first fully autonomous humanoid machine; prior to his accomplishments as a neuroroboticist, Hugo was awarded the Eisner Prize for Physics for his co-discovery of gravity-well travel; see also *natural analog*

Infinitude: a reference to the whole of creation in terms of dimensions, domains, planes, realms, spaces, times, lengths, breadths, heights, and depths; see also *Ancient Heights*

Infinitude's End: the end of the dimensions, domains, planes, realms, spaces, times, lengths, breadths, heights, and depths wherein and when only the Godhead may dwell

Jerusalem: the Old-Age name of the Old City at the heart of the Old City District

Jesus the Christ: the name and title of the only Son of God, the Lord of heaven and Earth; He is known by many other names, including Mashiyach, the Coming One, the Word of God, the Angel of the Lord, the Seed of the woman, the Avenger of Blood, Alpha and Omega, and the King of kings and Lord of lords; it is through one's freewill decision to believe that this Entity is the only Son of God, that He took the form of a man and came to Earth, and that He died for the sins of the world and rose again to eternal life and glory, that one's spirit is born again to everlasting union with God in Christ

Julius: a blind merchant who resides in the Old City District

Just War Act: a Supreme Assembly-approved act that placed restrictions on the type of military actions nations may employ during the course of future wars; specifically, the Just War Act criminalized so-called "faceless" or "safe-distance" wartime tactics and mandated the deployment of ground-based troops in sufficient number to defend the local citizens from the retaliation of rebel factions; the deployment of non-sanctioned tactics constitutes a breach of inter-system law, carrying with it severe penalties for the nation that employs them

King of Terrors: a title ascribed to Drakon

kingdomless kings: a term used in reference to the solar-system's ten most powerful terrorist leaders who Akathartos, the three unclean spirits, plan to lure to the Valley Esdraelon with a promise of kingdoms of their own if they will battle alongside Warlord Chuwl and his entity-armies against the armies of men from the north and the south in the Last War of the Age of Man

L5 Transfer Station: an enormous, wheel-shaped construction situated at Lagrangian point number five, the midway point between the earth and the moon; L5 is home to more than twenty million people and serves as the transfer point to all galactic destinations via the method of gravity-well travel

lake of fire: a place that exists within the trans-dimensional latitudes of the Ancient Heights; the location wherein the Great Beast of the Sea and the Great Beast of the earth, among others, are prophesied to be cast at the end of the Age of Man, where they will experience eternal suffering for their rebellion against the everlasting love and sovereign will of God

Lamphere, Jack William: an eccentric entrepreneur-businessman and founder of the Church of Cosmic Harmony

Land, the: an ancient term used in reference to the region of the Old City District

Last War: a war prophesied to take place in the Valley Esdraelon to the north and west of the Old City District that pits Warlord Chuwl and his supernatural armies, as well as the kingdomless kings and their followers, against the armies of men from the north and the south

Law of Redemption: an ancient law recorded in the Book of Leviticus in the Scriptures of Truth, which relates to the redemption of land or property; also called the Right of Redemption

Lawgiver: the title given to Mosheh, one of the two Esezan or Lived who enter the camp of the Qanah in the last days of the Age of Man; see also *Mosheh*

Lawless One, the: a title assigned to Warlord Chuwl, as recorded in 2 Thessalonians 2 in the Scriptures of Truth; see also *Great Beast of the Sea*

Leb Kamai (*leb-ka-MAY*): the ancient name of the land beneath the City Center megalopolis

Legends of Angelore: a term used in reference to the supernatural creatures, powers, and entities that were created during the Days of Angelore and experienced many legendary exploits therein, and that are again manifested within the earthly and spiritual planes of existence during the last days of the Age of Man

Leukos (*lew-kos*): the name of Warlord Chuwl's horse-entity; the word *leukos* translates to mean "white"

Lie, the: a term found in 2 Thessalonians in the Scriptures of Truth that refers to the strong delusion that will possess those who turn away from the eternal love and sovereign will of God during the last days of the Age of Man

Life, Book of: a supernaturally authored book containing the names of those who, during the course of their mortal existence, have made the freewill decision to believe that Jesus is the Christ, the only Son of God, and that He died for the atonement of their sins and rose again to eternal life and glory; the names of the faithful were recorded in this book before the foundations of the world were laid, and they are prophesied to inherit eternal life in Christ

Light of men: a term used in reference to Mashiyach, as recorded in John 1 in the Scriptures of Truth

Lived, the: a term used in reference to Lawgiver Mosheh and Prophet Elijahuw, the two witnesses who enter the camp of the Qanah and prophesy there during the last days of the Age of Man

locust-entities: a term used in reference to the locust-like entities that Drakon is prophesied to free from the Pit of Shachath at the sounding of the fifth trumpet during the dawning of That Great Day, as recorded in the ninth chapter of the Revelation of Jesus Christ in the Scriptures of Truth

Lord Desolator: a title ascribed to Warlord Chuwl

lower levels: the name of the street-level environs of City Center where the less-affluent reside and utilize Old-Age era combustion-engine vehicles for transportation in lieu of aircars

malak (*mal-ak*): an ancient word that translates to mean "messenger," "ambassador," or "angel," specifically, one sent of God

Man of Sin: a title ascribed to Warlord Chuwl in 2 Thessalonians 2 in the Scriptures of Truth

Marah (*mar-AH*): a reference to a people who reside in the Old City District; the word *marah* translates to mean "to be," "cause to make bitter," "to rebel, "to be disobedient," or "to grievously provoke;" hence, the Marah are known as the Sons of Disobedience; they have been at war with the Patron for many centuries

Mashiyach (*maw-SHEE-akh*): an ancient-tongue word that is translated "the Consecrated One," "the Anointed," or "the Messiah;" used solely in reference to the Coming One, the Word of God, Jesus the Christ

Maveths (*maw'-veths*): black-winged creatures of ancient origin, this breed of entities is prophesied to fight in allegiance to Warlord Chuwl in the Valley Esdraelon against the armies of men from the north and the south in the Last War of the Age of Man

Michael: the Great Prince or leader of the seven archangels

Millennial Age: the term for the age that is prophesied to succeed the Age of Man; this age is prophesied to commence with Mashiyach's consummation of His wrath upon the unrepentant, His reclamation of the title deed to the earth, His consecration of the millennial temple, and the establishment of His personal reign and rulership of mankind for the thousand years; see also *Age of Man*

Millennial Temple: a term used in reference to the temple that is prophesied to be the dwelling place of the Shekinah, or the presence of God, during the thousand-year millennial reign of Mashiyach; see also *Ezekiel Temple* and *Fourth Temple*

Mistress of Sorceries: an ancient term used in reference to a city which is prophesied to exist at the end of the Age of Man and which personifies all that is provocative, forgetful, or ignorant of the things of God

Mosheh (*mo-SHEH*): the name of one of the two entities known as the Esezan, or the Lived, who enter the camp of the Qanah in the Old City District and are prophesied to prophesy there 1260 days; known as Lawgiver, Mosheh has the power to call down fire from heaven, to prevent rain from falling on the earth, and to bring many plagues upon the earth and its inhabitants; Mosheh is from an old tongue word meaning "drawing out of the water"; see also *Lawgiver*

most holy place: the innermost sanctuary of the temples of God that have been constructed throughout human history; where the Shekinah, or God's presence, dwells

mounted armies: a term used in reference to the 200 million mounted entities that are prophesied to come at the time of the release of the Four at Perath at the sounding of the sixth trumpet during the dawning of That Great Day, as recorded in the ninth chapter of the Revelation of Jesus Christ in the Scriptures of Truth; the mounted armies fight in allegiance to Drakon; see also *Four at Perath*

Nachash (*naw-KHASH*): an ancient-tongue word meaning "to hiss," "to whisper a magic spell," "to prognosticate in the capacity of a divine enchanter," "to learn by experience," or "to diligently observe;" also translates to mean "snake" or "serpent;" it is a term the Nine Orders use in reference to Drakon; see also *Strongholds of Nachash*

Nadach (*naw-dakh*): ancient entities in appearance like men clothed in tattered garments, yet they are denizens of the trans-dimensional domains and masters of the mystic arts of the times and the spaces; with a thought, they possess the power to banish and condemn men to imprisonment within the temporal and spatial expanses of the Abode of Spirits; they fight in allegiance to Drakon and Warlord Chuwl

Name-Giver: a title given by the Nine Orders to the archangel Gabriel, the messenger who instructed Mary of the name she was to give to her unborn Child—Jesus—as is recorded in Luke 1 in the Scriptures of Truth

natural analog: the term used to describe the quantum logic brain Dr. Xavier Hugo reverse-engineered from a human brain; each molecule in this synthetic system does exactly what its natural analog does in the carbon-based system and is interconnected to the surrounding elements in precisely the same manner; every Peacekeeper war machine possesses the natural analog as its artificial brain; see also *Xavier Hugo* and *quantum logic brain*

Nephilim (*nef-hil-im*): an ancient word meaning "feller," "tyrant," "champion," "warrior," or "giant;" like mighty men of old in appearance, these magnificent offspring of the sons of God and the daughters of men fight in allegiance to Drakon and Warlord Chuwl

Nine Orders: a term used in reference to the Nine Orders of Angels: the Seraphim, the Guardians of the Sacred Glade, the Thronos, the Dominions, the Archomai or Principalities, the Exesti or Origins, the Virtues, the Watchers, and Archangels

Northern Federation of Nations: a federation of six nations with a large northern nation as its head that dissolved following the loss of five-sixths of their armies at the hands of the Peacekeeper war machines during the Great War; its member-nations subsequently joined the Eastern League of Nations, strengthening its military and political might

Ocaba, Vaughn: the sovereign overlord of the Great City Confederation; a former war hero, Ocaba chaired the Senate committee that commandeered Dr. Hugo's creation, Emissary, and mass produced it, creating an army of mechanized warriors; he was also the chief negotiator in the forging of the Divided Temple Peace Accord, alongside his information minister, Aden Xyan

Old City District: a small, ancient, war-ravaged district at the westernmost end of the territories of the Great City Confederation and near the northernmost tip of the Sandfill of Arabah; the district is under a state of quarantine due to the age-old violence between the Patron and the Marah

One, the: a title ascribed to Mashiyach

Optinet: the solar-system-wide communications and information dissemination system of near-infinite computational power; Optinet was created by scientists employed by the Cathian Church and under the direction of Archangel Sycuan the Third; through it, computational power reaches a point of singularity that is nearly indistinguishable from omniscience; Optinet became operational in the year 2451; its transponder serves as the mark by which the citizens of the earth and the inhabited worlds buy and sell goods and services; see also *DayStar, Sycuan the Third Archangel,* and *touchpad*

Origins: one of the Nine Orders of Angels; see also *Exesti*

Outer Darkness, the: the ancient name of the place reserved for the eternal suffering of the unrepentant in second death; see also *ghenna*

Patron: an ancient-tongue term used in reference to a people who reside in the Old City District; they are the descendants of Judah, the chosen people of God; they are at war with the Marah

Peacekeeper war machines: an army of mechanized soldiers in the employ of the Great City Confederation; Peacekeepers were mass produced from Dr. Xavier Hugo's creation, Emissary, whose original design purposes were exploited by then Senator Vaughn Ocaba at a Senate Appropriations Committee hearing in the year 2442

period of silence: a term used in reference to the four-hundred-year-long periods wherein the Godhead did not speak to humankind; the first recorded period of silence occurred between the writing of the last book of the Old Testament in the Scriptures of Truth, and the writing of the first book of the New Testament; the second recorded period of silence occurred between the removal of the faithful and the Hindering Spirit from the Earth, and the beginning of the seven-year long Tribulation period

Phelps, Anton: a Coreland Corporation laboratory supervisor

Pit of Sands: see *Shachath*

Principalities: one of the Nine Orders of Angels; see also *Archomai*

Prophet: the title given to Elijahuw, one of the two Esezan or Lived who enter the camp of the Qanah in the last days of the Age of Man; see also *Elijahuw*

Qanah (*kaw-naw*): a reference to the rebellious faction of freedom fighters who reside in the catacombs beneath the Old City District; the word *qanah* translates to mean "to procure by purchase" or "to redeem;" hence, the Qanah are known as *the Purchased* or *the Sons of the Kingdom*

quantum logic brain: the term used to describe the synthetic brain each Peacekeeper war machine possesses; created by Dr. Xavier Hugo, these ingenious synthetic systems are composed of machined molecules that utilize photons, or particles of quantum energy, as the means by which information is relayed and disseminated; see also *natural analog*

Quarantine, the: a reference to restrictions placed on exiting the region known as the Old City District due to the violence which besets the Land; the Quarantine was instated by Sovereign Overlord Ocaba following the renewal of violence between the Patron and the Marah and the dissolution of the Divided Temple Peace Accord

Raguel: one of the seven archangels

Raphael: one of the seven archangels

rapture of the church: a term used in reference to the removal of the faithful—those who during the course of their mortal existence have made the freewill choice to believe that Jesus is the Christ, the only Son of God, and that He died on the cross and rose again to eternal life and glory—along with the entity known as the Hindering Spirit from the earth over four hundred years prior to the end of the Age of Man; according to the Scriptures of Truth, there are prophesied to be three time periods between the rapture of the church and the Second Coming of Jesus the Christ to establish His millennial kingdom: an introductory period of preparation of unknown length, a period of peace of three and one-half years, and a period of great tribulation for three and one-half years

Ravelle, Spirit-Son: the priest or spirit-child (also, spirit-son) of the Cathian Church; also a terrorist leader and one of the ten members of the kingdomless kings Akathartos plan to lure to the Valley Esdraelon with a promise of kingdoms of their own if they will join Warlord Chuwl and his entity-armies in battle against the armies of men from the north and the south in the Last War of the Age of Man

Realm of Man: a term used in reference to the terrestrial plane of existence within which mortal men reside and wherein the creatures, powers, orders, breeds, beings, and entities of the Realm of Spirits occupy at certain times and in certain places

Realm of Spirits: a term used in reference to the realms of existence wherein the creatures, orders, and entities referenced in the Scriptures of Truth, dwell, worship, war and die; see also *Abode of Spirits* and *Ancient Heights*

Rebellion of Man, the: see *Fall of Man*

Red Planet Colony: the first and largest human settlement on the surface of the planet Mars, located between the geologic structures of Tharsis Montes and Valles Marineris

Redemptive Plan: a term used in reference to Mashiyach's eternal plan to redeem the fallen race of man; see also *Fall of Man* and *the Atonement*

Remiel: one of the seven archangels

Return of the King: a term used in reference to Mashiyach's prophesied return or Second Coming to the terrestrial plane of existence in order to establish His millennial kingdom, as is prophesied in many books within the Scriptures of Truth

Return, His: see *Return of the King*

Revelation of Jesus Christ, the: a book found in the Scriptures of Truth

Revelationform Chuwl: a term used in reference to the form that Warlord Chuwl is prophesied to don at his ascension from the Pit of Shachath

revival: a period of divinely-inspired renewed religious interest and restoration following a period of religious ignorance and forgetfulness

Risen Beast of Shachath: one of many names given to Warlord Chuwl

Ruwach (*ROO-akh*): ancient entities whose allegiance lies with Mashiyach; Ruwach are equal part mind, spirit, and wind; their existence is referenced in Zechariah 6 in the Scriptures of Truth; the word *ruwach* is translated from the old tongue to mean "wind," "breath," or "violent exhalation;" figuratively, the word means "life, anger, unsubstantiality;" by resemblance, it refers to a spirit, but only a rational being, including its expression, functions, and properties— air, anger, blast, breath, cool, courage, mind, tempest, whirlwind; see also *Four Spirits of Heaven* and *Legends of Angelore*

Sacred Glade, the: a term used in reference to the garden within which the firstborn of God's creation dwelled; see also *Garden of God*

Sandfill of Arabah: the name of the place where the men and machines relocated the Eastern Desert to make room for the construction of the Great City Industrial Quadrant; located near the westernmost border of the Great City Confederation and to the east of the Old City District, the Sandfill of Arabah was once a sea comprised of highly salinated waters

Sands, Gallina: a Guild Protectorate investigator

Sariel (*sar-ee-el*): one of the seven archangels

Satan: one of the many names given to Drakon

satyrs (*sa-tires*): an ancient breed of entities that resemble hairy goats; they dwell within the trans-dimensional domains, realms and planes of existence and their allegiance lies with Drakon

scalers: cosmic topographers and gravoastronavigators responsible for making gravity-well travel possible; they are the mappers of the space-time grid

Scripture of the heavens: a supernatural message connected with every constellation and every remarkable star; preserved in the imperishable signs of the zodiac, their accompanying decans or minor constellations, and the ancient names of the stars within them; the Scripture of the heavens constitutes the sacred text of the Church of Cosmic Harmony; see also *Church of Cosmic Harmony, Celestial Sphere of the Heavens Sanctuary,* and *Galactic Spirit*

Scriptures of Truth: a term used in reference to the book known as the Holy Bible in its uncorrupted form

Second Coming: see *Return of the King*

Seraphim (*ser-ah-FIM*): one of the Nine Orders of Angels; fiery, six-winged, serpent-like entities with human-like hands and feet and human-like voices; they are prophesied to battle alongside the Seven of the Supreme Order, the other Orders, and the whole Host of Heaven against Drakon and his entity-armies in the War of the Third Heaven; see also *Legends of Angelore*

seven last plagues: a term used in reference to the seven bowls of wrath which are prophesied to be poured out by the seven archangels upon the worlds during the twilight of That Great Day

Seven of the Highest Order: a reference to the Archangels

Seven Spirits of God: ancient entities whose allegiance lies with Mashiyach; also known as the seven lamps of fire that burn before Mashiyach's throne in heaven and as the seven eyes upon the Lamb as He exists around His throne in heaven; the existence and description of these entities is recorded in the Scriptures of Truth in Isaiah 11, as well as in the first, third, fourth, and fifth chapters of the Revelation of Jesus Christ; see also *Legends of Angelore*

seven trumpets: a term used in reference to the seven trumpets that are prophesied to be sounded by the seven archangels during the course of That Great Day and which are prophesied to signal the commencement of unparalleled change and destruction upon the physical universe

Shachath (*shaw-KHATH*): a reference to the Pit of Shachath, a lightless pit of infinite depths located somewhere on the earth; Shachath is prophesied to house the locust-entities until their heralded king, Drakon, frees them; it is also the place from which Warlord Chuwl is prophesied to arise after donning his revelationform appearance and the place where That Great Serpent of Old is prophesied to be held for the thousand-year millennial reign of Christ; the word *Shachath* translates to mean "a pit," "a trap," "a ditch," or "a grave;" figuratively, it means "destruction" or "corruption"

Shachath, Pit of: see *Shachath*

Shekinah (*shek-in-AH*): a word from the ancient tongue that translates to mean "the presence of God"

sheol: the ancient-tongue name for the abode of the dead, depicted as being located in the deepest place of the earth; often used synonymously with death itself

Sheshach: another term for Babylon that comes from Jeremiah 25 and 51 in the Scriptures of Truth

shield of faith: a term used in reference to one of the armaments which Mashiyach directs the faithful to don as a part of the whole armor of God in defense against the wiles of Drakon and his legions of evil, as is recorded in Ephesians 6 in the Scriptures of Truth

Shining One: one of the many names given to Drakon

Simon: a member of the rebel faction of freedom fighters known as the Qanah

Smith, Quellin: a brilliant physicist working in the field of particle physics

Son of God: a title held solely by Mashiyach

Son of the Most High God: a title held solely by Mashiyach

Sons of Disobedience: a term used in reference to the Marah; see also *Marah*

Sons of Levi: a term used in reference to an order of priests who existed in the Old Age of Man

Sons of the Kingdom: a term used in reference to the Qanah; see also *Qanah*

southern quadrant: a largely agrarian quadrant located beyond the southern gates of the Great City megalopolis; the people who dwell there are known as the Ur, having been named after the Ur River, which flows throughout the quadrant and which has the Great River as its source; the Ur are a people who have shunned the technological innovation and opulence of modern times and who cling rather to the simple, largely forgotten ways

sovereign overlord: the title of the leader of the Great City Confederation of Nations

space-time grid: a map of space-time curves and their destination points; see *gravity-well travel*

spirit-war: a term used in reference to the on-going war that takes place within the dimensions, realms, planes, and domains of the Ancient Heights between the supernatural creatures, powers, breeds, beings, orders, and entities who dwell therein; spirit-war pits those whose allegiance lies with Drakon, against those whose allegiance lies with Mashiyach

Spoiler: a name ascribed to Drakon

Strongholds of Nachash: a fortified location beyond the Great Barrier in the deepest darkest abysm of the Infinitude; also known as the Strongholds of the Serpent; see also *Nachash*

Supreme Assembly: the all-powerful judicial governing body of the Great City Confederation

Supreme Council of Churches: the all-powerful organization governing the doctrine and affairs of the religions that exist upon the earth and the inhabited worlds during the last days of the Age of Man

Supreme of Creation: a term used in reference to the archangels

Supreme Order: a term used in reference to the archangels

Sword of the Spirit: a term used in reference to one of the armaments which Mashiyach directs His faithful to don as a part of the whole armor of God in defense against the wiles of Drakon and his legions of evil entities, as is recorded in Ephesians 6 in the Scriptures of Truth; the Sword of the Spirit is the Word of God

Sycuan the Third, Archangel: leader of the all-powerful Cathian Church; twelfth in a succession of archangels to sit upon the vaunted Throne of the archangel at Cathian Prime; spiritually, Lord Sycuan is known as the Great Beast of the Earth and the False Prophet; he commissioned the Cathian scientists to create Optinet, the solar-system-wide communication and information system of near-infinite computational power; see also *Optinet*

Temple Mount: a large stone mount located at the heart of the Old City District and situated several meters above the surrounding land; once the ancient foundation for a large architectural structure, the Temple Mount is some thirty-four acres in extent and was constructed using archaic building techniques nearly six thousand years ago

Tempter, the: a name ascribed to Drakon

ten horns of the Beast: a term used in reference to the ten kingdomless kings, the ten terrorist leaders and their followers, who Akathartos plan to lure to the Valley Esdraelon to war alongside Warlord Chuwl and his entity-armies against the armies of men from the north and the south in the Last War of the Age of Man, as is prophesied in the sixteenth and seventeenth chapters of the Revelation of Jesus Christ in the Scriptures of Truth; see also *armies of Akathartos*

ten horns: a term used in reference to the ten nations that are prophesied to be part of the end-time confederation of nations

Testaments, the: a term used in reference to the Old and New Testaments, which comprise the Scriptures of Truth

Testimony of Jesus: the testimony that Mashiyach accomplished during the time of His First Coming by His sacrifice and death upon the cross and His resurrection to eternal life and glory; see also the *Atonement*

That Great Day: the period of time of unknown duration which is prophesied to commence at the moment the terrestrial sun becomes black as sackcloth of hair, the moon becomes like blood, and the stars of heaven fall to earth as a fig tree drops its late fig when it is shaken by a mighty wind, as is recorded in the Revelation of Jesus Christ in the Scriptures of Truth; that Great Day is prophesied to climax with the return of Mashiyach to the earthly plane of existence and to end with the founding day of the Millennial Age; see also *time of Jacob's trouble*

thousand years, the: a term used in reference to the millennial reign of Mashiyach, which is prophesied to commence following His return to the terrestrial plane of existence and the consummation of His wrath upon the unrepentant, His reclamation of the title deed to the earth, His consecration of the millennial temple, and the establishment of His personal reign and rulership of mankind; the commencement of the thousand years would mark the end of the Age of Man

throne room at Cathian Prime: the ornate room located at Cathian Prime wherein lies the Throne of the Archangel, the seat of power of the leader of the all-powerful Cathian Church

Thronos (*THRON-os*): one of the Nine Orders of Angels; the Thronos are the Third of the Nine, Masters of Thrones and Kingdoms, and their appearances are like those of sphinxes, with women's heads and lion's bodies and tails; they are prophesied to battle alongside the Seven of the Supreme Order, the other Orders, and the whole Host of Heaven against Drakon and his entity-armies in the War of the Third Heaven; see also *Legends of Angelore*

time of Jacob's trouble: a term found in the Book of Jeremiah in the Scriptures of Truth, which refers to the great tribulation, which is prophesied to plague the worlds during the course of That Great Day; see also *That Great Day*

touchpad: a personal data storage and transmittal device with links to Optinet; see also *Optinet*

trans-fluidic skin: the term used in reference to the aqueous dermal layer that covers the forged beryllium-alloy exoskeleton of all Peacekeeper war machines; its mercurial properties enable Peacekeepers to measure light from their surroundings and generate hard-light constructs around their body in order to alter or camouflage their appearance; see also *hard-light constructs*

Tree of Knowledge of Good and Evil: the name of a tree that exists in the Sacred Glade and whose fruit is prophesied to bring the knowledge of good and evil to those who eat of it

Tree of Life: the name of a tree that exists in the Sacred Glade and whose fruit is prophesied to bring the secret of eternal life to those who eat of it

Tribulation, the: a term found in the Scriptures of Truth that is used in reference to the catastrophic events prophesied to befall the earth, the inhabited worlds, and the universe at large during the last seven years of the Age of Man

Truth, Book of: a term used in reference to the Scriptures of Truth

Tyne, Emma: an accomplished neuroroboticist and director of the Artificial Intelligence Agency

upper levels: the name of the highest level environs of City Center; where the ultra-rich live, work, and play

Uriel (*yer-ee-el*): one of the seven archangels

Valley Esdraelon: a wide valley that rolls against the coastlands of the Great Sea to the north and west of the Old City District; prophesied to serve as the battlefield for the Last War of the Age of Man

Virtues: one of the Nine Orders of Angels; masters of divine power and mighty works, these ancient entities appear as decarnate conflagrations roiling upon the blackened expanse; the Virtues are prophesied to battle alongside the seven of the Supreme Order, the other Orders, and the whole Host of Heaven against Drakon and his entity-armies in the War of the Third Heaven; see also *Legends of Angelore*

War of the Third Heaven: a supernatural war that is prophesied in the twelfth chapter of the Revelation of Jesus Christ in the Scriptures of Truth; this future war pits Drakon and his legions of evil entities against Michael, the Great Prince of the Archangels, the Nine Orders, and the whole Host of Heaven, and is prophesied to take place within the trans-dimensional latitudes of the Ancient Heights; see also *Final War*

Watchers: one of the Nine Orders of Angels; noble warders of the children of men, these ancient entities are prophesied to battle alongside the seven of the Supreme Order, the other Orders, and the whole Host of Heaven against Drakon and his entity-armies in the War of the Third Heaven; see also *Legends of Angelore*

wheels, whirling: the mysterious entities that accompany the Guardians of the Sacred Glade, one for each of the four living creatures; as is recorded in Ezekiel 1 and 10 in the Scriptures of Truth, the appearance of the wheels is like sparkling beryl, and their workmanship is as if one wheel were within another wheel; a substance akin to burning coals exists within the confines of the wheels, and their rims are lofty and filled with eyes around and within; the burning coals within their inner wheels are often times referred to as oracles of fire and are believed to be the vessels wherein all mysteries of the Infinitude are chronicled; see also *burning coals, Guardians of the Sacred Glade*

whole armor of God: the spiritual armor that Mashiyach instructs His followers to don in order to quench the fiery darts of Drakon; in total, this armor entails the girding of one's waist with truth, the putting on of the breastplate of righteousness, the shodding of one's feet with the preparation of the gospel of peace, the taking of the shield of faith, the donning of the helmet of salvation, and the wielding of the Sword of the Spirit, which is the Word of God

Wisdom: a term used by Drakon in reference to the Scriptures of Truth

Word of His Testimony: see *testimony of Jesus*

Worthless Shepherd, the: one of the many names given to Warlord Chuwl; see also *Great Beast of the Sea*

Xyan, Aden (*Yan, Aden*): Information Minister to the Sovereign Overlord of the Great City Confederation since 2451; to those upon the earthly plane of existence, he is a man who hails from the Western nations who is an expert in information technology; for reasons unknown, he has lost the use of his legs and is bound in a wheelchair, and his right eye has been re-engineered

Zion: an ancient name for a region of the Old City District that is both literal and symbolic

Who Is this King of Glory?

Who is this King of Glory who Satan, the Dragon, and his armies of evil entities are plotting so feverishly to defeat, and why do they believe it is so critical for them to defeat Him?

He is Mashiyach, the Anointed One, the White Horseman, the King of kings and Lord of lords. His name is Jesus the Christ, and He is the One whose birth is celebrated at Christmas, whose death and resurrection are celebrated at Easter, and who has promised to come again in power and glory to destroy all those who have chosen to rebel against His eternal love. No wonder the Great Serpent of Old seeks to defeat Him!

This mighty, awesome King of Glory is real, and He wants you to be part of His kingdom—so much so that He committed the ultimate sacrifice: He died so that you could live eternally with Him.

Are you ready to receive Jesus as your Lord and Savior?

> Nor is there salvation in any other, for there is no other name under heaven given among men by which we must be saved.
>
> —ACTS 4:12

To learn more about Him, go to
www.NeverNight.com